Leigh Makes Three

GRACE PEARCE

Copyright © 2022 Grace Pearce

This book is a work of fiction. The characters and events portrayed in this book are fictitious. Any references to real things, real events, real people, or real places are used fictitiously. Any similarity to real persons, living or dead, business establishments, events, or locales is coincidental and not intended by the author.

Cover design and illustration by Laura Theriot Parker

All rights reserved.

ISBN-13: 979-8-3557-0662-3

For my husband: I choose you every day.

PROLOGUE

When your brother tells you he's getting married, laughter should probably not be your first response.

But that's what I did—I laughed hard. He couldn't have been serious. I really thought it was a joke the first and second time he said, "I'm getting married!"

He couldn't blame me for thinking it was a joke. He'd never been in a serious relationship in his life.

And he met her on a plane of all places.

Six. Months. Earlier.

That's not a real thing—meeting the love of your life on a plane. And people don't normally get engaged within six months. Right?

I was sitting there on the phone in my office, fresh out of a *five-year* relationship, not in my right mind.

"Leigh, I know it's been a bad week for you, and I am sorry. But I'm serious. I wanted you to hear it from me."

"Owen, I've been on juice cleanses longer than your relationship."

"Katie isn't a green juice that makes me gag."

I retched, my grip around my work phone tightening. I had

shameful emotions rising into my throat. He shouldn't be getting married before me. "You're making me gag!"

"Besides, you've never been on a six-month juice cleanse," he said. "Actually, have you ever been on a juice cleanse?"

I swiveled in my chair to look out the window and partly so my voice wouldn't carry out my office door. Deep down, somewhere in the folds of my brain, it knew it was not being nice. But I ignored that.

"Not the point. Would you like me to play Things That Are Longer Than Your Relationship?"

"Not particularly," he said.

I rolled the dice anyway.

"Our betta fish's lifespan."

"Thanks to me."

"My cell phone's battery life then."

"I don't think it would last that long even if you never picked it up once."

"Waiting for a flight at the airport."

"I'll Venmo you one hundred dollars if you can tell me you've been on time to the airport once in your life."

I paused. Dammit, I couldn't. That would have been good beer money.

"Pumpkin spice lattes."

"You hate that flavor, so don't pretend you know how long they're offered for."

"My childhood dance recitals."

"Those things sure felt like six months, and somehow I still didn't fall asleep."

"You get the point."

"You sound ridiculous. She wants you to be the maid of honor."

I laughed harder and swiveled back around. "Where are *her*

friends?"

"Co-maid of honor."

I scoffed as Emma walked by my office door and poked her head in. I looked up at her with wide eyes and mouthed, *Come back later*. She raised her eyebrows at me and turned around.

"I really am sorry about Dylan, but come on," Owen said.

Oh, we were going there that soon—*I Don't See This Going Anywhere After Five Years Dylan. It's Not You, But I Don't See Myself Marrying You Dylan*. It hadn't even been a week since he'd packed up and moved out, leaving me with a broken heart and without a couch.

"I'm sorry, who?" I shot back.

Owen chuckled. "You're better off. Seriously though, be happy for me."

Two pangs hit my heart.

One was in response to his first sentence. He'd said it so casually—almost like *everyone knew it but you* would be the next thing that came out of his mouth. I couldn't bring myself to call it out. I didn't want to hear his idiotic opinion, and I was sure it was only his opinion.

The second pang I verbalized. "Of course, I'm happy for you, Ow. And I like her, I do. But you don't really do serious relationships."

"She's different," he replied.

She's hot, I thought. The kind of hot that made you question your own sexuality—unless your type was already tall, skinny, blonde females with legs for days. She looked like she lived in a spin class. Then the way she dressed—you couldn't help but look at her cleavage when she faced you and the bottom of her butt cheeks coming out of her jean shorts when she turned away.

As a heterosexual woman, I could appreciate how gorgeous she was, but I felt like a moron when I'd glance down involuntarily.

There was no way she didn't notice.

"Well then, she's a lucky girl. I really am happy for both of you, and I'd love to be the *co*-maid of honor," I said sincerely.

"Thanks, Leigh. I love you."

"Yeah, yeah, I love you too. I'm excited! This is going to be fun."

Recalling this conversation makes me squirm. So no, I didn't have to be such a bitch to him. Don't judge me. There were worse things in the world than my older brother (by eleven minutes, and he never let me forget it) getting married—before me. But I was just *off* from love that particular week, thanks to an unnamed person. I really needed to buy a couch because sitting on the floor on pillows and blankets to watch TV only made me angrier with each passing day. I was happy for Owen beneath all of that.

After he hung up, I placed my work phone ever so gently down on the receiver. So quietly that Emma heard it from her office next door.

"What's wrong?" she asked as she walked into my office.

"Owen's getting married!" I exclaimed.

She sat down in the chair across from my desk. "Owen who?"

"Owen, Owen!"

For the record, she laughed harder than I did the first time I heard it.

"April Fools'?" She glanced at my calendar on the wall where November was written at the top. "Or is Owen Owen a celebrity or band I don't know like Duran Duran or something?"

"More like JoJo," I corrected her.

"Richie Rich?" she said unsure.

"Zsa Zsa… Gabor. How many more can there be? There's only one Owen Owen in the world. And he's getting married to Katie."

"Wow!" Emma said. "I'm happy for him. She's totally out of his league. It's about time he had a serious relationship."

I rolled my eyes. I don't know what girls saw in my brother, but according to every single girl in high school, he was *so hot*. He had zero trouble in the girl department and dated every single one of my friends, except Emma. We practically grew up together. She'd admit he was hot, but they also kind of saw each other as siblings—thank God.

Emma gasped. "Do you think Wes is going to be his best man?"

"I don't know, probably."

That hadn't crossed my mind yet, but it wasn't a completely unpleasant thought. I hadn't thought about Wes in a long time.

"God, I haven't seen him in forever," Emma said. "You think he still looks as good as he did in college? Where's he living now?"

"I think he's still in Nashville, but I haven't seen him in a couple of years. He works for his dad."

We'd all worked for Wes' dad in college. He was the reason that Emma and I went into advertising. However, Nashville didn't have a large advertising market like New York did. So, we'd both moved there as soon as we graduated from Vanderbilt.

"Oh. Well, I'm sure you'll be in the wedding party, so lucky you. College crush eye candy."

"I'm sure he's still with what's-her-face. And I already forgot. I'm *co*-maid of honor!" I laughed.

"Is that an actual thing?"

"Apparently. I'm sure she was just trying to be nice. I'll help her *real* maid of honor wherever I can."

"Did you swallow a bitter pill?"

"Ugh," I whined, still stuck in heinous-bitch-mode. "I never imagined Owen would get married before me. He's in and out of relationships like he's at a drive-thru. I dated Dylan for five years. I thought we would have been married by now, to be honest. Instead, I'm single, and Owen is engaged. Bizarro world."

"That's what you think now, but when you meet the next guy, you'll probably thank Dylan for breaking up with you. Depression now, realization later, happiness in the end."

"God, I hope so." I glanced at the clock on my computer. "Shit, we're almost late."

Emma popped up, and I followed her and her red eyelet dress out my office door and down the hallway flanked by glass to our conference room. Our high heels clacked along the floor in a pattern—hers heavy and dull, mine delicate and hollow—both a strange contrast to our personalities.

The conference room was the only room in the office without glass or windows, so when I shut out the sun behind me it became the mundane room it always was: four white walls and a wooden table illuminated by ugly fluorescent lights.

"Cute dress, by the way," I remarked. "You look so good in red." Her long dark brown hair, which I was always jealous of, was pulled back in a ponytail almost to her mid-back.

"Thanks!" she said, pulling her ponytail over her shoulder as she sat next to our friend and co-worker, Jack, who nodded in agreement. Lila and Stephen, our two other team members, were sitting across the long rectangular table from us.

"Now that we're all here…" our boss, Daniel, started. Emma and I gave him a meek smile. We weren't technically late. We had one minute to spare. "We have some exciting news. HMH will be acquiring Omega Advertising, which is based here in New York. In six months, we will be making room for some of their employees here, and I hope everyone will be welcoming to the new faces. We'll be getting two new team members. We'll need to clear out the two vacant offices for them. Does anyone want to volunteer?"

I raised my hand slightly to get back in Daniel's good graces. "I will."

"Thanks, Leigh," Daniel said. "Let's go over this week and

what's on everyone's schedule."

Emma, Jack, and I all exchanged glances. This could be fun. The three of us were the only ones sub-thirty. Everyone else was pretty boring. It wasn't their fault though. They were all married with kids. The older I got, the more I realized no one actually ever *feels* like an adult. We're all still kids at heart. The only difference is we become kids with bills, kids with responsibilities, kids with kids. Kids who still need their mommies or daddies to tell them how to buy a car or a house. That shit is confusing.

I whispered to Emma, "Will you help me buy a couch after work? I don't have my mom here to help me."

It was time I got my bony ass off the floor. It hurt watching TV, and maybe it would improve my mood.

CHAPTER 1
SIX MONTHS LATER

Buying a new couch really had been therapeutic. Emma and I found one of those huge deep ones where you can curl your whole body up on it and sink down into it. It hugged me every night, comforting me, and soaking up my tears. It probably smelled like salt. I spent a lot of time on it in my newly single life. I watched every chick flick I could find, so I had to start watching the foreign ones with subtitles. Although, it's really hard to watch movies with subtitles—I would just read them the whole time and never actually watch a majority of the movie—but it was more annoying to watch them dubbed with English, as their mouths moved out of sync with the sound.

I was embracing my newfound freedom and independence, even if it wasn't what I wanted. Dylan never watched a single chick flick with me, so I had a lot to catch up on.

I thought Dylan was the one. That we'd be in Owen and Katie's place before them. You should know after being with someone for five years. Two years really. Maybe even one. God, maybe even six months in Owen's case. I met Dylan soon after moving to New York. He'd been bartending while going to nursing school, and

Emma and I frequented the bar where he worked. He made me laugh and would slip me and Emma a free drink here and there. He'd talk to us all night, and when he wasn't, his green eyes would glance over at me.

A year later he graduated and moved in with me; four years later he moved out. I don't think he cheated on me because that's not his personality, but I do think he broke up with me for her—the doctor he was dating within a few weeks. I'd bet good money he emotionally cheated. He was giving himself to another while I was sitting at home on his couch.

I hadn't dated anyone in the last six months. I'd never been a big casual dater. I liked to date people I'd developed somewhat of a friendship with already. It made things harder, especially as I got older. But it's not like I was marking off each day on the calendar with a huge red X to keep a running total of how many days it'd been since I last had sex. It's not like I needed to see one hundred and eighty-one of those lined up all next to each other screaming at me to get a life.

The two offices across from mine had turned into makeshift storage over the years. Boxes, prints, magazines, and poster boards had slowly built up around the desks as we finished another project. I imagine that's how hoarders feel. It was always just one more thing—what's one more thing? But then, pretty soon, we couldn't access the desks.

Over the course of the prior week, I'd cleaned out the offices, cursing at myself for volunteering, and put everything in our real storage downstairs in our office building. The rooms had transformed without all of the boxes piled high, so I admired my hard work from my desk instead of daydreaming—like I had been all morning—about my sex life like it was on an episode of a game show with a loud buzzer sound that goes off and lovely red Xs that flash across the screen when you get an answer wrong. Owen and I used to watch game shows when we were kids and scream our answers at the TV.

Name a day I had sex in the last week.

Friday. Bbbeeehhh X

Saturday. Bbbeeehhh XX

Sunday. Bbbeeehhh XXX

Technically, that's a trick question because the answer is none.

Our offices had blinds, but everyone loved to see all the light bouncing around through the glass walls from everyone's huge office windows, so we mostly kept them up.

In the summer, my favorite time of day was around 9:03 in the morning. The sun would finally peek around a skyscraper across the street and be high enough to come straight through my window. It would hit the metal edge of my whiteboard on the wall and reflect into the glass flower vase I kept on my desk. From there it would break into a million sunbeams across the room. I'd watch them every morning, wishing I could somehow feel them, hold one in my hand. Then they'd slowly retreat in the same path they came in from as the sun went behind another building. I was playing with the sunlight on my fingers when Jack interrupted me.

"Have you met them yet?" he said, leaning against my doorway.

"No, they were in Daniel's office when I got here. Have you?"

"Briefly. Two guys. One's a nice, older guy named Andre. One of them is a tall, blond Greek statue of a man!" Jack said excitedly.

That piqued my interest. "Young?"

"Our age, I would guess. Wes something. I definitely get a straight vibe." Jack crossed his arms in disappointment.

How common of a name was Wes? Wes was in advertising, but Wes lived in Nashville. It must have been a different person. I was sure there were lots of tall, blond Weses who worked in advertising in the world. He didn't even look like a Greek sculpture. He looked like Wes Adams. It couldn't be Wes Adams.

"Wes Adams?"

"Yeah, that's it." Jack eyed me. "You know him?"

"I know *a* Wes Adams. But he lives in Nashville. There's no way."

There was absolutely no way. It's like when you typed someone's name into social media to stalk them and you could have never imagined there were so many people with the same name. You can't even find the person you're looking for, and it's frustrating as hell. I already knew there were fifty-nine results when you searched my name on my one account, so odds were anyone would find me.

"This Wes Adams is gorgeous," Jack replied. He looked to his side down the hallway, smiled wide, and looked back at me.

He's coming, he mouthed.

We were silent for a minute as I heard Daniel introduce Complete Stranger Wes Adams to Lila and Stephen. Their footsteps came closer and stopped in front of Emma's doorway, but I still couldn't see them.

"Wes, this is—" Daniel started.

"Emma?" Not So Complete Stranger Wes Adams said in confusion.

Jack's eyes went wide as he watched me dive under my desk. I never claimed to be an adult, remember?

"Wes!" Emma exclaimed.

"You two know each other?" Daniel asked.

"We went to college together," Emma explained. "It's been forever! Five years?"

Wes laughed a little and confirmed, "Five years. It's good to see you."

I hadn't heard that laugh in so long, but it was muted—subdued. Not how I remembered. A surge of unwelcome want flooded my body. I wanted to hear it fully. Hear it how I remembered when I used to make him laugh.

"Then you must know Leigh too," Daniel said, putting two and two together. I could feel his presence come into my doorway.

"Oh, she went to get some coffee," Jack covered for me with an amusing tone. "But I'm sure she'll be excited to see you again, Wes. Too funny!"

"It is," Daniel agreed. "I'm happy you will have some friends here. Let me show you the conference room and the break room, and we can go back to my office. You can see Leigh later."

"*So* good to see you!" Emma chimed in. "We're happy you're here."

"Thanks. Happy to be here myself," Wes replied as their footsteps started down the hallway, getting further and further away.

Oh my God. Oh my God. Oh my God.

"Oh my God. Oh my God. Oh my God," Emma hissed, coming around the wall that separated our offices. "Where's Leigh?!"

Jack chuckled. He must have given me away because a few seconds later Emma kicked my desk, and I heard my door close.

I poked my head out to see Jack and Emma sitting in the chairs across from my desk, laughing at me with their eyes.

"Jack, I will rip that clip-on bowtie right off your neck if you don't quit smirking at me like that."

"I would never wear such a thing, so go ahead and try," he challenged me. "But I don't want to choke to death until I hear this story."

"No story," I lied, returning to my chair. Back to the adult version of myself.

Jack looked at Emma for confirmation. Emma laughed. She wouldn't keep her mouth shut, even if I begged her.

"No *big* story. It's stupid," I explained. "We made out once in college. We were drunk. Nothing more to it."

"Hot and heavy on a pool table," Emma added.

It was definitely that. The four of us were at our lake house in North Carolina; me and Emma, Owen and Wes. We'd been swimming all day in the lake, bouncing on the water trampoline, and paddle boarding. Emma had gone to sleep, and Owen was passed out on the couch upstairs. We'd all been drinking too much. Wes and I were wide awake, so we decided to play pool. We were flirting with each other, letting our hands linger on the other. *He started it, and I couldn't help myself.* We'd been glancing at each other all day, and I'd always had a crush on him. We were kindred spirits, but he was always off limits. All of Owen's friends were. Owen made that clear from the beginning of time.

What's up with that bullshit double standard, by the way? Owen certainly didn't follow his own rules.

I finally beat Wes after losing the first two games. I can't remember how we ended up in the position we were in. My back was up against the table, and Wes was standing close in front of me, holding his pool stick vertically off the ground.

"You just got lucky," he'd said. He let his pool stick fall to the ground, and like a lightning bolt, we were making out. He picked me up, while I straddled him, and put me on top of the table. His large hands were all over me as they made their way under my shirt. My small hands were all over him as they made their way under his shirt. He was kissing my neck, and I'm pretty sure he was about to take my shirt off because he was gripping the bottom hem, and I felt his hands slide up the sides of my stomach. Then something upstairs made a thump, and he sprang back. He looked towards the ceiling where the noise had come from, shook his head at me, and walked out. We never spoke about it.

"Did you incorporate the balls and sticks?" Jack said, bringing me back to the present moment.

"Billiards *is* my fetish. All that soft green wool."

Jack nodded. "I bet he's a good kisser. All six foot four of him. I'd wrap myself up in wool with him if he wanted."

"Of course he is, but whatever, that's beside the point. He's my brother's best friend. We never talked about it after that, and we never will."

"Sooo much sexual tension wound up in there," Emma joked. "Leigh doesn't date her brother's friends, but he dated all of hers."

"Owen would flip his shit if he knew, so I don't think Wes told him either," I pointed out. "And Wes started dating that girl shortly after. They've been together forever, so it's a moot point. Story over."

Emma and Jack both snorted.

But that happened sophomore year of college. Like, eight years earlier. Two years short of a decade. I hadn't held on to it, and I knew he hadn't either.

"I have to get back to work, slackers. Slogans don't write themselves." I waved toward the door.

"Leigh Sullivan: More Than a Friend, but Less Than a Girlfriend," Emma retorted.

"Leigh Sullivan: Master of a Flirtationship," Jack continued.

Emma hit Jack in the arm as they stood up. "Leigh Sullivan: Is She Just Being Funny or Does She Want to Rip My Clothes Off?"

"Leigh Sullivan: Ignorer of Sexual Tension Who Goes On Pretending It Doesn't Exist," Jack said as he opened the door.

"Leigh Sullivan: The Girl Who Was Alone Because Her Two Best Friends Died Tragic Deaths," I called as they turned down the hallway.

How long did I have until Wes emerged from Daniel's office?

—

THIRTY-THREE VERY short minutes was how long.

The first ten minutes I spent fixing my shoulder-length brown hair so it looked like I'd effortlessly just woken up with curls so beautiful. I wanted to look halfway decent. I hadn't seen Wes in over two years. I dug around in my purse for something to put on my lips, but all I found was some lip balm that had probably been there for years. At least it would make them a little shiny. I pinched my cheeks like I'd seen girls in movies do, knowing that wouldn't translate to beauty in real life. But this was Wes. I had to try everything.

The next fifteen minutes I spent feverishly texting Owen.

Since when does Wes live in New York City?

He replied: I think it's been a year. Why?

And you never thought to mention that? Sketchy AF.

I didn't realize I needed to keep you in the loop on when and where my friends move. Again, why?

I wondered why Owen really never mentioned it. It seemed like something that would come up in conversation. I wished I could hear the tone behind his text messages and gain more insight into his frame of mind. I felt I would have been able to hear it in his voice if it was something he had purposely withheld from me, purposely keeping us apart.

You are talking to Wes' new co-worker.

No way! Y'all are the ones acquiring his company? Small world!

I'd say it's about as big as a pinprick at this point.

Tell him I said hey. Can't wait to finally see both of you at the couple's shower!

The wedding festivities were *finally* about to begin. And yes, I'd come around since I'd first found out. I wasn't a heartless, marriage-hating troll, and Owen seemed really happy—a happy I'd never seen before.

I'd been planning this couple's shower with my co-maid of honor, Kathryn, and I promise I had fun doing it. Even from afar.

I was confirming the alcohol order and headcount (wishing

Kathryn would have given me the headcount by person so I could see if Wes was bringing a plus one) when his voice pulled my head out of my computer.

"Well, well, well. Isn't this a coincidence?"

Wes was standing right inside my office, and he looked just as good as I'd seen him two years ago. His blonde hair was styled to the side with a part, and he looked handsome in a stylish gray suit that matched his gray-blue eyes. Aside from his looks, he always was my favorite of Owen's friends because he was a genuinely *good* guy.

I hoped I looked just as good—not like he'd remembered me one way, but then when he saw me, I'd suddenly aged two years, replacing the youthful two-year younger image he'd had of me in his mind. I always did that with celebrities. I'd watch their old movies, so they stayed the same age in my mind, frozen in time, for years. But then randomly, I'd see an interview of them from the week before and realize: damn, they're old.

The other new co-worker walked behind him into his new office across from mine. I glanced at his salt and pepper hair on the back of his head, but I was homed in on Wes.

"Hey, Wes!" He had to have known Emma already told me. I smiled brightly at him and hesitated. Should I stand up and hug him? He wasn't making any move to come further into my office.

I narrowed my eyes at him instead. "I don't believe in coincidences. Are you stalking me?"

He shrugged. "I figured getting a job here would save me on gas money. It's a long drive from Nashville to watch you through all these windows."

"So that *is* you on the corner every day with the binoculars. I thought so."

"Not just any binoculars; the Stalk Master HD with night vision," he countered.

"And just how long *have* you been in New York?" I asked.

"About a year now," he replied. "I can't believe it's already been that long."

"I can't believe I didn't know. Owen never mentioned it. I would have shown you around and everything."

"Not surprising. You know how he is."

"Yeah," I laughed, though I wasn't sure what he was referring to. Was it his forgetfulness, his lack of communication, or his protectiveness over me?

"I'm excited about the new job though. You like it here?" he asked.

"I don't think anything else can live up to Adams Advertising, but it's a close second. We've got a great team. You'll make it better, I'm sure."

"I meant New York, but you can keep up with the compliments." His mouth pulled up at the corners for a slight second before relaxing.

"Oh," I laughed. Me and my big mouth. "I love New York. Not as much as I love giving you compliments though."

What the hell was I saying? I could have stopped after I said New York, but I didn't know when to shut my mouth. The surge of wanting to make him smile again, hear that laugh from his throat, was stronger the second time.

"Your sarcastic ones are better," he replied.

My brain pulled the lever of its slot machine and whirred. "Backhand complimenting my compliment. Nicely done."

He laughed his real laugh. Ding, ding, ding. Triple sevens. An MRI of my brain at that exact moment would have been as bright and colorful as an actual slot machine hitting the jackpot.

"I'll leave you to it. I need to get settled in over there." He tilted his head toward the office to my left. "It's great to see you again. It's been too long."

I nodded at him with a smile and said to his back, "See you… all the time now!"

All the time. Literally.

I could see his left arm and shoulder come in and out of view from my desk as he moved in his chair. And occasionally, I'd see half of his striking face.

I was going to turn into an actual stalker. I'd already glanced over at him a hundred times in the first hour. The other new co-worker, Andre, came and introduced himself to me which gave my eyes and brain a much-needed four-minute break. Not long enough though. I probably cut my glances in half in those four minutes, but not completely.

Luckily, Daniel came and got Wes in the second hour to go over our accounts with him in the conference room. I needed him out of my line of vision because I couldn't stop thinking about him between my legs while I was on that pool table.

I was finally able to focus back on my computer and the logo I was working on for Rawesome Sushi until there was a short knock on my open door.

"Leigh, will you please get Wes up to speed with what you're working on?" Daniel asked me.

"Yeah, of course."

Wes stepped around him as Daniel said, "When you're done you can move on to the others," before he walked off.

"Where do you want me?" Wes asked me.

Across my desk, was my first thought.

"If a chair will fit, you can bring it around here," I said instead because that's more socially acceptable.

He picked up a chair easily and placed it close beside me to my right before sitting and bringing his scent of cedar and vanilla with him.

"Rawesome Sushi? That place is great," he remarked, looking at my screen.

I straightened back up after I realized I'd leaned into him slightly. "For sure! It's my favorite," I said, surprised he knew it. "I'm revamping their logo and digital marketing for their expansion and remodel this year. I'll be sad when it isn't a hole-in-the-wall sushi restaurant anymore."

He nodded in agreement, eyes on the screen. "Something isn't right about that."

"The expansion or the logo?"

"Both," he said. "That circle is off."

I studied the screen for a second. "I know, but I can't figure out what it is about it. We've settled on the circle around their name, but I'm having trouble making it cohesive."

"What about this?" He leaned in close to me as I looked slightly over my shoulder into his face, but his eyes stayed on the screen. I tried to nonchalantly look back toward the computer—like I didn't want to keep staring at his handsome face. I was so close that I had him under a microscope.

He gently took the mouse from me, his hand briefly gliding over mine as I took it away and into my lap. I looked back at the screen as a shiver traveled up my arm and down my body. Is that what sexual tension felt like? Or was that just what it felt like to be touched innocently by a male for the first time in one hundred and eighty-one days? I wondered if he felt anything, but I guessed he hadn't because he'd probably had sex with his girlfriend lots of times in the last one hundred and eighty-one days. And it was probably way hotter than our pool table escapade.

"The bottom of the R could create a wave and go around here into the circle," he said as he roughly drew what he was saying.

"I told you you'd make us better. I like the wave. It gives it some movement," I confirmed as the full circle he drew came to a close and balanced everything out. "That Adams touch."

He smiled—close to my face—and wrapped his hand around my arm. "Here, I'll give you some."

"Ow!" I screeched, making Wes jump back with a look of horror before realization set across his face.

"Watch your back, Leigh," he warned me.

I smiled sweetly. "So, I'll be working on the digital advertising for the expansion this week and next if you want to help me. I still have to put together all the mood boards. I'm presenting it to them in two weeks."

"Sounds great."

"You're still going to the couple's shower next weekend, right?" I asked him.

"I wouldn't miss it. What day are you flying in?"

"Friday afternoon. You?"

"Same."

We both eyed each other. How many non-stop flights from New York City to Birmingham, Alabama could there possibly be in a day?

"Flight 1022 at 3:29?" we both said in unison.

"Are you sure you're not stalking *me*?" Wes questioned.

I raised my eyebrows at him. "Depends. Does hacking into your email qualify as stalking?"

"Hardly. You want to meet at the airport by the check-in desk?"

"Sure," I replied a little shaken. We could be friends apart from Owen, right? We were co-workers now. It wasn't like I was pushing it. I never pushed it all four years of college, but I also never spent eight hours every day with him Monday through Friday. Being friends was almost a must now.

He pulled a yellow Post-it Note off the pad next to my computer, reached across my desk for a pen, and scribbled his number down. He held it out to me between two of his fingers. I slowly slipped it out. Wes Adams' phone number. I had Wes

Adams' phone number, and it would shortly be in my phone. I wondered why sharing phone numbers had never come up once in the four years we spent at Vanderbilt together.

"Don't call me in the middle of the night and breathe heavily into the phone before hanging up," he smirked at me.

"Not my style. I'm more of a thousand text messages in one day kind of girl."

"Who wouldn't like that?" He shrugged his shoulders with a laugh. "I'm sure texts from Leigh Sullivan are a treasure. All right, I guess I'll head over to Jack next. Put time on my calendar for whenever you're working on Rawesome."

He stood and put the chair back in place using one arm. He had one of those bodies that was naturally lean, but I never remembered him working out in college. Maybe it was his height or his genes, but he always looked so toned without trying.

"See you… all the time now," he parroted me as he walked out.

I eyed my wall calendar where I imagined the entire page with a big, thick, red X covering the entire month of May. I felt like the doctor in my own twisted scenario, but all I wanted was to feel that shiver again.

Twenty seconds on the clock.

Name a body part of Wes' I couldn't stop thinking about.

What was my current heart rate?

Name a feeling I was experiencing right below my belly button.

Name a chemical surging into my brain.

How soon was too soon for me to fill up Wes Adams' calendar?

CHAPTER 2

That night Kathryn and I had a marathon phone call going over logistics. If you've ever thrown a shower before you know how much goes into it.

The shower was at my parents' house. Of course, my mom was more than happy to offer. We'd catered it from Mike's Famous Bar-B-Q, and I ordered the alcohol from a local liquor store. Don't come at me about which barbecue place is the best in B'ham. You ask ten different people, and you'll get ten different answers.

Kathryn was going to meet us Saturday morning to help with everything, and we'd have Emma there to help since she was staying with me. Emma might have been from Birmingham, and we might have worked together, but why not have a sleepover with your best friend whenever you could? Besides, we drank.

Kathryn confirmed the photo booth the day before, and I'd gotten coozies and banners printed through my advertising connections and shipped to the house. I couldn't wait to see the party come to life. And, again, I liked to party in general.

After I got off the phone with Kathryn, I texted Emma.

Is there a co-maid of honor award?

Definitely not. Still not sure that's even a real title, she responded.

Maybe you can create the category on The Knot and crown me the winner.

You wouldn't win it if there was one. You laughed when they asked you, remember?

I scoffed out loud and replied: I was having a bad week that week, remember? I'm the best twin sister a twin brother could ask for.

Not when you're crushing on his best friend.

He has a girlfrienddddd of seven yearsssss, I reminded her.

Doesn't hurt to look at him. And smell him.

I didn't respond, so she kept going.

And innocently touch him.

Check out his ass when he walks out of your office.

Ask him to open a bottle so you can watch his forearms flex.

Ask him to reach something on a high shelf so you can admire how tall he is.

Have a sex dream about him.

I ended it with an eye roll emoji and a goodnight.

But I won't lie to you. I totally thought about him naked before I went to sleep, trying to force my subconscious to bring it back after I fell asleep. Maybe it would satiate my pent-up lust. One could only hope. It didn't work though. I only woke up wondering if he would be better than my dreams.

Wes was in my office every day for the rest of the week. He really did smell good. And I couldn't help but look at him. Everything Emma said—just… yes. We worked together to create boards for social media and print advertisements along with a presentation for the upcoming meeting. We'd finalized our logo, and it looked great on paper and the screen. I'd forgotten how good he was at his job.

Soon, my office got too small for all our materials and maybe us. We'd been maneuvering around my office in a tight space, trying to give each other room and move out of the other person's way—never touching. I'd slide by him, he'd sidestep. I'd sit, he'd stand. I'd bob, he'd weave. I was convinced he could feel how tightly I was wound, like a compressed spring ready to pop out of a Jack-in-the-Box at any moment. Wes controlled the crank. I kept looking at his hands, wanting him to touch me innocently, but at the same time not wanting to be the doctor.

He'd lean down to say something to me, our eyes connecting. He'd hold something out to me, and I'd contemplate brushing my fingers with his. He'd take off his jacket and roll up his sleeves. He'd loosen his tie. He'd lean over, making his forearm muscles tighten. He'd lean back with his hands behind his head and his elbows out to the sides. He'd bend over to tie his shoe. He'd hover over me as I sat at my computer, his tie brushing against my back until he'd take it off completely. He'd stare out the window. He'd fidget with the blinds. He'd sit against my desk. He'd scratch the back of his neck. He'd run his hand through his hair. He'd shrug. He'd smile. He'd laugh. He paced every corner of my office. He sat in every chair. He leaned on all four walls.

My office was now bursting at the seams with Wes Adams being Wes Adams. Every nook and cranny was full. I could write a book of all the innocuous things this man did in my office that made me feel not so innocuous things.

Seven more bright red Xs got crossed off across seven squares in my mind. Maybe I just needed to get laid, as guys so aptly say, and relax a little bit from all the built-up frustration.

We moved to the conference room the next week, where there was more room. It also helped that it was lifeless. My spring decompressed slightly, but I was still aware of his slightest movements. Emma defused the tension a little when she helped us put the final touches on our presentation on Thursday, and by the end of the day, we were ready for the meeting.

"This is good," Wes said, standing back and looking around at our materials we'd set up around the room before looking at me. "*You're* good. You're *too* good. You're going to market your best-kept secret into a hot new restaurant."

"Don't make me cry," I replied as I put my hand on the back of his upper arm without thinking. The energy I had from finishing the project gave me a temporary mind lapse, but when I connected with him, he only transferred more energy up my arm like I'd connected myself to a twelve-volt battery.

Emma eyed my hand from where she was sitting as I quickly took it back. "You're *both* too good," she said.

I shot her a look because I knew she wasn't talking about the project. "Okay, let's go through it one last time. We start with the new logo. Show them the two variations of it."

Wes nodded. "Then move on to the color schemes, which you are seriously the best at."

I pointed at the first board, trying to not look flustered from the compliment. "Social media advertisements and print advertisements."

"Do you have the demographics already?" Wes asked.

"Yeah, we've done the research. And we'll do certain subway lines and bus stops. I'll let them know our suggestions at the end."

"Are you doing radio and television?" Emma asked me.

"They wanted to hold off until closer to the reopening date on that." I looked down at my watch. "Wow, today flew by. I didn't even know it was six already."

Wes glanced at his watch. "Long day that felt like ten minutes."

Emma smiled at him like she was thinking something cheesy: *time flies when you're having fun, huh, Wes?* I knew it was more than likely dirty, not cheesy: *six to midnight, huh, Wes?*

"I'm taking off the whole day tomorrow, so we'll still meet you at the airport?" I asked.

Emma furrowed her eyebrows for a brief second. I forgot to tell her that tidbit.

"Yeah. Does two hours before sound good?" he replied.

"I'm usually running down the terminal as they're saying my name over the loudspeaker and warning me I have two minutes to board, but yeah, two hours sounds great."

Wes laughed, and my heart felt like it was placed under the nozzle of a Soda Stream. That laugh with those lips curved up and his gray-blue eyes that suddenly turned bluer did a number on me.

—

"DID YOU JUST forget to mention he was on the same flight as us?" Emma questioned me after work as she picked up her lemon drop from the bar to take a sip.

I had refused to let Dylan take our bar away from us. He hadn't worked there in years anyway. It was surprisingly spacious for New York City and had a young professional vibe. The brick-lined walls, circular barstools bolted into the ground, and wooden slats along the underside of the bar made me feel cozy. And not to mention the hooks. There is nothing more annoying than going to a bar and finding out after you sit down that they don't have hooks underneath to hang your purse. When that happens, I always wonder if they employ any women.

I shrugged. "I forget to mention a lot of things. I'm a vault of secrets, unlike my very best friend. And it's a total coincidence that came up when we were talking about the shower."

"I can be a vault of secrets. For instance, I've never told Owen you made out with Wes."

"And you never will," I replied, narrowing my eyes at her.

She locked her lips with an imaginary key and flicked it to the side. "Maybe we can finally figure out his girlfriend's name though. Did she move with him to New York?"

"Hasn't come up."

"Is that because you don't want to bring it up, so you can go on pretending she doesn't exist?" Emma teased me.

I shook my head as I took a sip of my cosmopolitan. "I'm not going to be the doctor, Em! We have a strictly professional relationship with a light friendship on the side."

"Your favorite," Emma said with a smirk.

"You got me there," I laughed. "But it's only a friendship because of Owen. Even if he was single, Owen would totally hate me if I tried to go for him. That has to be why Wes never told him about us. I don't want to come between them."

All through high school and college, I'd constantly heard remarks from Owen about how I better not try anything with his friends. He'd invite them over to swim, and he'd say, "No checking them out." He'd have a guy friend spend the night and he'd say, "No flirting with him." One time I overheard him telling a friend, "No way. Don't even think about it. She's my sister." So, I figured he was also telling all of his friends the same thing. In high school, I dated a few guys who weren't friends with Owen and a few from other schools. In college, my dating pool became so much bigger. I didn't have to worry if the guy I liked was friends with Owen or not. I had a few shorter relationships, and one that lasted a year, but nothing serious enough that I thought about marriage—until Dylan.

I was such a stellar sister though. I didn't complain when Owen went for my friends. Granted, Owen never came between me and my friends. It was known he was a casual fling guy, so none of the girls ever had any high expectations. They all secretly hoped they might be the one to make him change his ways, but they'd never get mad at me for anything he did. And he did a lot of stupid things. One of my friends he broke up with through a text message. One of my friends he dumped and turned around and asked her best friend to prom. Like literally turned around right there in the hallway. Of course, the best friend said yes though. I guess we're all stupid in high school.

Maybe that's just one of those innate differences between men and women. It's harder for men to look past those types of things—things like knowing one of your best friends is screwing your sister.

Emma lifted her lip up on one side. "Owen Shmowen. He'd get over it."

"I'm way too good of a sister."

Emma almost spat her drink back into her glass. "Do you actually believe the things that come out of your mouth?"

"You'll never know, will you?"

"Speaking of vaults, what else have you not told me?" she chided me.

"You'll never know, will you?"

"You crack eventually," she stated. "If there's anything in there, I won't have to wait that long."

She was right. We really didn't have any secrets between the two of us. We told each other everything. Even if I decided to suppress it, it would come to the surface at some point. I couldn't think of anything at that moment I hadn't told her. Maybe except for how Wes made me feel occasionally, but I was holding on to that for the time being.

"How was it working with him the last two weeks?" Emma asked me.

Crrrrack. So I didn't make it as long as I thought I would. "Sexually frustrating, to put it mildly."

Emma gasped. "Shocking. I thought your vault was so secure."

I ignored that. "God, everything he does incites me! Even when he just stands there. I'm aware of every move he makes like he's doing it in slow motion just to torture me. It's not fair." I pouted. "I wish I would have met him before Owen. Maybe then I would've had sex with him in college. I can't get that damn pool table out of my mind."

"We're not in college anymore. What say does Owen have if you both liked each other and wanted it?"

"I don't know. Owen and I have never really talked about why he feels that way. I just know he does. Why are we talking about this? He was pretty serious with that girl the last time I saw him. I don't want to play 'what if.' New subject."

"Okay, what's the plan for tomorrow?" she asked me.

"Kathryn's coming over Saturday morning. We can do the lights and decorations tomorrow night ourselves. Tables, chairs, and flowers the next morning. The photo booth guy will take care of that. Food and alcohol should be delivered closer to the party, and we can set all that up when it gets there. Good plan?"

"Adequate plan."

"I hope Owen and Katie love it. We worked hard to put all of it together."

"Have you ever thrown a bad party?"

"You do have a point."

"And don't forget to pack your swimsuit. I want to swim. It's finally hot enough," she said.

"We will definitely squeeze in some pool time," I confirmed.

Sullivan Pool Parties were a major thing when we were younger. My parents were always so laid back. They allowed me and Owen to have parties as long as no one drove drunk and we cleaned up after ourselves. We'd have a party almost every weekend during the summer, even if it was just a few people. In college, it became a smaller group—me and my friends with our boyfriends, Owen and his friends with their girlfriends.

"Don't wait until the last minute to pack either. Now we have to be there two hours before!" Emma lectured me or maybe scolded me. We ran down terminals together like we were competing in a track and field tournament.

I held up three fingers. "Honor. I won't."

"You were a terrible Integrity Scout."

"It's not my fault our troop leader had zero sense of humor," I said.

"She was madder that it rained. That toilet paper was stuck to her trees and bushes for weeks."

I rolled my eyes at her. "I was twelve. It's not like I checked the weather app every morning."

My mom had given me enough hell about that the following day after she hung up with Mrs. Troop Leader Whose Name Escapes Me Now. She had texted my mom a video from her security camera of me repeatedly throwing the toilet paper into a tree near her front porch. I was grounded for a week. I learned my lesson though—I made sure to cover my face after that.

"When I grow up, I'm going to be a badass troop leader mom. My badges will be epic. The Cosmo Badge."

"The Slutty but Not Too Slutty Halloween Costume Badge," Emma joked, but I was an expert on it. There's a fine line that I would conquer every year through high school and college.

"The Drunk Tattoo Badge."

Yes, I got a drunk tattoo one night in college. It was the night before we were leaving for our lake house in the mountains—*that* trip with Wes actually. It's my favorite place on earth, so I decided to get a picture of teeny tiny mountains with a little sun poking up above them on my inner hip. It's just simple, black, unfilled lines, and it sounded like a good idea at the time. You can only see it when I'm naked, so whatever.

"Besides, you weren't a model Integrity Scout either," I added.

"I know how to keep my face off camera."

Don't let Emma fool you. She was the sneaky one—the real one you had to watch out for. The one you wouldn't think would toilet paper her troop leader's house (even though I did talk her into that one), who wouldn't have that sense of humor, who wouldn't take Molly at music festivals and dance in the EDM tent. She got away with way more than I did. When we were younger, we pretended like we were really part of a set of triplets.

"I'm always your fall guy—fall girl. What would you do without me?"

"Not have as much fun, obviously," Emma conceded. "I escaped high school without ever being a suspect for the freshman glitter incident thanks to you."

"I appreciate you doing that when I at least had an alibi."

On the last day of freshman year, Emma put an envelope on each of our teachers' desks—filled with glitter. I was a suspect until our principal realized I'd been in P.E. the entire period, seen by my teacher for all sixty minutes of class, during the time frame the envelopes were handed out. Emma placed them there. I only helped her stuff them. No one ever knew it was us, but we heard from each class about the look on the teacher's face when they opened it, thinking it was a nice end-of-the-year card.

We were always in on everything together—sneaking out, pulling pranks, getting fake IDs, going on impromptu road trips to music festivals—but for some reason, people on the outside always thought it was me. That I was the instigator. But a few of us knew the truth—Emma was a rare art form. I was lucky she was my best friend.

We've grown up *a little* since then.

Emma finished her drink and slid it toward the bartender, so I tipped mine back and drank the rest, before doing the same.

"Early night?" I pouted.

She nodded. "We can't sleep until noon."

"Says who?"

She made a face at me.

"Joking!" I exclaimed like I'd never joked a day in my life. "I pinky promise I will be up at eight a.m., packed by ten, and in the cab you pull up in at noon."

And for once in my life, I actually was.

CHAPTER 3

I hadn't been home since Christmas five months earlier, and I missed my parents and Owen. We didn't see each other as much as we wanted to.

Owen stayed in Nashville after we graduated. He didn't fall in love with advertising like I did and majored in finance instead. He did investment banking. I didn't pretend to know what that was. Numbers are boring. My parents were retired and still in our childhood home that was too big for just the two of them.

We broke our mom's heart when we told her neither of us would be moving back to Birmingham after we graduated.

She sobbed into the phone when Owen and I called her to discuss it. Owen made me break the news to her. He said it would sound better coming from me, but that was really him trying to pull the female card on me because I knew he was too chicken.

She'd always worried we wouldn't and even first cried about it when we were applying to colleges.

"You're never going to move back," she had said through her tears. "This is just the first step."

I guess she was right, but I thought she was crazy at the time.

Ultimately, she was happy that we were happy because she

knew how much Owen and I loved the cities we lived in. She still held out hope we'd move back one day when we conceived and popped out a few babies.

Now, we had this wedding that would bring us together more than just the major holidays and multiple times over the next few months.

As Emma and I pulled up to the airport, I opened my new message screen and sent my first ever text message to Wes.

I'll scream bomb to get everyone to run toward you. You detonate.

As I was getting my luggage out of the trunk, he replied: **My first Leigh Sullivan jewel, and you've also given me the gift of having the authorities monitor my texts.**

Don't say I never gave you anything. I'll always remember you for getting me to the airport on time. You here?

Of course. Standing by check-in.

Emma and I wheeled our luggage in through the sliding glass doors of the airport, and there he was, head above everyone else's, waiting near the end of the line for us. He smiled when he saw us come through the door, and it almost took me by surprise seeing him so casual in his navy chinos and heather gray Vanderbilt T-shirt.

"Hey, you two," he greeted us when we were within earshot.

"Hey, yourself!" I said. "Wes out in the wild."

"You're by yourself?" Emma asked, looking around. I gave her a sidelong glance trying to tell her not to say anything else, but she never listened to me.

He let out a confused laugh. "Uh yeah, who else would I be with?"

"Your girlfriend. What's her name again?" she continued, ignoring the imaginary duct tape I was slapping over her mouth in my mind. I knew she could feel it.

"You mean Rachel?" he said. "We're not together anymore."

His words bounced off my eardrums, and two thoughts leaped

into my brain: *Duh, Rachel Cooper!* and *Does this give me permission to touch him?*

I couldn't tell if he looked uncomfortable. His hand went from his backpack strap to the handle of his luggage and back. He glanced down at his luggage and shifted his weight. I needed to save him.

"Do you have *the bomb* ready? I said, mouthing the words the and bomb, and his demeanor instantly changed.

He smirked at me. "You can be the one to explain to your mother why we missed this shower."

"She would love nothing more than to pick her daughter up from FBI headquarters," I said nonchalantly.

"After y'all." Wes held out his arm toward the back of the line. I followed the direction of his hand with Emma tight behind me. She nudged me twice with her elbow saying *you're welcome.*

We winded between the retractable stanchions to the front. I only know they are called stanchions because I googled it in line after calling them line seatbelts and getting crazy looks from both Emma and Wes. I thought it was an appropriate enough name, and when I challenged them to tell me what they were really called, they were dumbfounded. Who actually called them that? I honestly didn't think I'd heard the word in my life.

We checked our bags in before making our way through security with our carry-ons and down to our gate.

I looked at my phone clock as we sat down. "What are we going to do with all this time?!"

"Bring about world peace," Wes said.

"Cure cancer," Emma quipped.

Wes hit Emma's arm. "Run a marathon."

"Have a movie marathon," she said, hitting him back.

I rolled my eyes at them. "This game isn't as fun as you clearly think it is."

"It's funner!" Emma said.

Wes and I both laughed, but Wes beat me to it. "Not a word, Emma."

"I concur, but if you'd asked me thirty minutes ago which word, between stanchion or funner, was a real word, I'd have said funner. So, we won't hold it against you," I sympathized.

Emma stuck her tongue out at me with one side of her upper lip raised. "What game do you want to play, Leigh?"

"Heads Up!?"

"What's that?" Wes asked.

We both stared at him.

"Ellen's app," I said exasperated.

Wes looked at me confused. "Ellen who?"

"Ellen DeGeneres, that's who. We'll start with movies. It's easy." I pulled my phone out and navigated to the app to start. "Just tell me what I need to know to guess it. I have one minute to guess as many as I can. And we get competitive."

Emma and I used to play it when we'd come home drunk from the bars in Nashville—a favorite pastime. We'd be screaming in each other's faces, getting louder as the time ticked away.

I got *Toy Story*, *The Breakfast Club*, *Die Hard*, *Superbad*, and *Bridesmaids*, but I had to pass on *Legends of the Fall*. It was mostly Emma giving me the clues the first couple of tries.

"Okay, I get it now," Wes said after I went.

Emma got *Titanic*, *Avengers: Endgame*, *Men in Black*, and *Coyote Ugly*. She got stuck on *Lady Bird*.

"I watch a ton of movies," Wes smiled at us when it was his turn.

Wes might have been an amateur and not known what Heads Up! was, but he wowed both of us. He got *Parasite*, *Liar Liar*, *Elf*, *21 Jump Street*, *Napoleon Dynamite*, *American Psycho*, *The Parent Trap*, *Top Gun*, and *Ratatouille*.

They finally called our group for boarding after what felt like hours. We huddled together as we waited to scan our boarding passes. We walked down the jet bridge together before I stepped onto the plane making sure to do so with my right foot first (some weird superstition I picked up somewhere I don't even remember).

I felt like Wes and I were dancing the tango. A very sensual tango involving no body contact. I'd move back as he moved forward. He would turn his foot and mine would go in the opposite direction. He'd turn his body and mine would follow in parallel.

That was until I tried putting my carry-on luggage in the overhead bin.

Emma put her bag overhead first and slid across the row into the window seat—all while graciously letting the old lady sitting in the aisle seat stay seated. As I was struggling above the old woman, Wes lightly touched my waist with one hand and wrapped his other hand around mine that was on the bag handle.

The seal broke. The dam burst. Did he forget we had some unspoken no-touching policy? Maybe it was an accident—but it felt like someone let go of the chain holding up a drawbridge, and it crashed down across the moat I had carefully built around myself. And now anything could freely come and go across. Did he feel that too?

"Here, let me," he said softly.

I stepped to my side. "Thanks!"

He slid the luggage in and stepped back so I could get around him. "I'm four rows back. Have a fun flight."

"I'll switch if you want to sit together," the old woman offered him as I scooted across her. Choosing crotch or ass is life or death.

"Yeah? That'd be awesome. Thank you," Wes responded. She stood, and Wes pointed out his aisle seat behind him.

"Aren't you tall!" she remarked as she looked up at him from practically his waist.

What is it about tall muscular guys? Evolution? Like a human male's peacock feathers. They are stronger, can protect us, make us feel safe. Why do we still feel this in the twenty-first century? But I guess it was the cavewoman in me because, damn, when I looked up at Wes' eyes a foot above mine, I could start a fire within me with two sticks.

"Yes, ma'am," he chuckled.

"And so handsome," she added.

Wes smiled. "Oh, thank you."

I turned my neck toward Emma and crossed my eyes. She smiled for a quick second before pointing with her eyes and eyebrows to turn back around.

My neck craned back the other way to see Wes' shirt slightly lifting as he put his suitcase above us, exposing the bottom of his light happy trail, and making me want to reach out and run my thumb up it. I dug in my purse for my headphones and made a hardened face at Emma. She made an O-face back, tucked her long hair behind her ears, then plugged one end of her headphones into her ears and the other into her phone.

"That was nice of her," Wes smiled at me as he sat down.

"Do you want me to switch spots with her? She was obviously into you. You could be like Owen and meet the love of your life on a plane."

"I do love older women. Maybe she's looking for a sugar baby."

I'd lick sugar off of Wes at this point.

My phone dinged in my lap. I resisted looking at Emma when I saw her name across my screen. I turned my phone away from Wes to read it.

That happy trail leads to happier things. And you can thank me later for the girlfriend question.

There was still Owen.

I laughed under my breath and sat back. My arm grazed Wes',

which was on the armrest, reacquainting me with goosebumps.

Emma put her head against the wall and closed her eyes. Emma never slept on planes, so I knew what she was doing. Wes leaned over to dig in his backpack, and his thigh pushed itself into me slightly. His legs were too long for the little box space of a coach seat.

"You should have bought a first-class ticket so you could fit," I said into his back.

"You're telling me," he replied over his shoulder. "I can't find my headphones. I swear I packed them."

I held out one of my earbuds to him. "Want to watch a movie? I'll let you choose, or have you seen all of them?"

I was only being a nice person. Anyone else would have done the same in my position—the position of being a headphoned seatmate seated next to a non-headphoned seatmate. Not the position of being a sex deprived woman who wanted to share a pair of headphones so she could have an excuse to lean into her semi-friend. I was the former, not the latter.

"I'll have to peruse the movies before I decide on something so crucial." He looked up to my screen and swiped through the very limited list before smiling at me. He swiped through them again as we started to taxi onto the runway. "First we need alcohol."

He grabbed a notebook and a pen from his backpack and started scribbling. I read over his shoulder as he wrote out the rules of a drinking game.

We'd taken off by the time he was finished.

"Too many?" he glanced at me.

"Definitely not. How many beers do you think we need for that?"

"Three's too many, right? Two each?" he guessed.

I reached over and ripped the page out of his notebook. I nudged Emma awake and held the page in front of her face. "You in?"

Her eyes glossed over the paper. "Does a bear shit in the woods?"

I cracked a smile and pressed the button for the flight attendant.

"We need six… Michelob ULTRAs?" Wes looked at us to confirm, and we both nodded. "Michelob ULTRAs," he said with confidence back to the woman who came to help us.

"Six?" she questioned us like we were crazy, probably trying to decide if we were going to cause trouble.

I tried to pull out my most responsible face.

"Six." Wes held out his card to her between his pointer and middle finger, reminding me of the Post-it Note with his number on it that was in my desk drawer.

"Where are you staying?" I asked Wes as the flight attendant eyed us and walked away.

He furrowed his brow and looked at me with a sidelong glance. "Y'all's guest room."

The blood in my body momentarily turned into slush like a frozen strawberry daiquiri. Another thing Owen forgot to tell me. But maybe that meant there really wasn't a plus one that he'd gotten with his invitation. No other girl was going to come out of the woodwork.

"Oh, fun!" was all I said as my blood resumed pumping at a normal speed.

My phone dinged again.

That bed sure gets cold all alone.

I elbowed Emma's arm invading my armrest. Isn't it common knowledge that the middle seat gets the armrests for their sacrifice?

The flight attendant came back a minute later with six cold beers and handed us two each. I put my tray table down for my beers and slipped the piece of paper with the rules into the pocket so we could see them as we watched. I plugged my headphones into my TV, while Emma plugged her headphones into her TV, and we both pressed play at the same time.

I offered Wes my left earbud. He accepted it and leaned in a little closer to me as he slipped it into his ear and *Mean Girls* started to play.

We were one drink in by the time the movie was halfway through.

Wes shifted his arm and let it fall from where he had it propped up on his elbow across the armrest. His fingers were dangling right above my leg before I thought they made contact with my skin. Just for a split second—like when you think a bug is crawling on you, but when you look down, there's nothing there—his fingers were a ghost bug. When I looked down, his fingers weren't touching my leg. I questioned if they actually had.

The next time someone was called stupid, Wes flicked me with his middle finger, telling me to drink. Then he picked up his own beer with the same hand.

Transforming into the doctor was the last thing on my mind now. He opened the floodgates. I leaned a little bit to my left, as innocently as I could, and our upper arms connected. His body heat was the perfect temperature—warming me just enough but not too hot. We watched the rest of the movie, never breaking contact until the movie ended, and we chugged what we had left.

When the credits started rolling, we still had another twenty minutes until we'd land. Emma purposely turned to look out the window while she listened to music.

I crossed my legs toward Wes, letting the side of my calf touch his shin. I thought I saw his eyes look down where we were connected and flash some kind of eureka moment.

"Is *Mean Girls* your favorite movie?" I asked him.

"What's not to love? I've seen that movie more than twice, not including just now."

My brain continued a list it had started nine years ago. It already had many line items of things that drew me to Wes, but there had been a long hiatus in adding to it.

√ A man who doesn't always complain about chick flicks.

"Did you know there's a *Mean Girls* Broadway show? Do you go see musicals?"

He looked at me confused. "Are there people that don't?"

√ A man who sees plays.

"What's your favorite?" I asked.

"*Wicked*. Hands down."

My eyes lit up. I moved my foot up and down a little against his shin. I didn't really know why I was doing that at this point, but I didn't care if he noticed I was flirting with him. I wanted to make him flirt back. I wanted to feel that rush—a rush only Wes could give me.

"And then Idina Menzel turns around and does *Frozen*," he added.

√ A man without children who knows who sings *Let It Go*?!

"Who are you?" I laughed.

Then he did it. He reached his hand across my crossed legs, rested his hand on top of my thigh, and squeezed.

"I don't reveal my secrets," he joked, taking his hand back. "But I will tell you I know that because of my two sisters."

I raised my eyebrows at him. "Do you have a lot of secrets?"

I could think of at least one.

"Doesn't everyone?"

I thought about it and realized Emma probably knew all my secrets, and if she didn't know something, it was only because I forgot to tell her. I wondered then who he told about the pool table kiss.

"How tantalizing!"

He smirked at me, his voice playful. "They wouldn't be secrets if I told you."

"You must tell someone your secrets."

He nodded. "My older sister and Owen."

√ Close to his sister. I was trying hard to ignore that he brought up Owen.

"I imagine Emma knows everything about you," he added.

"She doesn't really give me a choice, or maybe I don't give her a choice," I mused. "What's your favorite thing to do in New York?"

Wes smiled at his feet.

"Oh, please tell me," I begged, resting my hand on his thigh and slightly shaking it.

"It's not a secret. It's silly," he explained. "When I have a free day, I go down to Battery Park and walk around in the gardens. Then, I go ride the carousel."

I laughed. Was this boy for real? Emma and I did that all the time 'in our youth.'

"Are you going to put that in your pocket to make fun of me later?" he asked.

"No! I'm only laughing because Emma and I used to get high and go ride the carousel at night. I love that place. We haven't done that in a while. We adult now—you know, sort of."

Wes laughed and nudged me with his arm. "Don't grow up too much."

Uh oh. A weird breeze blew through my body. I recognized the feeling that I hadn't had in over five years almost immediately. It was the feeling when you realize you like someone more than you previously thought, and it was more than just a physical attraction. It all just came rushing back in the blink of an eye.

Suddenly, we hit turbulence, forcing us to break contact. I uncrossed my legs at the suddenness.

Was this my life now? I was living for the next moment Wes

and I touched. While not completely guiltless, Owen wasn't there to watch it. And how much could I get away with without it looking like he was the sun in my own personal solar system?

It wasn't *my* fault. He opened the pressure-sealed lid like he opened a Snapple. You can screw the top back on, but now all you do is play with the safety button and listen to it softly pop again and again. After you read the fact, of course: Leigh Sullivan just realized sexual tension was most definitely a thing, whether it was one-sided or not.

CHAPTER 4

What is it about being home? That feeling you get when you step into your parents' house is not easily recreated elsewhere. The house you grew up in, even when it's not technically your home anymore, just feels like *home*.

As we pulled up in our Uber, I looked up at our white house sitting on the hill. The columns stretched high to the roof, and my mom had painted the door black since the last time I'd been home. I got the chills like the house was playing the crescendo of its song for me.

Or is it not really the physical house? Maybe it's whatever house your parents currently live in, regardless of if you've ever lived there. Maybe it's the feeling that you're not a kid with responsibilities or bills or whatever anymore. You get to partly feel young again. Mom and Dad are going to take care of you—make you a sandwich, maybe fold some of your laundry.

I even get a version of that feeling when I walk into Emma's house, so it must transfer to your best friends' houses. And I imagine it could transfer to your significant other's parents' house—if you like them.

"What is it about this house?" Wes said as I unlocked the door.

"Best feeling," Emma agreed when we walked into the foyer.

It wasn't just me.

"Leigh?" my mom's voice called from the kitchen, reverberating into the foyer. She rushed in with a face of pure joy. "Leigh! I'm so happy you're home. I'm going to cry." She brought me into a huge hug.

"Please don't, Mom. But I missed you too."

"Emma," she said, releasing me and bringing Emma into a hug.

"So good to see you, Nancy," Emma said.

My mom moved on to Wes. "And Wesley."

Wesley and Leigh. I'd never put that together before—Ley and Leigh. Like my (girl) friend from college, Jordan, who had a boyfriend named Jordan. I always wondered if they added Jordan to every sentence they spoke when they were alone together: "Pass me the ketchup, Jordan." "Sure, Jordan." "Thank you, Jordan." "You're welcome, Jordan." I wouldn't have been able to help myself.

Wesleigh. What a great couple name! I thought like the complete psycho I was.

"Mrs. Sullivan. It's been too long," Wes said as he bent down to hug her.

"Nancy, please! How many times do I have to tell you?"

"Nancy," he corrected himself. "Thank you so much for letting me stay."

"You are welcome any time. I'd like y'all to come more often, honestly. Owen and Katie should be here in a little while. Make yourselves at home! I need to finish cooking dinner. Your father's still at the store."

"Do you need any help?" Wes offered like the complete gentleman he always was.

I rolled my eyes at Emma. That was supposed to be the beauty of being at your parents' house, so I wasn't going to offer. Besides,

Uber Eats was probably my most used app. Does anything about my personality scream chef?

"No, no, of course not," my mom replied. "Go have fun."

Wes nodded, and I reached down to grab the handle of my suitcase slowly, trying to will Wes and his core virility to step in and help me.

Honestly, it was probably more his instinct to do the right thing and nothing to do with me trying to compel him. But I was rewarded anyway.

His hand came between my arm and the side of my chest, his fingers lightly wrapping themselves right above my elbow.

"Leigh," he said with a short laugh that was saying *let me and my manly arms touch you, flex their forearms for you, and relieve your gorgeous girly arms from having to lift something so heavy*. At least, that's what I heard. His mind was probably just saying my name because he's a man, and men aren't that complicated.

He picked up my and Emma's suitcases and started up the stairs. We followed, and I watched his chinos hug his ass with every step. He stopped in front of my door and put our luggage down for us in the hallway. He turned toward me, and we did that awkward sidewalk dance. He stepped to his right, I stepped to my left. He stepped to his left, I stepped to my right. We both laughed, and Wes reached out his hands and grabbed softly around my biceps before sliding them down to my elbows. I could feel my hair stand up, and I wondered if he could feel it poking his palms. He pulled me in a little closer and twirled us together one hundred and eighty degrees. I was dizzy from the half spin. Okay, that's a lie. No lying. Wes made me dizzy for other reasons than a spin.

"Thanks, we would have ended up in a never-ending loop. Stuck in a gif," I laughed.

"Who doesn't love a good gif?" he said amusingly before turning to go back downstairs to get his luggage.

So true. Why did I like everything that came out of his mouth? You can express every feeling ever in a gif—there's a perfect one for every situation.

"It's so thick, I'm having trouble seeing either of you," Emma expressed behind the closed door of my room.

I shot her a look. "Shh! He will hear you."

I put my suitcase in the corner and sat on my bed to admire my room—the high school version of myself. I ran my hands over my pink floral comforter as I studied my photo collage on the wall to my right. It was mostly me and Emma and me and Owen together with an occasional photo of a boy sprinkled in. My white desk and shelves were lined with trophies and medals from volleyball and debate. I still had most of my high school textbooks and yearbooks stacked on one shelf like unburied time capsules holding the past. But even unburied time capsules can be forgotten about.

"If you don't kiss him this weekend, I will," Emma joked as she lay down on the bed.

"No one's kissing anyone. Well, except for Owen and Katie and my mom and dad."

"Too bad. How long has it been now?"

"I don't know," I lied.

"We both know the answer."

"One hundred and ninety-two days, fourteen hours, fifty-three minutes, and seven seconds. Eight. Nine. Ten..." I *half* joked.

"Really too bad. Or maybe the longer this goes on, the better it will be when you finally get in each other's pants."

"Okay, Miss Six Days," I laughed.

"He's cute! I'm going out with him again next weekend," she told me.

Emma had good luck with dating apps. I did not. I ended up deleting mine because guys can be total dickheads—figuratively and literally. I received enough unsolicited dick pics in the four weeks I was on there to last me a lifetime.

"That's exciting. Is this date four or five?"

"Five."

Five was hard to get to with Emma.

"When do I get to meet him?" I sang.

"When I feel confident enough that he won't run away from your interrogations, *Mom*."

I shrugged. "I feel protective over my Emma. So sue me."

"My very own Owen," she laughed.

"I am nothing like him."

Emma shot me a skeptical glance. "If you say so."

"Hellllooooo?" Owen's voice bounded up the stairs.

I ran out my door, down the steps, and into his arms as I cried, "Ow!"

My mother had already gotten to him first. That sneaky mom thing where they hear every creak the house makes—making it way harder for you to sneak out at night. And Wes must have been downstairs talking to my mom because he was standing next to her. That sneaky good guy thing—talking to their friends' moms.

Owen laughed and hugged me tight, neither of us wanting to let go. I eventually did to hug Katie. Then my dad walked in the front door, and we started all over again. We were *that* annoying family.

"Dinner's ready," my mom said eventually, herding everyone into the dining room.

We sat around the large wooden dining table and passed around the salad, spaghetti and meatballs, and French bread as we talked. My mom poured everyone a glass of wine. Owen told us about his financing world. Katie told us a story about some famous doctor she met in her job as a pharmaceutical rep (only adding to the stereotype that they are all gorgeous). I told them about the Rawesome Sushi project the three of us were working on. Emma talked about the latest musical she and I went to see. My mom asked Wes about his old job, if he liked HMH Advertising, and how his dad was doing. She asked Emma about her parents. My dad, always the strong, silent type, mostly listened.

It felt good to be there, surrounded by people you love, who love you in return with no questions asked.

Eventually, we were full to our throats with noodles and bread. Emma and I excused ourselves (with another bottle of wine because we were never too full for that), so we could hang the lights in the backyard.

We started on the left side of the roof, attaching them with small nails and heavy-duty tape as we went around with the only step stool I could find. It was starting to create a starry effect, but we still had a lot more to go. When half the bottle of wine was gone, we reached the pool house at the back of the yard, and I glanced inside through the window to see Wes standing at the sink helping my mom do the dishes.

I wasn't sure what emotion I felt hit my heart. Pride, maybe. Batshit crazy pride for my non-boyfriend who was just my co-worker and brother's best friend. It should be Owen feeling proud that he was friends with someone like that—he probably was in a boy type of way (you know that weird way guys' emotions come to the surface differently than girls').

I needed to have my head examined.

I kept watching him through the window, smiling and laughing, as he talked to my mom. She would occasionally poke her head over where I could see her face through the window too. She was always a classic beauty, and I hoped I would look half as good as her when I was her age. Her reddish-brown hair was shoulder length and full, curled slightly in on the ends, and her bangs would fall over her eyebrows sometimes before she'd brush them back.

Dylan never did stuff like that. He was selfish. Selfish with his time, selfish with his emotions, selfish with his possessions, and even selfish in bed. He would never watch a rom-com with me. I tried to drag him to see shows, but he said they were too long and too boring. He never wanted me using his stuff, even if it was something completely meaningless. And when he came to my parents' house, he would sit on the couch and hardly talk to my family. He had made me laugh in the beginning, but he got more serious as time went on and got annoyed with my sarcasm more than he laughed. Maybe that's what Owen meant when he said I was better off. I'm probably making him sound worse than he was. We did have fun together—it's true that opposites attract. We'd go to concerts, we ate out constantly, and we walked around exploring every inch of New York. He'd even cook elaborate meals for me sometimes. But I don't think he got me.

As far back as I could remember, my mom and dad always had fun together. They laughed a lot—even their fights sometimes ended in laughter. They loved each other, so much occasionally, that Owen and I would get grossed out when we were younger. We'd make faces of disgust when they kissed or tell them to stop when my dad grabbed her ass. We'd tell them, "Don't be gross! Y'all are too old!" But my mom would always say that the key to happiness was staying young with someone.

I'd never considered what that really meant until her words started ringing in my head while I stared at Wes. I think that was the first time I started to feel glad Dylan broke up with me.

"Sticky eyes," Emma commented when we finished the pool house.

I rolled my very sticky eyes at her. "Gazebo next. It's going to look beautiful."

I positioned the step stool under the gazebo, but I couldn't reach, and Emma was shorter than me. I couldn't reach it standing on the chair either. The wooden beams were at least twelve feet high.

We were both staring up at it when the back door opened.

"Need some help?" Wes called.

"Yes!" Emma said.

Wes walked over to us, but the ceiling was still just out of his reach when he stood on the chair.

"I bet you could reach it on Wes' shoulders, Leigh," Emma suggested not so innocently as she sat down in a chair. She thought she was so clever, and I sprang my eyes open at her and mouthed, *Screw you.* She knew I was happy about it though.

"She's probably right," Wes said. "Want to try?"

I nodded my head as he crouched down. I slipped my legs around his neck, and he placed his right hand on my thigh as he used his left hand against the chair to stand up before placing it on my left thigh. I wondered if he could feel the temperature increasing through my jean shorts against the back of his neck as heat cascaded down between my legs. That should not have been turning me on. Emma was right, and as we moved together beneath the ceiling, his fingers would occasionally curl or brush over my skin, and a few times he strengthened his grip around me.

I was feeling bold. I placed my left hand over his as he stepped around a chair. "Don't drop me."

"What, like this?"

Wes dug his fingers into my thighs as he suddenly tipped me far to the side making my stomach bungee down to the floor and a stupid giggle escape my mouth.

"I got you. You're about as heavy as a leaf," he said as his fingertips brushed over my skin a few times before coming up slightly to lace through mine.

Harmless flirting was all it was. No one could see us. Owen was inside, and Emma's face was glued to her phone. I thought then that he could feel the sexual tension as much as I could. We were taking what we could get, when we could get it, from each other.

I didn't want that light-hanging task to ever end, but eventually, we came to the last section.

"Where's your phone?" Wes asked me.

"Uhhh." I looked around. "Over there on the table. Why?"

He didn't respond. Instead, he walked quickly over to the pool and threw me into the deep end as I laughed like a maniac, before he jumped in beside me.

I loved how he could manipulate my body with ease—pick me up off his shoulders like I was an actual leaf.

When I surfaced, Emma was looking over at us smugly.

I flipped her off as I treaded water. "You too, Emma. Jump in or I'll make Wes come pick you up."

She threw her phone down on the chair and dove into the deep end. After a minute Katie and Owen came out the door with a case of cold beer.

"I thought I heard a splash," Owen exclaimed. He pulled off his shirt, and Katie followed suit. Emma looked at me with her eyebrows raised, challenging me to do the same. I shook my head at her. I didn't want to compete with Katie's boobs. Not a game I'd win.

Owen and Katie jumped in and swam to the shallow end.

"Chicken fight?" Owen narrowed his eyes at me. It was our favorite pool game when we were kids. But now all I could think about was being back on Wes' shoulders.

Wes swam beneath the water toward me. I felt his head against the back of my legs as I spread them a little, so he could pick me up. He placed his hands back on my thighs and now our wet skin was gliding together like a granite curling stone on ice.

Owen popped up out of the water with Katie on his shoulders, and Wes and I won the first round. Owen held up Emma who beat me. Then Emma won again with Katie on Wes' shoulders. In our last round, I beat Emma, and I held up my arms triumphantly. Wes high-fived me before he picked up his feet from the bottom of the pool and we both slid beneath the surface. He ran both of his hands down the entire length of my legs before squeezing my ankles. I had shaved that morning, but the prickling he was leaving in his wake was standing up every hair I had on end, and I'd have to shave again the next day. I slid off of him, immediately craving the contact.

Owen passed around beers, and he and Katie swam over by the steps and talked by themselves, so Wes, Emma, and I took turns on the diving board. On his second turn, Wes pulled off his shirt that had been clinging to every curve of his muscles.

My eyes became molasses, stuck on every body part he slowly revealed as his shirt came up higher. When it came up over his head and arms, his abs and upper body tensed at the slight increase in effort required. I had to put my tongue back in my mouth.

"I've never been so happy to be a fifth wheel," Emma whispered to me. "You should take off your shirt too. I promise he'll look at you the same way."

I shook my head at her slowly, still in my trance. "I can't help but look at him."

"Katie distracts Owen so much, he will never notice."

I glanced over at them. Owen didn't give a damn about what the three of us were doing. Katie was straddling him under the water as they talked and kissed.

"They'll be leaving shortly; you can guarantee it. They're practically having sex over there," Emma said under her breath. She narrowed her eyes. "Ew, maybe they already are."

"Ew," I laughed.

Like clockwork, Owen said, "We're going to go up. Goodnight y'all." They walked out of the pool, grabbed a few beers, and made their way inside.

Emma jokingly winked at me. "I won't make it so obvious

when I go up, I promise."

I rolled my eyes at her and looked over at Wes drinking his beer next to the diving board. "He would never kiss me. Guy code."

"He already has."

Is staying away from your best friend's sister a normal rule between guys or part of the stupid douchebaggery rules of guy code? Wes wasn't a douchebag. And once guy code is broken, does it cease to exist? I wasn't privy to the rules of being a guy.

The three of us drank and played various pool games like handstands and washing machines. That had always been my and Emma's favorite together when we were kids, and we were remembering our youth being back there. We sat on the steps and talked for another ten minutes before Emma asked us if we wanted another beer as she got out of the pool.

She came back and held them out to us. "I'm going to go use the bathroom."

She wasn't coming back.

"The lights look great," Wes said, opening his beer.

"Thanks for helping," I replied.

"You were born to throw parties. I think you came out with a party hat on and a party horn in your mouth."

"Even newborn Leigh loved a good party. Maybe my mom drank too much alcohol when she was pregnant with me."

Wes laughed. "That is so wrong. Your mother is a godsend."

"She's alright," I said sarcastically before I nudged him with my knee under the water. "She adores you though. Doing her dishes, talking to her."

"I probably adore her more. She was really there for me after I lost my mom. I came here a lot with Owen after she passed." He shifted his leg back into mine, leaving it slightly against me.

"I'm so sorry, Wes. Owen told me about that. How long has it been?"

"Two years." He looked down into his beer and paused. "Sometimes it still feels like yesterday, but it gets easier each day."

"I'm sure she was a great mom." I was so bad at serious conversations. I never knew the right thing to say without being sarcastic.

"She was." He looked back up at me and nodded. The pool lights made his eyes appear a deeper blue. He took a sip of his beer, breaking eye contact. "You know, I took care of her for a year when the cancer got worse."

"No, I didn't know that."

"To make it even worse, that's when Rachel cheated on me. She blamed it on me not being around enough at the time. Can you fucking believe that? I wasn't around enough for her while I was taking care of my dying mother. Supposedly, the guilt was eating her alive. Or so she said, but she didn't tell me until a year after my mom died because she didn't want to 'pile it on.'" He laughed morbidly under his breath. "Anyway, I had to get out of Nashville."

My heart picked up speed at the intimacy of the conversation. He seemed to think Owen had told me all of that, but of course, he hadn't. Why did shitty things have to happen to good people sometimes? And vice versa. I had only just become aware that he was playing with my left ankle bone. I wasn't sure how long he had been doing it because I couldn't remember feeling him start. His thumb was rubbing over it, then circling around it. I wasn't sure he even knew he was doing it. He was staring into the pool.

"You didn't deserve that. If she couldn't recognize that you were carrying out one of the greatest acts of love, then that's on her. Taking care of someone like that is probably one of the hardest things a person has to do in their life. It's selfless."

He ran two of his fingers up and down over my Achilles tendon. "I'd do it again in a heartbeat. To be with her again, but it's hard having to remember her like that. I'm glad I got the opportunity to show her I could be an unselfish version of myself." His eyes made contact with mine, and he quickly pulled his hand back, making a small splashing sound. "Sorry, this is depressing."

I shook my head, and a shiver ran down my spine.

"Are you getting cold?" he asked me.

"No," I sort of lied. I wasn't sure what the shiver was in response to. Maybe I was a little chilly, but Wes was plucking the strings of my heart, playing my emotions like they were notes.

He shifted on the step, breaking our legs apart. "So, can you believe Owen is getting married?"

I laughed. "Nope. It pains me to say I laughed when he first told me."

"Classic Leigh!"

"I'm not that terrible, am I?"

He looked over at me with a smile. "Of course not. You make everything better."

Was that a drunken slip of the tongue?

"I know I hurt his feelings. But I was having a terrible week. My boyfriend had just broken up with me, and he bought the couch that we had in our apartment." Wes shifted to make eye contact when I said 'broken up', the look of eureka back in his eyes. No wonder. He didn't know I was single, but he probably guessed it on the plane. "So, when he moved out, he took it with him, which only fueled my anger every day I had to look at that empty space." I laughed at myself and how different I felt now. "So, I was a bitch to Owen for no reason. God, even thinking about that conversation now makes me upset at how I acted. I never thought he would get married before me."

"I didn't think Owen would *ever* get married," he smirked. "But they're great together. I'm really happy for him."

I nodded at him and sipped my beer. "If he's into hot girls, and that sort of thing, then I guess she's perfect for him."

"Have you given up on guys?" Wes joked. "What happened with him? Dylan?"

Hearing him say Dylan's name brought no emotion, other than the exhilaration I felt realizing Wes always remembered my boyfriends' names.

"I'm fairly certain he dumped me for a sexy neurosurgeon, so who can blame him?"

"Well, brain surgery *is* sexy, but I'm sure your brain is sexier," Wes quipped. "Did you love him?"

Then he dropped a compliment like that on me but didn't give me enough time to acknowledge it before he asked me a question. Probably just drunken slip #2 of the tongue. We'd been drinking since three-thirty in the afternoon.

"I did," I confessed. "But now I realize it's more complicated than that. I think I thought I did—thought I wanted to marry him. Surprisingly, thanks to something Owen said."

Wes nodded like he understood. I think that might be a universal feeling for people who have found someone better after being completely heartbroken.

"No dating luck of your own since then?" he asked me.

I snorted. "No. I did the app thing for, like, a month. I won't be going back to that. I could fill an album with all the dick pics I got right after the first hello."

Wes laughed. "Do girls even like dick pics when they come from a consensual sexual partner?"

"I'm sure they exist," I said with a shrug. "I've never met one though."

"I tried that too when I first moved to New York—not the dick pics—the apps. Didn't last very long. I didn't find anyone I wanted to hang out with after a few dates."

"Maybe I would have had more luck if I'd found guys like you on there."

I couldn't make my mouth stop fast enough once I realized what I was saying. Drunken slip #3.

I tried to follow up quickly like Wes had done. "Emma meets nice enough guys on there."

"Where'd she go?" he said, realizing she hadn't come back from the bathroom.

"She probably got tired."

If he was connecting the dots in his mind, he didn't let it show.

"What time is it?" he asked.

"I don't know. Late?"

Wes rose from the step and went over to where I left my phone on the table hours before.

"It's after two," he said, shocked.

"Big day tomorrow," I exclaimed, standing up.

We looked at each other and hesitated before we both started picking up the beer cans scattered around the pool. We threw them in the outside trash, and Wes picked up his cold, wet shirt and unplugged the lights for me. Everything suddenly turned blue from the lights around the sides of the pool. We made eye contact, his smile causing my stomach to spin like a Tilt-A-Whirl. I felt the hesitation again, the strain. He walked over to the light switch and turned off the pool lights. Everything went black.

I walked toward the door with him close behind me, exceedingly aware of his presence hovering behind me, as we walked through the dark living room, up the stairs, and into the hallway, passing every picture hung on the wall of me and Owen at every age. I hesitated at my closed door for the briefest of seconds. I didn't even know what I was going to do or say. I just didn't want to go into my room. I just wanted to be with him a moment longer. But ten pairs of Owen's *Mona Lisa* eyes were staring at me from every photo on the wall.

"Goodnight," Wes said, leaning down toward my ear. He ran his hand down my right arm as he stepped around me.

"I'd tell you a dick pic joke, but I don't want to seem cocky," I said softly.

He chuckled as he walked further down the hall. The sound was music to my ears.

"Good. I wouldn't want to laugh too *hard,*" he said without turning.

"Goodnight, Wesley," I whispered.

I LAY NEXT to Emma, who was snoring softly, for forty-five minutes. I kicked her gently, so she'd roll over and stop. I would never be able to go to sleep with her making a racket. But I couldn't fall asleep anyway.

I picked up my phone and stared at the screen contemplating my life choices. He might still be awake, and I was okay with making some bad ones.

I texted Wes: **Me at 3 a.m.**

I followed that with a gif of a woman singing at the top of her lungs.

Five seconds later he sent me a gif of Patrick Star sitting in bed eating a hamburger.

And you're a *SpongeBob SquarePants* fan?! You're a gift that keeps on giving, I said.

Wes replied: **I watch it alone on Saturday mornings. Don't tell anyone.**

My vault is so secure I have to sing a song to unlock it. I thought you didn't reveal your secrets.

Then I hesitated over my keyboard deciding how forward I wanted to be.

I chose: **Tell me another one.**

It was flirty but left it open for him to respond in the way he wanted.

He took it further: I didn't want to come upstairs.

Then why did we? I responded.

I don't know. Maybe multiple reasons. Tell me one of yours.

I was sure one of those reasons was Owen. The others could possibly be that we worked together, or we were at my parents' house. And how could I pick just one secret? I had an unlimited supply involving him going back to freshman year of college when Owen first introduced me to him.

I went with: I stalked you on social media in college.

The time I spent trying to see where he was, where he was partying with Owen, and who he was seeing is something I'd rather not admit.

You are obsessed with me.

How topical! I replied about his *Mean Girls* reference.

I'm a topical guy. I'm guessing you're full of secrets, only your hair isn't that big.

You only get the one, I told him.

He followed with: I can be patient.

We were full-on flirting at this point, and I had a sudden urge to pull the reins. He must have had the same feeling.

Do you still always stay up this late? he asked. Wes and I were always the night owls.

Hard to turn this brain off. But I should probably try. Lots to do in the morning!

Night.

I stayed up for another thirty minutes wondering if this was worth jeopardizing Wes and Owen's friendship. If something went sideways, could they still be friends? But what if it could be something more? Was it worth it to try?

CHAPTER 5

In-Person Kathryn was not the same person as On-the-Phone Kathryn. She was spunk. She was sass. She was boss. And I was there for it.

She ordered the men around (even my dad), directing them where to put the tables. She made them unfold every chair and place them exactly how she wanted with a certain spacing that took her forever to decide on. When the alcohol arrived, she had them carry the heavy boxes to the bar and set all the bottles out arranged in a certain order.

When Emma came back with the flowers, Kathryn inspected each one before deciding which vases went where.

Emma and I hung the banners (that we didn't get around to the night before) I'd had made across the pool house and the gazebo, and above the front door. My mom had bought a big diamond ring door hanger. Emma laid out all of the silverware and plates while I put the coozies in a basket on the bar. One side said *Owen's Sullying Katie's Good Name*. The other side said *But Katie Still Harts Owen* with a heart around Harts. The best puns I could come up with from their last names.

The photo booth delivery guy arrived, and Kathryn spent

fifteen minutes telling him how she wanted it set up so the backdrop would be just right. At one point, I saw Wes say something to him under his breath, and the guy laughed.

When the food arrived, Kathryn had them place the food in a certain order so it was cohesive as you moved down the buffet. Kathryn ordered Wes and my dad to get the cake from inside and put it on a certain table.

She started to make Owen go get the balloons from her car but changed her mind because he was canoodling with Katie under the gazebo. She spun around and pointed at Wes, who dutifully went out to the car and came back with six huge bunches of balloons. I questioned how she fit them all in her car and drove to the house, but if she'd gotten into an accident, it wouldn't have mattered because she would have been wrapped in bubble wrap.

Katie instructed Wes where to put each one, and when he was done, she stepped into our back doorway to admire everything. All the men held their breath.

She pointed at a balloon bunch and nudged her finger to the right. Wes picked it up and dropped it a foot over.

She studied everything again before giving everyone a nod of approval.

"Looks great guys!" she said loudly.

All of their shoulders relaxed in tandem.

"I need a shower after that workout," Wes declared and went into the house.

Emma and I went upstairs to get ready. We stood in front of my mirror, me in front doing my makeup on the ground, her standing behind me straightening her hair. Then we switched places so she could do her makeup, and I could curl my hair.

"Which dress should I wear?" I held up a flowing floral spaghetti strap dress and a royal blue princess cut dress with a low back.

Emma bounced her brown eyes between the two. "Blue, definitely. You have a sexy back."

"So, the floral one then?"

"No! Really, the blue one."

I gave in and slipped the blue one on. Emma put on a red shift dress.

"You and red are meant for each other," I remarked. Her tan skin, dark hair, and brown eyes contrasted so well with it. I pouted. "I need a color."

"In that dress, Wes will be the one with sticky eyes tonight. Y'all both need to stop resisting." She shook her head at me. "I can't *believe* y'all didn't kiss last night. My exit was phenomenal. Did he even notice that I didn't come back?"

"Not until I mentioned your name."

"Well, that was your first mistake," she joked as she opened the door.

"I think my one hundred and now ninety-three-day streak I have going is messing with my head," I said quietly.

If I hadn't been on this sexual sabbatical, would these feelings even be bombarding my brain, my heart, and my sexual organs?

We made our way back downstairs and into the backyard. It was just starting to get dark, and the yard was already full of people. When we stepped through the doorway, Wes looked up from where he was sitting with the groomsmen under the gazebo. He was leaning forward, elbows on his thighs, with a beer in his hands. He'd changed into a white button down and khaki pants and the lights I'd hung were cascading a yellow hue over him.

Our eyes weren't just sticky, they were superglue.

"Told you. I'm some sort of magician," Emma whispered softly near my shoulder. "If you think he can't take his eyes off you now, wait until he sees the back of your dress."

"Excuse me," a woman's voice said behind me, ripping my eyes off Wes in an almost painful way.

"Sorry," I replied as I moved out of her way. I turned to Emma. "I need a drink."

This push-pull wasn't good. We couldn't keep doing it. I knew myself too well. I would push the boundaries and hope to get away with a little more each time. Hell, I was already in the process of doing that.

I poured myself a glass of white wine at the bar and turned to talk to Emma, but my eyes glanced right back to Wes. We made eye contact again, but this time we looked away at the same time. *That* was a look filled with guilt.

Is there a weird word I don't know about for the unexplainable and involuntary way someone's eyes dart to things they shouldn't look at? You know you shouldn't look at it, but it's the only thing your eyes can now focus on, and you can't figure out why you can't stop. Like a car wreck or Katie's cleavage. Whatever that word is, it was happening to me. Or us.

Because every time I glanced at Wes, he was glancing at me. We'd move around the party, completely separate but always aware of where the other one was. I'd be talking to someone by the pool house, and he'd be at the bar. I'd be in the gazebo, and he'd be talking to someone at a table. Buffet versus yard. Yard versus buffet. Inside versus outside. Outside versus inside. Yes, even through the window, we caught each other's eye.

I was playing a sick twisted game of not wanting to come between my brother and his best friend but wanting to really fucking badly.

"Leigh, this party is amazing," Owen said, walking up from behind and putting his arm around me like he caught my stream of consciousness. "Thank you so much! As usual though. I think I just realized I wouldn't have been cool in high school if my name wouldn't have been attached to your parties."

I put my head against his upper arm, laughing at his lie. He knew girls who weren't me thought he was hot, which is why he was actually cool in high school. He wasn't the modest twin.

And he wasn't the tall best friend, but it was close. There was this picture in my parents' living room that Owen absolutely hated of me and him in eighth grade. It was from our spring break beach trip, and I am towering over Owen. Like at least five inches. And I'm only five four. The following summer Owen hit some insane growth spurt, and he entered high school over six feet.

"Of course. I'd do anything for you, Ow. Is Katie having fun?"

We both glanced back at her in her white dress talking with a few bridesmaids and admiring some of her gifts. She was holding up a Dutch oven like she was a natural domestic wife. Maybe it's all the home and kitchen wedding gifts that turn you into a cook. Eh, probably not. Naturally, I wanted a ruffled pie dish, but I would never actually make a pie from scratch. I'd just be a wife who admired everything sitting in my cabinets.

"She's in wedding heaven. Between you and me, it's a little insufferable really, but I'll put up with it for her," Owen laughed.

"Look at you sacrificing. I'm so happy for y'all. I really am sorry for the way I acted when you first told me. It's so nice to see you finally in love."

"I think I love her too much. Is that possible?"

"Nope, not possible." I paused. "Well unless you, like, kill for her or something. I wouldn't be happy about being interviewed for the documentary they'd make about you."

"Make sure you paint me in a good light. It's all for love."

"Well, I'd say anything they wanted me to as long as it came with a big enough check."

"Fair. As long as y'all got rich while I sat in prison, I'd be content."

"I want to love someone too much," I pouted.

"How are you doing since the Dylan breakup?"

If only he knew.

Well, Ow, I thought. *I've moved on from that Dyl-weed to your winsome Wes of a best friend. Are we cool if I just bring my sexual fantasies with him to life? Good? Good.*

"Good," I stumbled. "I'm good, I promise. You were right. I think I am better off."

He winced. "*I'm* sorry I said that. I was mad you laughed at me. I shouldn't have thrown that in your face like that. Especially that week. Have you gone on any dates recently?"

I shook my head. "Nope. Six months and counting."

"Don't worry about it. I know you're going to end up with someone better than him. You deserve a lot more than he gave you."

"When did you become so wise, big brother?"

He shrugged. "It happens."

"Did all of you know he wasn't the one for me and just neglected to tell me?" I asked, remembering I suspected that he felt that way.

"I wouldn't say that. But I think we all thought he wasn't good enough for you. Plus, he hardly talked to us. You know Mom hated that."

"Alright, so the next guy will have one characteristic—talk to mom. Doesn't matter if he's boring or ugly or a deadbeat."

"Don't compromise on any, Leigh! Haven't you been listening to what I've been saying," he teased me. "If you want my honest opinion, you need someone just as fierce and loyal as you. Someone who appreciates your little Leigh things. And it *has* to be someone I like. Why do you always date guys I don't like? Can't one of them just be cool?"

My eyes glanced to Wes. He was everything Owen described, but a feeling of disloyalty overcame me. We both were being disloyal to Owen, weren't we?

But Owen and Wes had those strange man crushes on each other. I knew that's not what he meant. He wouldn't be thrilled if he knew I liked his best friend, but Wes did pretty much fit Owen's description to a T. Owen just didn't realize who he was describing.

"I love you, Ow," I said as I hugged him.

"Love you, little sis." He looked back at Katie and then looked back at me with wide eyes. "I'm getting married!"

I pushed him away. "Go back to her. I know you want to."

He walked backward for a few steps before turning around and making his way back to Katie. I smiled as he brought her into a hug and kissed her.

I found Emma and dragged her into the photo booth. We stood at a high table afterward, laughing at the four pictures, when her eyes glanced behind my shoulder. She stopped mid-sentence as her eyes went wide. She looked back at me, took a sip of her drink, and started walking away.

He was coming.

Wes' beer, in his left hand, was the first thing I saw in my peripheral vision. He rested it on the table next to my arm, keeping his hand wrapped tightly around a coozie where I could only see *Owen's* like the universe was telling me that Owen had already called dibs. He stood angled to the left slightly behind me. I didn't look up.

"What are you doing to me, Leigh Sullivan?" he said with his voice low in my ear, the meaning behind it worming its way into my heart. My eyes searched for Owen, but I didn't see him.

"*I'm* not doing anything to *you.*" My veins started pumping fire through my body instead of blood, telling me what I really wanted was to be doing anything and everything to him.

"Oh, it's all *my* fault?" he said with an amused tone.

"Yes," I whispered accusingly.

There it was, out in the open—us acknowledging whatever was going on between us, and us acknowledging that whatever it was, it shouldn't be happening.

"Did you wear this dress just to torture me?" His hand lightly rested on my shoulder.

Wes created this special ASMR within me—one that my body reserved only for him. I could feel it start in my scalp and move down my spine, as the waterfall started to flow.

I shook my head. I wanted him to run his hand down my back, but I wasn't so lucky.

"Okay, then," he said before turning and walking away.

What the hell was that? He was the tortuous one.

Thank God all the guys went out after the shower. But he had already become my drug—I was addicted to anything he would give me.

Emma and I were flipping through our old yearbooks in my room reminiscing about high school.

"Look how young you look. We were like babies," Emma laughed.

"I know!" I cried. "Isn't it weird to look back and think about how cool we thought we'd be in college; how old we would be? And now here we are five years post-college, and we still feel like children?!"

I took a picture of my senior photo with my ridiculous senior quote, "My brother hijacked my quote," and sent it to Wes.

So cringe, I added.

Emma eyed me as I texted but didn't say anything. She flipped through the pages. "Here's one of us in the cafeteria," she said, pointing to a picture.

"Why did we think our hair looked good like that?"

My phone buzzed.

You were a 2000s fashion icon!

I sold my soul to my mom so she would buy me those low-rise jeans.

I looked up and turned the page to senior superlatives. I scanned them, bringing back so many memories.

I texted Wes: **Guess what my senior superlative was.**

"Of course, you won prettiest hair," I said to Emma as I ran my hand over it. "It's like silk."

"Don't get your hand grease all in it," Emma said, swatting my hand.

I rolled my eyes at her and when I read Owen's—biggest flirt—when Wes texted me back.

Biggest life of the party...?

Most likely to get away with anything. That one should have gone to Emma though.

Also fitting. What was mine?

Best eyes? I guessed.

Nope, tallest. So original.

A minute went by while Emma and I were laughing through the list as we read them out loud.

My phone buzzed again. He was peeling the layers back just as much as I was.

You like my eyes?

I smiled that goofy smile that people do when they are texting someone they like.

Emma called me out, "I know that smile."

"Shut up," I grumbled at her.

Of course. Gray is the rarest eye color, I replied.

Emma and I finished flipping through our senior year before moving on to junior year. I kept glancing at my phone, but Wes didn't respond.

I couldn't help but wonder if that was on purpose, designed to leave me wanting more, or if it had something to do with Owen being around.

LEIGH MAKES THREE

—

WES WASN'T ON the same plane back with us to New York. That was probably a good thing because Monday morning I was sitting at my desk refusing to look at him. I wasn't sure if it had to do with being in public or at work. I guess, for me, it was more about trying not to drag myself down deeper.

I scooted my chair in so close to my desk so I wouldn't see half of his body through the glass. Even when I had to shift, I couldn't see a sliver of his arm.

I had to worry about my meeting with Rawesome Sushi anyway. I had gone over my boards and presentation one hundred times, proofreading and rehearsing. I ate lunch at my desk, so I could go over everything one last time.

As I was gathering my things, Wes' voice pulled my head up. "I wanted to tell you good luck." He couldn't help but be polite, even when he could tell I was trying not to interact with him. He wasn't being overly friendly to me either. We stared at each other for a beat too long.

"So, are you going to tell me or just tell me you wanted to?"

That tug of a smile. That bluing of his eyes.

"Good luck, Leigh. Not that you need it," he said before going back into his office.

"Good luck!" Emma called from her desk as I passed her door.

Jack gave me a thumbs up as he passed me in the hallway.

I set up the mood boards Wes and I worked on around the conference room. I plugged in my laptop and pulled up the presentation on the projector screen against the back wall.

In front of each seat, I put a water bottle and the packets I'd printed out that morning. I made coffee in the break room and brought it back into the conference room with cookies and fruit I'd picked up that morning on the way to work.

I surveyed everything before sitting down to collect my thoughts. Even after years of giving presentations in that job and years of high school debate, I still got nervous at the thought of public speaking. But the pinnacle of that type of project was the best part.

And after I finished, I was confident I killed it. Wes' ideas brought everything together: the logo, the fonts, the colors, the essence. Really, he should have given the presentation alongside me. I was kind of mad I hadn't thought of it—not just to be in the same room with him, but because he deserved the recognition.

The owners, manager, and chef each shook our hands as they left our conference room, leaving me and Daniel alone.

"Great work," he praised me.

"Thanks, Daniel. I think they liked everything we've put together. I'm excited to work with them."

"He said he'll be in touch this week. Email that presentation over to them and copy me," he requested.

"Wes was a big part of the success, so he deserves every bit of credit as well."

Daniel nodded as he walked out.

Back in my office, I heard Daniel congratulating Wes on his hard work.

That night my phone dinged around midnight. When I saw Wes' name, my stomach unexpectedly plunged into a dunk tank I didn't know it was sitting above. Maybe he was only trying to be professional at work earlier that day. We were navigating uncharted territory.

He texted me a *Parks and Recreation* gif of Andy talking about how he was allergic to sushi.

Could you be any more perfect? *Parks and Recreation* **is one of my all-time favorites.**

I wished I could take it back as soon as I sent it.

Favorite character? he replied.

Jerry Gergich. Always the butt of the jokes, but never took it personally. My kind of person.

He liked my message and said, Mine's Ron Swanson. He's got that soft side under there.

I sent him a link to a website explaining what your favorite character says about your personality.

Is 'tallest' also 'biggest softy'?

I'm a softy at heart, but if you tell anyone I'll deny it, he replied.

Ooh, another Wes Adams secret. I'm going to need my own Wes Adams vault soon.

I trust you.

Oh, the implications behind that. It made my heart flutter like I was housing a hummingbird. The text message: a modern love letter. I would have loved to see Jane Austen's take on a flirty text.

But I'm no Jane Austen. The next thing I would have texted would've gone way too far. I had to put my phone away. We were in dangerous terrain. The pull was so strong between us—this was why we never gave the other our phone number. I was sure of it.

The next day we played the same card—Work Leigh and Work Wes. From the outside looking in, nothing was happening between us. We were already experts at having undeclared secrets, so what was another one? To anyone else, we were definitely not two people who had secret text message conversations in the middle of the night.

But neither one of us could stop.

CHAPTER 6

That night, I texted him first. I was already up to my neck in quicksand. I didn't think there was any point in trying to get out. I wasn't sure I wanted to. I tried to rationalize it. It's not like we were sexting. We were just having fun—innocent fun.

Would you rather eat old sushi or drink sour milk?

Old sushi, I think. Sour milk makes me gag, but I don't think I've ever smelled old sushi.

We took turns going back and forth.

Him: Would you rather burp butterflies or fart sequins?

Me: Burp butterflies. I would go around making people happy because who doesn't love butterflies.

Me: Would you rather everyone know your internet search history or read your mind?

Him: Internet search history. It's not that terrible.

Him: Would you rather change genders every time you cough or never drink coffee again?

Me: Genders. I've always wanted to know what it'd be like to be a guy, and I can't live without coffee.

> Me: Would you rather only age in your face or your body?
> Him: Hard one. I think body and I'd work out a lot.

> Him: Would you rather vomit on someone or be vomited on?
> Me: Ew. Vomit on someone because ew!

> Me: Would you rather completely chew off your own toenails or bite someone else's fingernails a little shorter?
> Him: Stranger = my own toenails because ew! A girlfriend = her fingernails because I could handle that.

> Him: Would you rather have no elbows or no knees?
> Me: I think no knees. I'd want to be able to bring my hands to my face.

We went on like that for over an hour.

See, innocent fun.

Wednesday night we played 20 Questions—the version where you have to narrow down the answer. We chose characters from various things. I started with Squidward from *SpongeBob SquarePants* and Wes got it in twelve questions. He chose Dwight from *The Office*, and I got it in sixteen questions. We went back and forth. I lost on Waldo from *Where's Waldo?* He lost on Hello Kitty.

More innocent fun, I told myself, rationalizing my addiction like a true addict.

Thursday night Wes texted me first. And it wasn't an innocent text, though it was disguised like one. It was the perfect opening to take things further.

> You're going to turn me into more of an insomniac than I already am.

Dopamine rushed to my brain. My toe played with the line as I thought about how to respond. I decided to put my whole foot over it.

I lie in bed and think about you too.

What do you think about? he pushed.

I pushed further. How much I want to know all your secrets.

He grabbed me and pulled me completely over the line. I'll tell you whatever you want to know.

I wanted to know everything there was to know about him. I didn't know where to start, so I decided to start slow, and I'd work my way in.

What superpower would you want?
Teleporting.

Biggest fear?
Stupid one is needles. Deep one is my dad or sisters dying of cancer.

I took it up a notch on the personal scale.
Last time you cried?
My sister's wedding nine months ago.

I dialed it back.
What's your guilty pleasure?
Macarons.

Did I want to start to turn it in a sexual direction this fast?
Your love language?
Quality time.

I told myself to go back, so I asked a deeper question.
Biggest regret?
Walking away from you on that pool table.

There it was. He worked it in himself. The unspoken became spoken (or texted). Guilt hit me like a semi-truck, but I kept going, the pleasure centers in my brain were hyperactive and overpowering the guilt.

Do you feel guilty about that night?
Yes.

Has Owen told you to stay away from me?
No, not me specifically. I've heard him say it to other guys.

I offered a secret: I think about it all the time. Who knew you were such a good kisser?
I don't think my sixth-grade girlfriend would agree. My turn.

Did you know you are a better kisser?
No.

How often do you think about it?
Every day since you walked into our office.

Were you purposely flirting with me on the plane?
Yes.

Did Emma purposely go upstairs?
Yes.

Do you feel guilty?
Yes.

Do you think we should stop doing what we're doing?
Sometimes.

Do you think we should go back to being strictly work friends before it's too late?
Do you? I asked back instead.

I didn't know the answer. Maybe that's what he wanted. We'd both dragged each other down; pushing the other to be the instigator. Knowing we both wanted it, but knowing it wasn't something either of us should be doing.

Friends? he asked again.

I relented. **Friends.**

Friday was just another workday. Rawesome signed off on all our ideas, and we congratulated each other like any two friends who worked together and never talked outside of work would.

That night, I relayed the prior night's text conversation to Emma (like I'd done all week) at the bar after work.

"Whyyyyy?" Emma chastised me.

"That's what he wants, Em."

She scoffed. "You should have never brought up the guilt."

"But we both feel guilty."

"Whatever. You could have turned that conversation into some hot sexting. I bet he would have even come over if you asked. You could have finally broken your streak."

"Do you think this is what this whole thing is? Just me being so seriously deprived of male company that I have to go after the forbidden fruit?"

"Do you think it is?" Emma questioned me.

"I don't know," I said. "At first, I thought it was. But then I started to realize how much I genuinely like talking to him, like before. It's like college but stronger. Now we have direct communication whenever we want it."

I glanced at my phone. Our relationship in college was like Halley's Comet. Now it was like the sunrise.

Emma raised her eyebrows at me. "He's pretty much the opposite of Dylan."

"God, did everyone in my life fail to mention what a dipshit he was to me?" I asked exasperated. "You're supposed to be the one to speak up."

"He wasn't that bad, and you wanted to marry him. You

seemed happy, even though he had no sense of humor whatsoever. You wouldn't have listened to me if I had said something."

I laughed. "You're right, but I wasted so much time. Now I realize and it sucks."

I glanced at my phone again.

"For right now, just be happy you didn't marry him," she pointed out. "Wes is like filet mignon, and Dylan is like ground beef."

"Lobster and a barnacle," I laughed.

"A sports car and a bicycle."

"A diamond watch and a sundial."

"A yacht and a dinghy."

"So true." I nodded my head at her. "Where is Logan taking you tomorrow on date number five?"

Emma grinned like an idiot. "A pottery class."

"A pottery class?" I slowly repeated. "You *like* him, don't you!"

She laughed and squeezed her eyes shut. "I do."

"Aw, he's your Patrick Swayze," I said sweetly. "I'm going to buy you a pottery wheel as a wedding gift when y'all get married."

"And I'll buy *you* a big fat 'I told you so' when you and Wes get married."

"Uh huh," I muttered then glanced at my phone for the third time.

"Staring at your phone isn't going to make him text you. You pretty much told him not to, and he's too good of a guy to disrespect that."

"Ugh, I know," I said angrily.

"You two make a good team at work. I wouldn't be surprised if Daniel keeps asking you to work on projects together, so you better be prepared."

"You think? Don't get my hopes up."

"Make up your damn mind," Emma said. "You either be with

him and deal with Owen or remain friends and don't do anything. But with both options, you stop being wishy-washy.

"I wish it were that simple. I can't help how I feel. I'm like that swinging thing with all the balls."

"The only balls that should be swinging near you are Wes'."

The bartender, who was cleaning a glass in front of us, laughed under his breath with me. Okay, I unintentionally set Emma up for that one.

But on a serious note—and how I really meant it—I swung out far to the left wanting nothing but Wes, but when I crashed back into the stationary balls…spheres, the force pushed me out far to the right, not wanting to hurt Owen.

—

WES AND I worked cohesively as good, innocent, not-attracted-to-each-other co-workers should. The next week we got a call from a new boutique hotel that was referred to us by the owner of Rawesome Sushi. They weren't happy with their current advertising agency and were looking to see some ideas in a time crunch. Daniel requested that Wes and I work together to put together logo concepts.

"Your office or mine?" I asked Wes in the break room as I poured my coffee into my 'Caution: Contents Hot' mug Emma had gotten for me for Valentine's Day.

"Fan of Emma's?" he said, eyeing her face on the side of my mug.

"Her number one fan," I corrected him, then chose for us. "Your office."

Maybe I could chill out some if I wasn't in my own habitat. Wes sat in his swivel chair while I took a seat in front of his desk.

The Claire Hotel would be opening next year around the corner from Rawesome. It was going to be a boutique five-star hotel, and they felt their current advertising agency wasn't capturing their look and feel. The hotel's concept was unique and beautiful. The photos they provided us had lots of greenery, lots of dark woodwork, and a bright patio and vibrant pool.

Wes and I brainstormed fonts and colors throughout the morning. Wes felt that their name in a striking unique font would work best. I felt that we should combine dark and light colors, and I was leaning towards olive greens, blush pinks, and various shades of deep and vivid blue-greens.

After lunch, I hung posters around Wes' office with my color schemes, and Wes printed out THE CLAIRE in fifty different fonts, hanging each piece of paper up with tape. Mid-afternoon, Daniel came and checked on our progress.

"I'm liking it so far," Daniel said, standing against the wall and studying our work. "You've gotten further than I thought you would. Can you have something ready that we could send tomorrow morning?"

Wes and I glanced at each other. We were both thinking the same thing: *tomorrow*? It was already almost five. Tomorrow morning meant staying late. But we were both too dedicated.

"Of course," we said together because that's what Daniel wanted to hear.

"Great. Can't wait to see it."

We got back to work as soon as he left.

I stood in front of my color palettes and glanced back at Wes. "Do you think this blue-green is too green?"

His eyes sprang up to my face from where I thought he was checking out my ass. He studied the wall. "Yeah, if you use it go a little bluer and a little darker. That olive green is perfect though muted like that. So perfect, in fact, *olive* it."

"*Olive* your puns are cheesy. And I'm sticking with that as the main color. Website, etcetera—olive green and super light green. Adding blush pink and light robin egg blue as a secondary palette. Masculine and feminine. Four final colors, I think. Hopefully, they like it."

"I like it."

Emma poked her head in the doorway. "Bye, y'all."

I waved at her, and Wes gave her a, "Later, Emma."

"I think we should eliminate these three fonts, for sure." I pointed them out on the wall.

Wes nodded, so I took them down.

My phone dinged. Emma texted me: Take him across his desk.

I laughed, but I couldn't help glancing at the desk. I threw my phone back down on the chair. One by one, each light around us went out, and we were alone in the office. The sun set, casting the office in yellows, then pinks, then reds, all bouncing off the glass like a prism. Slowly, it became dark, and Wes' office was illuminated by the fluorescent lights above us. Not a very sexy atmosphere.

We'd narrowed it down to two fonts, both very similar, but we weren't one hundred percent happy with either.

"It needs some kind of unique characteristic," Wes said, sitting back in his desk chair at the computer.

"What if we pull the serifs out a teeny bit further? And widen some parts of the C and R? Give it a little bit of edge," I suggested. I leaned down near his shoulder and pointed to where I was referencing on the screen. I brushed him (I'll admit now it was on purpose) with my chest. "Here and maybe here?"

His shoulders stiffened, but he didn't respond.

"No?" I said unsure. "Maybe pull the bottom of the C out a little further than the top too? I don't know. Fonts and logos are your thing."

"Leigh, quit doing that," Wes said under his breath. He shifted away like he couldn't stand the smell of me.

"Doing what?"

It took him a second to respond. "I guess being *you*."

"I'm not doing anything," I whispered.

"Like hell you aren't." He swiveled around in his chair, leaned back, and brought one of his legs to the other side. I was standing just a few inches from between his knees. He rubbed his hand over his mouth—one of his little manly things that completely fascinated me.

"I'm not doing anything," I said louder. I didn't know if I should be offended or not.

He shook his head and looked up at me.

"You're over there standing." He pointed toward the wall with his head.

"You're over there crossing your legs back and forth." He pointed across from his desk.

"You're playing with your necklace. You're putting your hair behind your ear. You're putting your hands on your hips. And you're hovering above me smelling like flowers or strawberries or coconuts or I don't know what. You are doing *lots* of things."

His gray eyes ran down to my waist before he looked me up and down from my waist to my knees.

"*And* you're wearing this tight skirt," he added as he reached out and played with the bottom hem.

I looked down at my black pencil skirt and his fingers rubbing the fabric between his thumb and pointer finger before he brought his hand back and rested it on his thigh.

"How can I work with you being you, all the damn time?" he groaned.

"Me? You do the same thing," I accused him.

"I don't know what you're talking about," he said.

"*You* roll up your sleeves. *You* run your hand through your hair."

He shook his head. "You lean over the desk and your shirt drops."

"You put your hands in your pockets making your pants tighter."

"Your clothes are always tight," he countered as he reached up and grabbed my hip.

"You cross your ankle over your knee and lean back," I said as he rubbed his hand over my outer thigh.

"You pick up your leg with those high heels and scratch your thigh right under the hem of your skirt." His hand found my ass.

I had never been that turned on from such minimal contact.

"You shouldn't have touched me on the plane," I whispered as he pulled me in closer to him.

He sat up in his chair, shook his head, and looked up at me. His eyes looked like storm clouds. "It started way before that."

"So, blame it on the acquisition," I said breathily as his left hand gripped me right above my knee. The feeling of his large manly hand wrapped around my lower thigh was mind-blowing.

He shook his head again and his hand came up my inner thigh. "Before that."

"Like college?"

Did he feel it the entire four years like I did?

He finally nodded. "You're driving me crazy, Leigh."

"I'm not meaning to. And you're driving *me* crazy."

"Not on purpose," he said, squeezing the top of my inner thigh with his left hand.

Never mind, the upper thigh was even better.

"We're at work," I said hesitantly. Stupidly.

His hands released me. "Do you not want this?"

"You know I do."

"But this is a mistake." It didn't sound like a question.

"A mistake," I repeated.

He nodded slowly and brought his hand back down, trailing my inner thigh lightly with his fingers. "Then we should stop, shouldn't we?"

I nodded slowly back. I couldn't read his face. His eyes were cast downward, and it looked like his eyelashes were resting on the tops of his cheeks.

"We probably should," I said, not sure what I was saying. *Should* we, but we're not going to? *Should* we, but we won't just once and deal with the consequences later? *Should* we, and we really were going to?

He stood up, and my hands immediately grabbed his waist and pulled him closer. I wanted to feel his body against me. That might be the only chance I ever got again, and honestly, it was glorious having that all up against me.

"I want your hands back on me though," I told him quietly.

He glanced down at where I was holding him and pushed me gently back into the desk. His eyes followed his hand as he brought it up to caress my throat before he ran his thumb over my lips gently. I parted them slightly, and my tongue darted out to feel his fingerprint on the pad of his thumb. He slid his thumb into my mouth, and I sucked it gently.

"Do you want to stop?" he asked in a gravelly voice as he took his thumb back and tucked my hair behind my ear. I pushed my cheek against his palm.

Wes brought his hand down to my open shirt and slipped his hand just inside of it, caressing below my collarbone. I shook my head slightly. "Not really. Do you?"

"Definitely not." He pushed me up onto the desk, and my skirt came up halfway as I spread my legs wider.

His hands glided up my outer thighs, pushing my skirt up higher, as I rubbed his forearms that drove me into a tailspin. He looked down at my lips and back up to my eyes.

"And what if we don't?" he asked, stepping in between my legs. Actually, I couldn't choose the best feeling. They were all the best. I liked him between my legs. A lot.

I repeated his words in my head as his fingers continued to run over my upper thighs. I played a quick game of mental table tennis.

I'd finally have your lips on mine again.

Do: 1. Don't: 0.

But Owen would be mad.

1-1.

I might break my never-ending streak.

2-1.

But Owen would be mad.

2-2.

I like you more than just a hook-up.

3-2.

But Owen would be mad.

3-3.

You might like me back.

4-3.

But Owen would be mad.

4-4.

You might be everything I'm looking for.

5-4.

But Owen would be mad.

5-5.

Owen would be mad.

5-6.

Owen would be really mad.

5-7.

His lips had come closer to mine in the middle of my game. I could've stuck my tongue out and licked him, but he was looking at me, waiting for my answer. Waiting for permission to blow up our lives.

But I couldn't get it out of my damn head, so instead of saying what I really wanted, I said something stupid while screaming at myself not to say it.

"I couldn't live with myself if I came between you and Owen," I whispered.

Wes closed his eyes and took a deep silent breath. "Then we'll stop," he said gently, opening his eyes. He stepped back and picked up his jacket from the back of his chair. "I like your idea about the C and the R. I'll finish it first thing in the morning."

With that, he left me sitting on top of his desk with my skirt almost around my waist and my heart pounding.

Even if it was a mistake—even if we *should* stop—I didn't want to, dammit. It's easier to ask for forgiveness than permission, right? But my conflicting thoughts were overwhelming. I didn't know how I would cope with myself if I ever drove a wedge between Wes and Owen. He was my twin brother, and I was being unfair to him. I shouldn't have been chasing after his best friend so callously. Or was he chasing after me?

Maybe we were chasing after each other.

CHAPTER 7

I woke up early for some reason that next Saturday morning, even though I'd gone to bed too late as usual, and I couldn't fall back asleep. Every sound outside kept me up, every thump in my neighbor's apartment. So infuriating.

I pulled myself out of bed in a hunt for coffee and breakfast, but suddenly bagels and nova salmon were shouting my name from across the city.

I texted Jack and Emma: If for some godforsaken reason you're up, I'm going to Nell Bagel.

There was no way I'd hear from them for hours.

When I emerged from the subway station, I made the two-block walk in the expensive athletic wear I bought because I promised myself I was going to start doing Pilates. Psh. At least I looked good in it, even if I wasn't getting actual exercise. Walking two blocks counted as exercise in my world.

An hour later, I emerged from the restaurant with a bagel and iced latte in hand because the line had been out the door, even at six-thirty in the morning, and I couldn't find a spot to sit. But that was fine with me because Greenacre Park was right around the corner. It had been so long since I'd sat next to the waterfall, and it was a beautiful day outside.

I looked at my phone to see if I had a response. Nope, but I did read the date and time.

June 1st. God, how was it already June? The halfway month of the year that loves to freak you out about how fast time is moving—how fast life is passing you by. Why when you get older the faster time seems to speed up? Maybe it's the monotony of life. Work, sleep, work, sleep.

I walked up a few steps into the magnificent space. It was almost strange that this little slice of greenery existed in the middle of New York with tulip tables and wire chairs surrounded by lush flowers and trees. And the wonderful sound the waterfall made hitting the stones and pool below. The park was probably the size of half a football field. Maybe less. And at that time there was hardly anyone there.

So, if you were going to run into someone you knew accidentally, you wouldn't ever be able to escape without them noticing you. I couldn't dive under a table or shrink back behind a tree.

Instead, I stood like a deer in headlights, hoping Wes wouldn't notice me if I didn't make any movement—as if I could blend into his peripheral vision. I should have kept walking like any old stranger.

To make matters worse, I was staring at the back of a blonde female head. Rachel.

Time wasn't going fast anymore. The next fraction of a second was almost eternity. My head was going a mile a minute. I was contemplating how to back up without him looking five degrees to his side. I was wondering why I felt a punch to the stomach because it wasn't my business what he did in his free time or whom he did it with. I wanted him to turn and look at me so I could talk to him. I didn't want him to turn and look at me because I knew I had cream cheese on my face from the big bite I had taken right before I saw him. I wanted him to turn and look at me and realize we both made a mistake. I didn't want him to turn and look at me because I had zero makeup on and my hair was in a messy bun. I didn't want him to turn and look at me because I didn't want to talk to him.

As soon as I decided to try to walk backward, like I could simply rewind, his eyes connected with mine. I didn't think it was happiness that flashed across his face, but he smiled anyway.

"Leigh awake at seven a.m.," he said like he was hallucinating. "Or have you just been up all night?"

My mouth was full of carbs. "Ha. Ha," I muttered in a very unladylike manner. Anything more than that and he'd have been able to see the food in my mouth.

The blonde turned to look at me. Not Rachel, but of course, she was beautiful. I tried thinking back to the brunettes Wes had dated. Were there any? Was blonde his type? No, there was a brunette sophomore year.

"Did you attach an AirTag to me without me knowing?"

I swallowed finally. "No, I injected a GPS tracker in you while you were sleeping."

"Is that why my shoulder is so itchy?"

Maybe I shouldn't have brought up some weird comment about him sleeping. I had never seen him in any position like that, and I caught myself wondering if I was purposely trying to muddy the waters in this girl's mind.

"Anyway..." I started as I fumbled with some napkins to wipe my mouth. I could feel my eyes frantically looking between them like I'd suddenly developed nystagmus. I needed to get out of there.

"Leigh, this is my sister Charlotte."

Now that he said it, they looked stunningly similar. Of course,

Wes' sister would be a blonde bombshell. She didn't look very tall though. I wondered if Owen had ever hit on her.

"Oh, it's so nice to meet you," I said. I was too far away to reach my hand out, but close enough where I could take a step or two. I awkwardly hesitated too long.

"You too, Leigh. Do you want to sit down?" She smiled at me and motioned to the chair next to her, never taking her blue eyes off mine.

Wes looked like he wanted to tear his hair out. Maybe I'm exaggerating.

"No, I don't want to intrude," I offered, shaking my head. "I'm sure y'all never get to see each other."

"Oh, please?" she begged.

How many times could we go back and forth? Would she keep insisting?

I shrugged one shoulder and sat as Wes carefully watched me.

Charlotte felt like she had to fill the silence that was looming between us. "How do you two know each other?"

"We went to Vanderbilt together," Wes said at the same time that I said, "I'm Owen's sister."

The look on Charlotte's face the moment she confirmed to herself what she'd done was subtle but there. Giddiness almost. Wes was looking at the waterfall. God, why did I sit down?

"I see that now. You two look alike," she commented.

Wes looked back at me. Did he see Owen when he looked at me? That thought had honestly never crossed my mind.

Our friends always made remarks when I made a certain expression or said something specific about how eerily similar we looked, but I didn't think we looked that much alike.

"Do you usually insult people when you first meet them?"

"Oh my God, no. I'm sorry," she apologized. "I didn't—"

"Charlotte, she's kidding," Wes told her.

"Oh," she laughed.

I gave her a small smile, telling myself to act normal. "Trust me, I've heard enough about how hot he is, so I guess I'll take it as a compliment. You also look like your brother."

"I'll definitely take that as a compliment," Charlotte smiled before looking at Wes.

Of course, you do. Look at him, I thought to myself as I stared at him for too long. He turned to look at some flowers like they were the most interesting thing in the world. His hard jawline was clenched.

"How long are you here for?" I asked her.

"Just until tomorrow. I drove in yesterday from D.C." She paused like she was deciding whether or not to continue. "To celebrate Wes' birthday."

"Wes!" I exclaimed. "You didn't mention it was your birthday."

He groaned. "On purpose."

"Is it today?"

Wes wasn't going to answer, but Charlotte stepped in for me. "No, it's Monday."

"Do not throw me a work party," Wes scowled at me.

I pouted and put my hand on his thigh. Seriously, what was wrong with me? "Why are you so difficult?"

He raised his eyebrows at me like he was asking me the same question back. Or that's what I wanted him to be asking me so I could confess I made a mistake. I quickly took my hand back.

"Well then, I won't tell you mine," I huffed.

"February eighteenth," Wes smirked.

For some reason, I was initially shocked like I had forgotten that I was a twin and that the other twin was his best friend.

I turned back to Charlotte. "Are you the older or younger sister?"

"Older," she replied. "By two years."

"Has Wes always been so altruistic?" I asked.

Charlotte laughed. "Yes and no. He would do stupid things all the time, but then he could never lie."

"Can we be best friends? Tell me more," I said before I realized what I was saying. We definitely didn't need an additional best friend in this already complicated shit show.

"Umm, one time, he threw this huge party. It got really out of hand and the house was trashed. But Wes cleaned up everything himself. My parents didn't figure it out until a week later when my mom found a cup in the bushes. One look from her, and Wes spilled his guts. He could've made up some little lie and she would've believed him. He's too honest. It tears him apart. Even when he tries to lie, he has a tell. His eyebrow twitches. Mom didn't know about that one." She reached out and placed her finger on the edge of his eyebrow. Wes ducked away.

"Good to know," I said at the same time Wes said, "Thank you, Char."

Charlotte just smiled this closed-lip smile at me. She knew about me. I could feel it. Was she trying to give me some key to Wes' mind?

"I'm sorry. I need to use the bathroom," she said, rising from the table. "I'll be right back."

There were no bathrooms in the park. She was going to have to find somewhere to buy something so she could use the restroom. I watched her walk further away, wondering if she did it on purpose.

"You don't have to stay," Wes told me. "She'll get over you ditching her without saying goodbye."

"You want me to leave?" I asked, looking back at him.

"No." He shook his head and sighed. "That's not what I meant."

"You can leave if you want…" I offered. "I came to sit by the waterfall and eat my bagel by myself."

He scratched the side of his face like he was trying to decide how to respond. I could hear his leg bouncing up and down beneath the table. He looked back at me and narrowed his eyes. "What are you trying to say beneath that?"

"Nothing," I said, but *I WANT YOU TO TELL ME YOU DON'T WANT TO LEAVE!* is what I wanted to scream, but the atmosphere was suddenly different—he was the hesitant one. Not me. His face was filled with uncertainty. Why could I not say what I wanted to say? Like I was tiptoeing around him.

Maybe because I knew I was an indecisive mess. I deflected. "What're y'all doing for your birthday?"

Wes gave me a hollow look. "Charlotte wants to go to the Statue of Liberty."

"Are you so self-sacrificing that you're going to do what your sister wants on *your* birthday?" I joked.

Wes shrugged. "I guess so."

"What do *you* want for your birthday?"

"Your bagel." He grabbed the paper it was sitting on and pulled it toward him.

"Hey!" I grumbled but let him.

Wes took a big bite. "So good," he said with his mouth full before sliding it back to me.

"Is that all?" I wasn't sure if I was truly curious or if I was trying to push him to say he wanted me, so I didn't have to be the one to do it.

"That's all."

The finality in his voice was striking. Was I just reading into everything he was saying? Or was he trying to convey a message?

I stared at his eyebrow, right where Charlotte had held her finger, but I couldn't see anything, or I didn't know what I was looking for.

SOMEHOW, WE STILL all ended up on the subway together taking the same line, me back to my apartment, and Wes and Charlotte to the Statue of Liberty.

It was packed, and I insisted Charlotte take the one open seat. Wes and I were standing next to each other, obviously trying to put as much space between us as possible in a crowded train. We were back to dancing the no-contact tango.

Charlotte and I talked most of the way. We talked about D.C. and New York. They had tickets to see a musical that night. She asked me about work. I told her how much Wes was killing it. She wasn't in advertising. She said she couldn't stand working for her dad no matter how much she loved him. She asked me about Birmingham. She told me about her husband and their new-ish marriage. She was hoping to start trying for a baby next year. She couldn't wait to see Wes become an uncle. Then, of course, she gushed about what a great brother Wes was.

Even while she talked, Charlotte would eye me and Wes. It was as if she wanted to memorize every move our bodies were making, catch each little tic.

Eventually, she left me to my own thoughts.

As much as I selfishly wanted Wes, I wasn't going to keep trying after I clearly told him to stay away—twice. He would think I was nuts—I *was* nuts. The dynamic of this entire situation was messing with my head. It was my own fault for messing it up anyway, and I was furious with myself. I was stringing him along. Wes wasn't a guy who needed to wait around for girls who couldn't make up their minds. I bent over a little and put my head into my arm, trying to erase my thoughts.

Suddenly, Wes grabbed me and pulled me into him, almost frantically. His large arm held me tight against him, my face in his armpit. My arm was against the hard muscles of his chest and abs. I could smell his deodorant mixed with the vanilla in his clothes. Manly, intoxicating. Everything happened so fast my mind was still catching up.

"Fuck. Off." His voice was scary. I didn't know who he was talking to. A few seconds later, his face was in my hair and he whispered, "Are you okay?"

I nodded my face into his chest. He was gripping me so tightly that I could hardly move. "What happened?" I asked, confused. My voice was muffled by his shirt.

"That guy was about to put his hands on you," Wes said softly. "Did he touch you?"

"No."

His muscles relaxed. "He's been leering at you the entire time. I hate the fucking subway. Don't you miss driving in a car?"

"I shouldn't have bent over," I said. "And yes, I do. Everything about it. Being by yourself, listening to the silence or your own music. Driving with friends. And not getting groped is a big plus."

"Leigh," he said, still holding me like he didn't want to push me back into the world, "don't do that thing where you take responsibility for someone else's actions like it's your fault. You can bend over if you want to bend over. That doesn't give someone the right to touch you."

"I know," I whispered.

As a female, of course I knew this. I had so many friends who had been groped on the subway and suffered in silence, trying to move away, trying not to make a scene, trying not to escalate the situation. And then they think, *What's the point in reporting it? They will never be caught.* I was close to joining them. It scared me to think I would have just stood there, maybe trying to move away from the guy, but not saying anything. It wasn't often I didn't open my mouth.

"He's over on the other side of the car now," he said seriously before letting the humor back in. "I don't feel like picking up an assault charge today, but I'm twice his size, so I will if he comes back."

I placed my arm around Wes' back. "Thank you," I whispered.

Even though he already had his arm around me, his embrace turned into a hug, and he nodded into my hair. A few seconds of silence passed. I wanted to ride every subway line underneath all of Manhattan and stay in that hug forever.

"Don't blame yourself. You didn't do anything wrong," he whispered.

He placed his chin on the top of my head. I started to wonder if he was trying to tell me something. Like what happened between us wasn't something I needed to feel guilty for.

But his voice interrupted my thoughts. "Okay, I'm going to let go now."

More words of finality—like there should have been a *you* in that sentence. The tone of his voice was definitely telling me this was over.

He stepped back, even though all I wanted was for him to keep holding me. His were the only set of hands I wanted touching me—I'd given him the right, and I screwed it up.

I knew that was the end.

But there was one thing I still had to do. So before I went back to my apartment, I stopped at the store. If he wouldn't tell me what he wanted, then he left it up to me. I picked up a small *Parks and Recreation* Ron Swanson figurine because he absolutely hated birthdays. On the back I wrote *HBD* and a smiley face, and on Monday morning, June 3rd, I placed it on Wes' desk before he got into the office.

A peace offering for being the unbalanced lunatic of a girl whose mind never shut off.

CHAPTER 8

June passed without any incidents. I slowly cranked my drawbridge back up. Instead of a moat, I built a wall between us—wallpapered with professionalism. We were friends, both on our best behavior, and we made a great team. We won The Claire account, which snowballed into five more clients: another hotel, a huge plumbing company, another restaurant, a club, and a bar. We put together digital advertising, websites, commercials, and social media campaigns. There were many late nights and quick turnarounds. We did so well, I should've asked for a raise because you know Wes was probably making more than me for doing the same damn job.

By the end of June, I'd been on three (!) unsuccessful dates with three (!) guys trying to get back out there. The very least I could say was that my streak was more than still intact, and I was more than ready to get the hell out of the city. My family and a few people from the wedding party were headed to our lake house, where we went every year for the Fourth of July.

I had a sneaking suspicion that Wes went a day earlier than me and Emma so he wouldn't have to sit on a plane with me again.

C'est la vie.

Emma and I pulled into the driveway that was already full of cars and exited the rental car we'd driven from Asheville.

The cool mountain air hit my nostrils as I breathed in the smell of sunshine, leaves, and wet rocks. Here's a crazy word I actually know—petrichor—but who knows why it's so pleasant. It was something that I always looked forward to, knowing it was there waiting for me as soon as I stepped out of the car. But I only got to enjoy it for a little while before I became accustomed to the smell of the air. Then I'd have to wait until the next time I came back to the mountains to smell it again.

We could hear everyone's voices coming from the screened-in back porch as we made our way into the house and out the back.

"Heyyyy!" everyone said in one form or another as we walked through the door. It was starting to get dark, and it looked like they had just lit up a fire in the stone fireplace. Even in the summer, the nights could get chilly.

Emma and I made our way around the room hugging my parents in the rocking chairs, Owen and Katie on the loveseat, and Wes, Kathryn, and Nick, one of Owen's friends, on the couch. I couldn't tell if the hug Wes and I shared was too long or too short. It was the first time we'd touched in a month.

Something felt different. We were outside of work. That wall I'd built between us fell as soon as we made contact like it could only stand based on necessity in the workplace. Or maybe it was just me as always, feeling too much when it came to Wes.

"Just in time for dinner. Steaks are almost ready," my mom told us. "I'll set the table."

"I got it, Nancy," Wes said as she started to stand up.

Half good guy, half trying to get away from me, I was sure.

My mom smiled at him like he had just said she'd won a million dollars. I recognized myself in her in a way and wondered if I looked that obvious when I looked at Wes. If I did, Owen would figure it out in less time than it took for him to propose.

Wes came in and out the door between the kitchen and the long table on the porch as he brought out the plates and utensils.

"What'd y'all do today?" I asked the room.

"Fly fishing," Owen said. "We caught some beautiful rainbow trout."

"Nice," Emma said. "Let's see the manly pictures."

We passed Owen's phone around to swipe through their trophy shots. I had seen hundreds of the same picture between my dad and Owen—holding the fish up with the biggest smile on their face. And every year it's the same picture—hat on, sunglasses on, fishing shirt on—but with each passing year, their faces were just a little bit older. I'd never seen a Wes one though. His made me want to fish with him; something I'd stopped doing because it was so boring and long. But I doubted it would be boring or long with Wes with all those opportunities for him to do a bunch of unintentionally sexy things.

"Don't swipe too far," Owen joked, but I was sure he was serious because Katie hit him in the chest.

Emma came to a halt with his phone in her hand. "Now I'm scared to swipe anymore." She tossed the phone back to Owen, who laughed.

My dad left the porch and came back with a platter full of steaks. "Let's eat!"

We all followed him inside to make our plates on the island.

Wes held out a plate to me and smiled. "Salad?"

"Yes, please," I replied, taking the plate from him. Our fingers brushed underneath it accidentally, and I tried to push it from my mind. We'd acknowledged there was sexual tension. Wasn't it supposed to go away after we acknowledged it? Why wasn't it going away?

He put some salad on my plate for me, and we continued down

the counter together. We were the last two out the door to sit down, and the only spots left were next to each other. We didn't sit next to each other on purpose.

"Can we go tubing tomorrow?" Katie asked Owen.

"Yaaasss," I interjected. "Katie, you're going to fall in love with this place."

"I already am," she exclaimed.

"And tomorrow's Thursday, so we have to go to bingo. You can't come here and not go to Thursday Night Bingo at the community center," I added.

Wes held out his beer to cheers me. "Leigh knows what's up."

I clanked my beer bottle back into his. "You only like it because you love older women."

Wes smiled slyly at me as he took a sip of his drink and placed his arm around the back of my chair. I felt the pull like we were magnets, but I resisted.

I turned back to Katie. "Five rounds, last round is blackout for five hundred dollars. But don't get it twisted. Owen won't split it with you."

Bingo got competitive when we were younger. I'd won only two rounds in the twenty years we'd been going up there. Owen had won three rounds and the jackpot twice. Wes even won the jackpot one year.

Owen laughed at me. "Well, you have to buy the alcohol if you win, so fair's fair. I'm not giving you any of my money. I'll share it with Katie, of course." He put his arm around her and kissed her on the side of the head before turning back to Wes. "Are you dating an older girl?"

Wes looked at Owen confused for a second. "Oh, no. Inside joke."

Emma covered her smile by taking a long sip of her beer. Owen glanced between me and Wes twice like he was deciding if he should ask what the joke was. But, of course, that's never advised when you aren't on the inside of the joke. Here we were—me and Wes in our circle with Owen on the outside. We had many more inside jokes than just that one. I wondered if he could sense that we'd become closer over the last month or so working together, and I studied his face for any hint of concern about it.

"You?" Owen asked me instead.

For a split second, I thought he was asking if Wes was dating me. I had no idea what I looked like because I felt a few emotions hit my face: confusion, guilt, and embarrassment. I tried to wipe it clean when I realized what he was actually asking me.

"I also love older women," I joked. "But I managed to go on three dates with guys my age this past month."

Out of the corner of my eye, I saw Wes twist his head a little too quickly at me. Katie glanced at Wes. Of course, I hadn't mentioned that to Wes. I didn't owe him anything, but I felt the hope rising in my chest. Had I made him jealous?

"I'm giving up on dating," I added.

"Oh my God, tell them how bad they were," Emma exclaimed. "Like, really bad."

I laughed. My dating life was humorous even to me. "Ugh, fine! Date number one. My co-worker Jack set me up with some guy that was a friend of a friend. He proceeded to pitch me his annoying-ass multi-level marketing energy and sports performance supplements. As soon as I got home, he slid into my DMs asking if I wanted to buy a starter kit and sell them with him. Like, what the fuck?"

"Leigh! Language," my mother chastised me like I was a child as everyone else laughed.

"Sorry, Mom, but seriously," I said before continuing. "Date number two. This guy asked me to dinner in the coffee shop line. I reluctantly agreed, even though I didn't want to, because I won't find love sitting on my ass… couch. He forgot his wallet, and I had to pay. I was highly suspicious he did it on purpose. Thankfully, he doesn't have my phone number or know my last name."

"Maybe you fed a homeless person. You can file that in the good deed column," Kathryn chimed in.

"So noble of me. And date number three. Another one of my co-workers set me up with a guy she knew who had recently broken up with his girlfriend. I thought that saying, 'third time's a charm,' had to come from somewhere, right? That's a big fat N-O. He got super drunk and was so rude to our waitress that I had to keep apologizing to her. He ended up apologizing to me before telling me he was still in love with his ex. I ended up getting up and walking out. The end."

"Oof," Nick joked.

I tipped my bottle toward him in agreement and sighed.

"But I'm listening to you, Ow. No compromising."

Owen laughed. "If you went on a second date with any of those guys, that would be what we call giving up on life."

I shrugged. "Or maybe it's just me. Anyway, enough of my horrible dating life. Emma has found her spirit soulmate."

Everyone turned to look at Emma, and she narrowed her eyes at me. "Yes, I like Logan. Yes, he took me to a pottery class, and he sat behind me on the wheel. No, we didn't kiss while at the pottery class. Yes, that's all I'm going to say."

"You should have invited him here," my mom said. "We would love to meet him."

"I told her," I said, exasperated. "She never listens to me."

"You never listen to me either, Leigh. Your loss," she shot back. It was my turn to narrow my eyes at her.

"Okay, who else?" she asked the table. "Kathryn? Nick? *Wes?*"

All three shook their heads. Katie glanced at Wes again. Emma put too much emphasis on his damn name.

"Nobody else is dating?" Emma joked. She looked over at my parents. "Nancy and George? Is there a good swinger community in the neighborhood?"

"Jesus, Emma," Owen laughed.

Of all the times to make a joke, my dad said, "What, Owen? You didn't see the upside-down pineapple in the kitchen?"

The entire table burst out laughing.

My mom hit him in the arm embarrassed. "George!"

"George with the zingers," Wes remarked. "Where have you been hiding those?"

My dad shrugged. "It's been known to happen."

I held my hand to my heart pridefully. "Like daughter, like father."

"Who wants dessert?" my dad asked loudly as he placed his hands flat on the top of the table. "We've got cake."

He rose from the table and brought back a big cake with Owen's and Katie's names on it, and we proceeded to eat the entire thing—all while my leg was a centimeter from Wes'. I nudged him slightly, only once, and when he turned to look at me, I held his gaze for just a millisecond too long, daring him to make the first move.

Again.

Again x3? Again x4?

How many moves had he already made? All I wanted was another shot. I wouldn't give him up that time.

—

"IF YOU WOULD listen to me, you'd be dating Wes right now," Emma said as we were lying in bed later that night.

I groaned.

"Also, don't be too alarmed," Emma continued, "but you two

aren't as sneaky as you think you are. I'm sure the guys haven't picked up on it, but Katie looked like she did."

I didn't know Katie well enough to know if she would mention it to Owen or not. "I noticed too. Ugh, all I wanted to do was lean back in my chair and feel his arm around me. It's so much harder outside of work. I don't have to be professional."

"Y'all are annoying."

My phone buzzed on my chest where it was lying face down.

"How much of your bingo winnings will you give me if that's him? I would bet an enormous amount of money he can't help himself after hearing about your dates down there."

"You think?" I said with my hand on my phone, pretending like I didn't practically challenge him.

"Am I ever wrong?" she joked, raising her eyebrows at me to check. "Jealousy is a powerful emotion."

I flipped over my phone and 'Wes Adams' appeared above '1 Message'. He accepted my dare.

Emma chuckled. "Would y'all just have sex already?!"

"Em, I don't *just* want to have sex with him. I like him."

"Even better," she said, rolling over. "Goodnight."

I swiped my phone open.

It's not you, his text said.

Feels like it is sometimes, but I'm sticking up for myself now, I replied.

I waited a few minutes before my phone buzzed again.

Good. You deserve to be appreciated.

By him? I thought. We were going to be right back to where we were a month ago in a matter of minutes if he would let me back in. I wanted to be appreciated by him.

Why are you such a good guy?

He responded, Am I? I'm texting my best friend's sister while I'm in the same room with him, and he has no idea. I'm also playing on a pool table where I made out with her once eight years ago, and he still has no idea.

I laughed under my breath. Yes, despite that, he still was.

Somehow you still are.

I was wide awake. I rolled out of bed and put on a sweater before making my way down the stairs and out the side door. I stepped down our stone steps through the tall trees and made my way onto our dock. The moon was hitting the still water, reflecting light on all the boats lining our cove.

The silence engulfed me as I lay down on my back to look at the stars. I listened to the sound of nothing before hearing a fish jump up and ripple the surface of the lake. The moonlight danced across the water as the tiny waves spread. I tried to breathe in the petrichor again, but there wasn't anything registering to my senses.

A frog started to croak on the shoreline, and I sat up to look toward the noise coming from somewhere near the rope swing in the tree. So many great memories on that rope swing.

My dad hung it the summer after Owen and I turned twelve. Our dog, Mabel (R.I.P.), used to bark at us when we would swing. One time I accidentally kicked her into the water, scaring the crap out of her, when she jumped in front of me mid-swing. One year, we set up a ladder so we could swing higher. Owen could do backflips off the rope, but I was always too scared I was going to hit my head.

I looked out across the water to the small island that sat across from our cove. Owen and I used to have paddle board races there and back from our dock. We'd also picnic on the shoreline sometimes and go to the other side to watch the older kids wakeboarding and waterskiing in the wider part of the lake until we were old enough to be those kids.

When we got tired of swimming, we'd get life vests and put them on like diapers. Then we'd float near our dock and watch the clouds.

There were so many things to do apart from the lake too. Owen and I had hiked every hike and seen every waterfall in a one-hundred-mile radius. Our favorite was going down the sliding rock like nature's water slide at the end of one of the hikes near there.

Every time I left that place, whether it was back home to Birmingham, Nashville, or New York, it took me weeks to pull my heart back into my chest because it was stuck there in North Carolina.

I looked up at the house. My parents bought it when Owen and I were seven. It held a lot of memories that spanned twenty years.

Their window on the main floor and my window on the second floor were both dark. The guest rooms on either side of mine had a lamp on, so I guessed Kathryn was still up with Katie. My brother's room in the basement, where Wes and Nick were staying, was bright, and the pool room next to his bedroom was lit up from the light hanging above the table. I could see Owen, Nick, and Wes moving around as they played. They kept laughing at each other as they drank their beers. My eyes attached themselves to Wes—leaning over, chalking his pool stick, scratching his arm, racking the pool balls. I got out my phone again and texted him.

And you're hot.

I looked back up through the window. He dug his hand in his pocket, turned around to face the window, and read my text.

He smiled that goofy smile that people do when they are texting someone they like. My stomach turned into a black hole, sucking up everything around it before exploding back inside my abdomen.

CHAPTER 9

I picked up my phone again and read his response from the night before for the millionth time.

Thanks :) but you're hotter.

I got a smiley face. A smiley face, from softy Wes Adams, that I watched him text me before Owen grabbed his shoulder, and Wes quickly shoved his phone back in his pocket.

I checked my swimsuit in the mirror again before walking down to the dock, where everyone was already on the boat.

"Waiting on you, Leigh," Owen called to me when he saw me coming down the steps.

"Keep your shirt on. I'm coming," I called back.

"That's the exact opposite of what I'm trying to do. I need a tan."

I stepped onto the boat and plopped down next to Emma in front.

"Took you long enough," she said.

I shrugged. "I had to shave my legs." I shoved my towel beneath the seat and put on my sunglasses.

Owen turned the music on as he pulled away from the dock slowly. He cranked it up when we got to top speed and the wind rushed over us as we made it to a wider section of the lake. Wes handed me and Emma a beer.

Thanks, I mouthed. He smiled. The music was too loud to talk.

Owen came to a stop and turned the music down. "Who's first? Katie and Kathryn?"

"Yay!" Katie exclaimed as she and Kathryn stood up and put life jackets on. They jumped into the water from the back of the boat and climbed up on the tube.

"Katie, just because you're my fiancée doesn't mean I'm going to go easy on you," Owen warned her loudly. "The whole point is for me to knock you off and for you to *try* not to get knocked off."

He didn't go easy on her, but she and Kathryn put up a fight. Owen did big loops around the middle with Katie clinging to the handles, her legs flying up behind her, before Owen brought the boat around to force them over the wake. Their tube flipped, throwing them both off.

Owen laughed as he came up slowly on the side of them bobbing up and down in the water.

"Round two?" Owen asked, and they both nodded as they tried to get their wet hair out of their faces.

I moved to the opposite bench at the front of the boat and lay down across the seat on my back with my eyes closed. I moved to the music Owen was playing and felt my body tilt as the boat turned in different directions.

Ice-cold metal hit my leg a few minutes later. I sprang my eyes open to see Wes holding a beer can against my thigh.

"Want another beer?" he asked me, smiling.

"Please," I laughed, grabbing it from his hand where it was still against my skin.

I sat up a little and bent my knees as Wes sat down at my feet. The balls of my feet found the side of his thigh.

He took a sip of his beer. "You gonna tube with me?"

"You gonna keep me from falling off?"

"No," he said seriously.

"Then we battle it out on two tubes. And don't forget I grew up doing this."

"Don't forget I'm stronger than you." He wrapped his fingers around my ankle and squeezed. "Which I suspect I'll need because it's the only way I'll probably get you off that tube."

"I've also been taking steroids in preparation for this moment," I said as Wes rubbed my ankle bone with his thumb. I couldn't wait to be alone with him. We both knew what was coming.

"I was wondering where that beard and low voice came from."

"Tolerable side effects to see your face hit the water." I curled my lavender-painted toes into him.

"All that for nothing then?" He pouted.

I broke first and laughed. "Probably."

Katie and Kathryn both screamed as they skidded across the water before going under.

"Who's next?" Owen looked up. "Emma and Leigh?"

Emma shook her head and pointed at us in her true wingwoman fashion. "They can go."

"We want two tubes," I told Owen.

"Always the difficult one," he said, shaking his head at me. As much as I annoyed him, he'd be the first to admit there is nothing quite like our bond. I grinned as he grabbed the extra tube tied to the side of the boat and attached it to the tower with a rope.

Wes and I sized each other up as we put on our life jackets and jumped into the water. I situated myself on the red tube and slipped my hands through the handles. Wes climbed on the yellow tube and gave Owen a thumbs up.

Owen slowly increased his speed, and our ropes became taut. He swung us to the left, and my tube crashed into Wes'. He kicked my tube.

"Child's play," I yelled as my tube veered back to the right and over the wake. I expertly maneuvered my body so I wouldn't flip. It usually took Owen a while to get me off the tube, but it had been a while since he and I had battled while our dad drove, so I was rusty.

We careened into the middle, and our tubes bumped before sending us in opposite directions. Owen turned sharply, sending Wes' tube into mine hard. Wes grabbed my handle and tried to flip my tube manually before I kicked him away and out of his grasp. I stuck my tongue out at him as we separated.

We went back and forth over the wake five times. On the sixth time, Wes' tube connected with mine, and I jumped from his tube to mine.

"Are you resorting to dirty tactics?" he exclaimed.

I smiled innocently at him and wrapped my leg with his before I whispered in his ear; "How dirty do you think I can get?"

"Apparently very dirty because that's even dirtier," he whispered back. He slid his right hand up my thigh and his fingers found their way to my swimsuit strings like he was going to pull them. "I can get dirty too."

I gasped jokingly. "I know you would never do that."

"You're right, so I'll do this instead." He wrapped his fingers around mine clinging to the handle.

I gasped for real and glared at him. "Don't you dare!"

"I knew I would need strength," he remarked as he pried my fingers off the handle and sent me flying up into the air because we coincidentally hit the wake at the same time. I belly-flopped into the water.

Actually, face-flopped—hard.

I surfaced and Wes was already swimming frantically toward me. "Oh my God, are you okay?"

My face felt like I'd fallen on a porcupine. I covered my left eye and laughed. "Yeah, but shit, that hurt. Is my face red?"

He winced when I uncovered my eye. "Just a little. Fuck, I'm such an asshole. I'm sorry."

"It's fine. I practically drove you to it," I laughed. "Besides, it was just luck I landed like that."

He reached his hands out beneath the water and found my hips, pulling us closer together through the water. "Seriously, Leigh, are you all right? I think I just gave you a black eye."

I nodded and entangled my legs with his as he cupped his hand around my cheek and softly ran his thumb below my eye. We stared at each other for a few seconds.

"You're going to need to ice that," Wes said.

Owen pulled the boat up next to us. "Man, that looked rough. You okay?"

"I'm good!"

Owen laughed. "That's going to bruise."

"I can't wait to tell people Wes punched me." I swam to the back of the boat and climbed in with Wes behind me. "Will you bring me back home really quickly so I can ice my face?"

"Sure," Owen replied.

"I'll go with you," Wes said, jumping off behind me when we reached our dock.

"You don't have to if you don't want to," I told him, but I wanted him to. Really badly. I said that more for the optics. Hopefully, he knew that.

Emma tried to pull a neutral expression as I telepathically told her to stall everyone from coming back.

"I want to, and I want to make sure you ice it correctly, so you don't go around telling people I punched you."

"Do you think I'm the first person to ever wish for a black eye?" I asked as we walked up the stairs to the house.

"You're the first person to wish for one so you can torture me."

"How many black eyes have you inflicted on people?"

"You will be my second. I pushed my sister into a door frame when I was five—and she let me live that down."

"Where's the fun in that?" I asked him as we stepped into the kitchen. He walked over to the pantry and grabbed a Ziploc before filling it with ice from the freezer. He wrapped a paper towel around it and handed it to me.

He went to the cabinet and got two Advil from the bottle, holding out his hand to me and dropping them into my palm. He filled a glass with water from the fridge and turned around.

He held out the glass to me. "Leigh, I'm sorry." His voice was apologetic and hesitant.

"Don't be," I said, taking the glass and swallowing the ibuprofen. I put the ice back on my eye. "I'll tell people I got it in that mysterious Illuminati ritual, only because you're so nice."

Wes' lips twitched up at the corners like he didn't want to smile, but I forced him to. He took a step toward me. "Put it around your eye, not on it like that. Twenty minutes on, twenty minutes off. And I'm going to make you do it multiple times."

I nodded at him as I pulled my one right eye off the corners of his lips. "Thanks for taking care of me."

"Of course," he said before adding, "But you're not making it easy."

"I don't make anything easy."

Our eyes studied each other for a few seconds, communicating silently about what we were actually talking about. Wes placed his hand over my hand that was holding the ice pack. He pulled the ice away from my eye with his long fingers.

"No, you don't," he said, tossing the ice gently onto the counter behind me and taking another step closer. "Are you going to make things hard for me now?"

"Depends."

"On what?" he whispered in my ear.

"If you meant for that to be a pun or not."

He chuckled under his breath and grabbed my hip. "I didn't."

"Well, I didn't ice my eye for twenty minutes like you said." I looked up at him, grabbed the waistband of his swimsuit, and pulled him closer. "That was less than a minute."

"You can start with twenty minutes off." He tucked my wet hair behind my ear. "And if I did mean for that to be a pun?"

I tipped my chin up toward him. His pupils dilated, and he bent his shoulders and lightly brushed his soft lips against mine slowly.

"Would you rather the pool table?" I joked.

He shook his head slightly and his lips came a half centimeter closer. Against my lips he said, "No, I want to do this in every room of the house."

"Please, can we?" I whispered. I wanted to walk into that house and have a memory of Wes on every piece of furniture.

He kissed me hard, his wet tongue parting my lips. This was what it felt like to deny yourself something—someone—for a long freaking time. My tongue connected with his, tasting beer and strawberries. He tasted just like I remembered. But this time, my emotions were heightened. His right hand found my other hip as I tightened my grip around his ribs, feeling his bones tight against his taut skin. He brought his mouth down to my neck, kissing me lightly along my tendon as I tipped my head to the side.

"That's a lot of rooms," I pointed out.

He pulled back and nodded. I opened my mouth, but he quickly brought his thumb up across my lips with a sexy half smile. "Do not make a joke about Owen's room right now."

I smirked against his thumb. I was absolutely about to do that. I licked his thumb. "You're no fun."

He brought his hand down my throat, his fingers tracing every beauty mark. He ran his palm down between my breasts and hooked his finger on my swimsuit in the middle. "You've been driving me fucking nuts in this bikini."

One finger snaked its way underneath the seam of my swimsuit and he brought it up under the triangle shape over my right breast.

"You're too far away." I brought my fingers down his sides over his warm skin and pulled him in even closer by the small of his back. It was risky that we were in our swimsuits, already half naked, but I didn't care. Wes and I weren't going to just make out. This had been building for almost a decade.

I stood on my tiptoes to get closer to him, and he kissed me hungrily. His warm tongue was sending fire down to my stomach. His teeth played with my bottom lip until he pushed me against the kitchen island. His kiss became rougher as he squeezed my ass hard and slipped his fingers beneath my swimsuit. His fingers massaged my glutes before he grabbed me by the back of the upper thighs and lifted me onto the island. My body flushed, and my heart picked up speed at the excitement of learning him. He liked it rougher than I remembered, and I wondered how rough he could get. The thought of exploring it sent sparks down between my legs. It was the opposite of his nonsexual personality.

His palms came up my inner thighs as he pushed them apart slowly. He kneaded his thumbs into my skin when he reached the top.

He planted kisses along my jawline as his hands came up to my breasts over my swimsuit. I reached down and rubbed him over his swim shorts, the front pulled out tight.

"Mm," he said against the bottom of my jaw. His hands found their way under my swimsuit, and he pinched my nipples causing my back to arch. His left hand came up and gripped the back of my head. His fingers twisted into my hair, and he pulled my head back, forcing me to look up.

"I love you being rough with me," I whispered, wrapping my

legs around him tighter, testing him and telling him he could take it further if he wanted.

"God, Leigh," he said eagerly, pushing harder against me. "Are you giving me permission to be rougher?" He needed to hear my consent out loud.

"Yes," I breathed out.

My hair came down harder with the force of his pull. Fuck, that felt good. His mouth and tongue came down my trachea, to the notch between my clavicles, before his wet tongue trailed down my sternum. He pulled up my swimsuit triangles and played with my right nipple between his fingers, while he licked my other nipple and sucked, gradually increasing the strength. My hands ran through his hair as he took my nipple between his teeth gently. I let out a small moan. He switched to the side, and I dug my fingernails into his upper back. I wanted to leave a mark that I could look at later—evidence of another secret we would now share.

His fingers traced up my spine and played with the strap right across my back. His fingertips slid underneath it, rubbing back and forth. His soft mouth came back up to my collarbone, his teeth skimming my skin, as his left hand slid between my legs. I moaned louder as he rubbed me, giving me the friction and pressure I'd been craving. The intensity he'd been building was swirling around in my lower stomach. His teeth sank into my shoulder gently, then harder, and my swimsuit became damper. He pulled my swimsuit to the side and ran his thumb over me a few times before inserting his middle finger.

"Mm," he hummed against my skin, wrapping his other hand lightly around the base of my neck. "You're so wet for me."

His voice was deep and close to my ear and hearing him say that made me wetter. Wes was way hotter than I could have imagined. He was nothing like my dreams, and it was an incredibly welcome surprise. I liked him taking control more than I thought I would. I wanted to give him total control.

"Take me any way you want," I whispered as his fingers glided over me, and he moved his other hand down to my breast. I leaned back with my hands on the cold countertop. I could feel his body respond with longing and urgency.

"Fuck, I want it all. How much time do you think we have?" he said huskily against my neck. His tongue was sending a tsunami down my body. He pulled back, and his hand found the strings dangling down my back. He wrapped one end around his finger in a spiral. He came toward my lips, but instead of kissing me, he whispered against them, "I'm going to drive you fucking nuts."

The way he said that so confidently—like he knew he could derange me with pleasure—I can't even begin to describe how it made my mind and body feel. I tensed my legs around his waist.

"You already are," I said breathily before he kissed me lightly on the lips. He smiled, and his fingers curved up around my jaw and held me solidly at the joints. The force of it was a mix between loving and powerful.

"God, I love kissing you." He pulled my face toward his, then he kissed me again softly as he started to pull the string of my swimsuit. When he pulled back, his eyes darted over my shoulder, and he leaped back faster than I'd ever seen another person move.

Holy Mother of God. Why would they all come through the front door? I pulled my swimsuit back down over my boobs. I didn't want to turn around and see everyone's faces staring at us in disbelief. At least Emma would be overjoyed. It was inevitable, so I might as well just get it over with. I pushed myself off the counter and turned around—to see Holy Mother of Leigh staring at us in total shock.

Wes stepped behind me, and I could hear him adjust himself. I adjusted my own swimsuit bottom.

It was a 'who speaks first?' standoff. My mom looked from me to Wes, then back to me. We stood there for another five seconds in silence.

I wondered at which point she walked in. How much of that did she see and hear? Is there anything more embarrassing than your mother walking in on you about to have sex? Okay, having her walk in on me *actually* having sex would be a whole lot worse. But I was still trying to decide if that was going to claim the top spot on my list of most embarrassing moments. It would replace the time I was sitting on the ground in front of my locker in middle school, curled into my sweatshirt because I was freezing, and my crush started tickling me, knocking me over, and causing me to fart in the process. Shit. I still cringe when I think of it. Which one deserves the top most-mortifying prize?

She spoke first, but only because she was trying to hide her smile that was peeking through her lips. "I'm sorry. I needed water."

"I thought you were golfing all day," I stammered.

"We decided to only play nine holes," she explained, leaving out the part we were all thinking—*which is why I just walked in on you and Wes about to have sex on my kitchen counter*. At least I was confident she didn't walk in on some of the earlier things we said. She wouldn't have stood there that long. But now, she was frozen; unsure if she should continue on her water venture or turn and walk away.

She chose the wrong one.

She walked around the island, beelining for the cabinet where the cups were.

"Mom, I—" I started before she cut me off.

"I don't need an explanation." Her voice was steady and reassuring. She pulled a plastic cup down from the shelf.

"Okay, well—"

"It's no one else's business." She placed the cup in the slot in the door and proceeded to take twenty thousand hours to fill her cup up before my dad walked in.

He smiled at all of us, oblivious to the fact that there was no oxygen in the room. "Great golfing day. Do you golf, Wes?"

"Yes, sir," he said, still positioned behind me.

My mom turned toward us and took a long sip of her water.

Wes couldn't help himself. "Mrs. Sullivan, I'm sorr—"

"Nancy!" she exclaimed, waving her hand at Wes, as I turned to glare at him. "And what do y'all want for dinner?"

"I vote for salmon," my dad interjected as he walked around my mom, patted her butt, and got his own water from the fridge. "Wes, you want to golf with me while you're here? Nancy is all right, but Owen is terrible. We could do the back nine tomorrow."

"I would love to," Wes responded.

I just stared at my mom the whole time as she tried to wipe the newly emerging glee from her face after it would reappear every three seconds.

I was trying to communicate to her through facial expressions that she needed to leave the kitchen and drag my dad with her, but she was off in Nancy la-la land, hoping Wes would soon become her son-in-law, that we'd have mini Weses running around, that we'd move back to Birmingham, and whatever else moms dream about when they are obsessed with their kids.

"Salmon it is," she remarked. "Are y'all going to bingo?"

I nodded at her. "Salmon sounds perfect. And yes, I'm going to go get ready."

Her eyes circled my left eye. "Do you have a black eye?"

"Oh, yeah, just a tubing accident. It's nothing."

Was it that bad?

I backed up into Wes who put his hands on my upper arms. He grabbed the ice off the counter, and we both turned together as we walked out of the kitchen and to the stairs in the foyer.

"We will never speak of this moment again," I hissed as I

stepped up on the first step.

Wes grabbed my hand, spun me around, and whispered, "I'd rather your parents not see how fucking hard you make me, but I don't care if they know about us."

"How much of that did she see and hear?" I asked him.

"She only saw me kiss you, and maybe she heard me say how much I love it, but I don't think anything else."

A wave of relief washed over me.

Wes reached behind me and grabbed my butt, pulling me against him with a devious smile. We were almost face to face with me on the step. His mouth hovered over mine. "You think they'll walk in here or did we traumatize your mom?"

"God, Wes. I want you so bad," I whispered against his lips and kissed him.

He squeezed my butt. "Good. Don't forget that when you look in the mirror," he said before putting the ice in my hand and turning to head down the stairs to his room.

CHAPTER 10

"B9!" the teeny old white-haired lady at the front called.

I scanned the B columns on my four cards and sighed. I looked over at Owen marking off two of his cards with his red dauber.

He looked up at me. "Ha!"

"You're such a gracious winner," I replied. "And you haven't even won yet."

Emma was not into bingo. I leaned over and marked her nines for her while she texted Logan.

"He could still fly here for the weekend, you know," I told her.

She shook her head. "I need to ease him into y'all."

"O72!"

I marked one off my card with my blue dauber. "I could argue that you're the craziest of us all. So, if he likes you, he'll like us."

Emma glanced over her cards. "Which pattern are we playing again?"

"Postage stamp. The little square in any corner," I reminded her.

"Right," she said and went back to texting.

"Ooh, I'm close," Nick announced to us.

Kathryn leaned over to look. "One more!"

I'd noticed her hovering near Wes at the couple's shower and eyeing him earlier on the boat, but he'd made it clear from his body language that he wasn't into her. Or maybe that was wishful thinking on my part. Of course, I hoped he wasn't into her. At least it looked like she'd moved on to Nick.

I turned slightly to Wes sitting on my right, trying to judge his body language toward me. His shorts were pushed up a little showing more of his muscular thigh. It was close to mine but not touching. He had his left hand wrapped around the front of his knee. He was bouncing his right leg up and down. I glanced up at his face and down to his lips.

The bottom of my stomach lurched, heat building between my legs, as I remembered his mouth on my body, his firm tongue pressing into my neck, his hands grabbing my boobs, and his hard-on rubbing against me. I wanted to hear his low voice say more dirty things to me. It was thrilling to know a side of him I'd never seen. Dylan was vanilla—what you saw was what you got. I had to take charge like I did with everything else. I'd never been in a relationship where I didn't have to, and I realized what I'd been missing out on. Wes was a scoop of sweet, a scoop of spicy, and a scoop of sexy. It made me need to take a cold shower just thinking about it.

What did his body language say? He was nervous? He was deep in thought? Did he actually like me, or did he think this was all a deep sexual primal desire thing going on between us? All I wanted to do was climb on top of him.

His phone laying on the table dinged. He looked at it and turned it face down.

"G48!"

"No cheating," he huffed, dragging me out of the daydream I was having about him pushing everyone's bingo cards off the table and taking me right there.

What would the look on everyone's face say if I just kissed Wes right now?

Wes: shock, then acceptance and he'd just kiss me back?

Owen: shock and anger?

Katie: I knew it?

Kathryn: jealousy?

Nick: indifference?

Emma: about fucking time!

Me: horny as hell because I'd lost count of the days at that point.

"You can't cheat in bingo," I pointed out.

"You can when you distract someone."

I laughed under my breath.

He glanced over at Owen, who was flirting with Katie, then leaned down to my ear and whispered, "I can't wait for us to be alone again."

We'd be lucky if we got another opportunity for the rest of the trip. Everyone was *always* around. Luckily, back home in a city of eight million people, no one was ever around. I ran my hand down to my own knee and reached my fingers out to graze his. He played with my fingers, interlocking his through mine. Then he grabbed them and pulled my hand over to his knee. He brushed his fingertips over my palm.

"G55!"

"Bingo!" Nick screamed, holding his fists up high in the air and startling me and Wes apart.

"Booooo," Owen and I said together at him.

"Come up here, young man," the old lady called to Nick.

Nick rose with his card and brought it to the front.

The woman checked his card before announcing, "We have a winner! That's one hundred and ninety-eight dollars."

Everyone clapped politely as Nick made his way back to his seat.

"If I had tomatoes, I'd throw them at you, but at least now you have to buy a case of beer on the way home," I said.

Kathryn squeezed his arm as they sat down.

The teeny old lady stood up at the front, dragging her metal chair across the floor. "Blackout will be the last game. Cover a full card for the five-hundred-dollar jackpot. Good luck everyone."

Our table tore off the previous game's paper cards to reveal our fresh sheets as the lady turned the metal cage to mix the bingo balls a few times.

"N33!"

We all collectively studied our N column.

"How does your eye feel?" Wes asked me after he was done.

"Pretty good. Can you tell?" I turned my head to give him a better view of it.

"I19!"

He shook his head and ran his thumb under it before he quickly took it back like he realized what he was doing, and he shouldn't be doing it. "Barely. Emma did a pretty good job covering it up."

My eye had bruised underneath and up the outer side. It wasn't swollen or puffy—just a nice purplish brown.

"Don't I!" Emma looked around me. "Thank you for noticing, Wes. It's nice to get some recognition for once."

I kicked her with my heel under the table.

"B3!"

Wes chuckled. "If only Owen was as good of a best friend as you."

Owen looked up when he heard his name and scoffed. "If you got a black eye, I'd punch your other eye to even it out for you."

"I would appreciate that," Wes laughed.

"N45!"

Owen shrugged. "What are best friends for?"

He'd probably want to punch him for other reasons that he didn't know about. Would Owen actually punch Wes? Wes had already told me before we left for bingo that he wanted to tell Owen something had happened between us, and I was adamant he didn't. He didn't have to be such a nice guy all the freaking time, and we didn't have sex. Guilt started to spin around in my caged chest like it was full of bingo balls.

"O69!"

Emma and I laughed under our breath like the children we were. But then heat started to rise to my face as I thought about doing that with Wes. He shifted in his seat, and I was pretty sure he could feel the warmth from the fire crackling within me.

"B1!"

I needed to distract myself. I turned to Emma. "Will you at least bring Logan to the wedding?"

"I've been thinking about asking him. Do you think that's too serious?"

"G59!"

"Why? Because it's in Nashville?"

"Yeah, staying in a hotel with him. Having him join the bachelor party, rehearsal dinner, and the wedding. It seems like a lot."

"No, it will be fun. Plus, that's so much time to hang out with him and get to know him better."

"I guess you're right. Y'all are going to scare him off though, so I'm sure I'll regret it."

"I27!"

She leaned in towards me and put her phone between us as she texted: **Do you want to come to the wedding in Nashville with me?**

Logan texted back right away. **Yeah, I'd love to.**

"Oh my God, he's in love with you," I screeched.

Emma giggled. *GIGGLED!* I'd never heard that sound come from her mouth in my life.

"Oh my God, you're in love with him!"

Emma only rolled her eyes at me. I could tell in her face she was telling me she was, but she didn't want to talk about it in front of everyone.

"G53!"

"Wait, in love with who? We haven't met him yet, Em. What if we don't like him?" Owen said from across the table.

"True," I said. "Are you going to break up with us?"

"You'll like him," she said to me. "And Owen, I don't care if you don't."

Owen laughed. "It's going to take a lot for me to like him, so he better bring his A game. No one is good enough for either of you."

"N40!"

My eyes darted to Owen as he pointed between me and Emma with two fingers. Owen had never really liked any of my boyfriends that much. Would he like my boyfriend if it was someone he already really liked before we started dating? What were Wes and I even doing? I hadn't expressed my feelings for Wes to Wes yet. Maybe he thought this was all about sex.

"O70!"

I whipped my head up at the old woman, realizing I hadn't been paying attention to the last few balls that were called. I scanned the board with the called numbers brightly lit up. I checked my cards carefully for any missing ones.

"B15!"

"Shit, I got distracted," I muttered to myself.

Wes eyed me with a smile. "Told you."

I looked around the table as I tried to hide my smile. "Katie, yours is half full. I hope you win. That'd be awesome for the honeymoon."

"O61!"

"Ugh, I would love that." Katie marked another one off. "We decided on Hawaii."

"I'm sure it will be perfect," I said. "Which island?"

"The big one. It has the beach and the city. Lots of things to do."

"For sure. That sounds so great," I replied.

"B13!"

Owen whispered something in her ear, and she started to blush. I was sure it was something about all the sex they would be having. Owen wasn't very sly. Well, at least he wasn't to me. I guess because we shared a womb for nine months and did almost everything together until the age of twenty-two.

"I16!"

I wondered if he could tell something was going on with me. Was I just as much of an open book to him? Or was it because I was a girl? The one who was supposed to be in tune—connected to the twin bond. I'd never hidden anything from him. I'd never had a reason to. Dammit, this was such a bad idea.

"B12!"

I looked at Wes' profile again. Dammit, I didn't care. I wasn't ready for Owen to know, and I couldn't let Wes go. I just didn't want to deal with the shitstorm that I knew was coming.

"N36!"

"How close are you?" I asked Emma, checking out her cards she'd been ignoring.

"Umm." She tore her eyes away from her phone. "No idea."

"Why did you even come?" I laughed.

"FOMO," she said. So many things can be explained with those four little letters.

"G49!"

"How close are you?" I asked Wes, leaning on his leg under the table and checking out his cards.

"Not remotely close."

I ran my hand up his thigh. Whatever, no one could see. He was pushed in all the way to the table. Owen and Katie were probably doing the same thing.

I frowned. "Aw, too bad. I'm not either though."

"N42!"

We scanned his cards together as I rubbed him over his shorts. I wanted to dominate his thoughts. I wanted him only thinking about me and the next time he'd be able to put his hands on me.

I pulled back and started scanning my own cards. I could see Wes smirking and shaking his head out of the corner of my eye as he stared at his bingo card.

"B7!"

I listened to Kathryn and Nick flirt for a few minutes, while the woman called G55, G48, O62, and I30.

I listened to Owen and Katie flirt for a few minutes while the woman called N44, B10, O75, O68, and I23.

I'd given up. I had more blank spaces than I had filled in spaces. Katie only had a few unmarked numbers. She started fidgeting in her chair, intensely looking up at the little old lady, holding her breath waiting for the next number.

"O66!"

Her smile widened as she marked it.

"G51!"

Her shoulders dropped.

"G46!"

She huffed.

"I20!"

She sighed.

"O64!"

"Yes!" she said under her breath.

"How many more do you need?" I asked her.

"Two," she exclaimed. "I'm way too invested at this point."

"N38!"

I raised my eyebrows, but she stayed still.

"N43!"

She pouted. I picked myself up a bit to see what she needed.

"I25!"

"Yessss!" She marked it off.

"What do you need? O73?" Owen asked, looking over. The whole table became invested in her last number.

We all looked up at the lady hunched over, rotating the lever.

"O…" It felt like a lifetime. "71!"

"Dammit," she grumbled.

"B4!"

Owen chuckled and put his arm around her.

"N31!"

"G58!"

"O…" We all held our breath. "73!"

"Bingooooo!" Katie screamed.

We all clapped excitedly. I didn't want to throw tomatoes at her.

"Wooo!" Owen called to her as she walked up.

She was smiling from ear to ear, super excited, as they checked her card and handed her the money.

She waved it in Owen's face when she came back to the table. "This is another excursion we can do in Hawaii! Will you put it in your wallet for me?"

"Yes, ma'am," Owen said, pulling out his wallet. "Nick, you have to buy the beer on the way home though. Rules are rules."

Rules are meant to be broken sometimes though, right?

—

I LOOKED AT the list on my phone. I needed cream of tartar, more butter, powdered sugar, vanilla, strawberries, and blueberries. My mom had everything else. I made a sugar cookie fruit flag cake every year for the potluck at our neighbor's house. It was probably the only thing I'd mastered in the kitchen.

I shifted the green hand basket onto my forearm as I looked for cream of tartar in the spice aisle.

"Do you come here often?" Wes said, walking up beside me.

I looked at him indifferently and went back to searching. "No."

"Playing hard to get." He lowered his voice. "I like it."

He brushed my hair back and lightly kissed me on the neck twice.

"Wes!" I exclaimed, even though I loved it.

"Leigh!" he joked and looked around at the empty aisle.

"What if Owen saw you?"

"You like the thrill a little, don't you?" He could read me.

"Beside the point."

"I want to tell him that something happened between us."

I shook my head. "I already told you no."

"It's the right thing to do."

"And if he punches you?"

"Then I'll deal with it."

"You're going to punch him back?"

"No," he laughed. "He's not going to punch me."

"And if it ruins your friendship?"

"We're all adults. I think Owen can handle it. And whatever happens between you and me is between you and me."

I shook my head again, faster that time. "No. I'm not ready."

"Are you going to say that every time I bring it up?"

"Probably," I huffed. "You didn't say anything to him eight years ago."

"That was college. I was an idiot, and we were drunk," he said.

"We haven't even had sex."

"I'm well aware."

I rolled my eyes at him.

"Your mom already knows," he reminded me.

"Don't remind me. And *she's* not going to say anything."

"Do you think she told your dad? He booked us a tee time for tomorrow morning."

His phone dinged in his pocket. I looked down at it, but he ignored it.

"If she did, that will be an awkward golf outing."

"How does one tell your dad he wants to tap that?" Wes said, raising his eyebrows and looking at my ass.

"He'd probably launch into a detailed explanation on how to tap a beer keg, so ask away."

I'd looked at every spice row fifteen times because Wes was being Wes. I finally spotted the cream of tartar on the top shelf. I stood on my tip toes trying to pull one out of the spice dispenser.

Wes chuckled, watching my fingertips spin it around, not able to grasp it. "Need help?"

"No." I stretched out higher.

"Are you trying to turn me on?"

"What?" I came back down on my heels. "No."

He stepped up behind me, his full body flush with mine. He reached up and grabbed it easily as he bent his head toward my ear. "If we weren't in a grocery store, I'd be all over you right now."

The tickle of his words cascaded down to my lower stomach. I pushed my butt against him, wanting him to say something else.

His right hand snaked around my waist and pulled me against him tighter. "You love it when I say dirty things to you, don't you?"

I nodded the back of my head against his chest and whispered, "What would you do to me?"

"God, so many things I can't even pick just one to say, but I'd definitely push you up against this spice rack." He pulled me in even tighter. "I want to make your whole body shake."

My body flushed. He was lighting the coals in the pit of my lower stomach.

"None of the other guys told you how badly they wanted you all the time?"

I shook the back of my head against his chest.

"Lucky for me then, that they didn't know how to please you." He brought his arm down and pulled my hair to the side. He licked the cartilage of my ear and bit it gently. "And the next chance I get, I'll be pleasing you more than just this."

He stepped back and dropped the cream of tartar in my basket. "Think about what I said about Owen."

Wes turned and started walking down the aisle, leaving me staring at his back, wishing I could pounce on him—until Owen walked by the end of the aisle, missing our transgression by ten seconds.

"There y'all are," Owen called.

"Hey, man," Wes said casually.

Owen looked over Wes' shoulder. "Leigh, did you get everything you need? Nick got the beer."

"Yeah, I think so," I said, looking down at my phone and trying to ignore how turned on I was.

All I was thinking was, *No, I definitely did not get everything I needed.*

CHAPTER 11

If I thought I was an insomniac before, I didn't know what to call myself now. A jellyfish, a dolphin, a giraffe, a bullfrog? I needed to research how these animals survived on little to no sleep.

Emma, on the other hand, was sleeping like a baby curled up in the fetal position. I was still a little drunk from the wine we'd all had at dinner and the case of beer we all shared while playing pool—thanks to Nick.

Wes and I had sat next to each other (on purpose that time), our feet finding their way to each other under the table every so often while we ate salmon. We were on the same team when we played cutthroat pool, so I didn't think it was that obvious that we couldn't stop staring at each other.

I picked up my phone and googled 'how long can a human go without sleep.' As I was reading that the longest documented time a person has ever gone without it was eleven days, Wes texted me.

Awake? Let's go somewhere.

He knew I couldn't sleep, not after what he'd done to my mind.

Did you forget this is the mountains and there is nothing open at midnight?

Nature is always open, he responded.

He did have a point, and we could get away from the house. **Meet me underneath the house in ten minutes.**

I got out of bed and slipped quietly into my bathroom. I fixed my hair so that it looked like I didn't try, and covered up my black eye as well as I could. I brushed my teeth again—in case—before I tiptoed down the stairs and out the side door.

Below the house, there was a storage room where we kept all our outdoor equipment: tubes, kayaks, paddles, paddle boards.

I unlatched the wooden door and stepped inside to wait for Wes. I rested my back against the side wall. A few minutes later, it creaked open.

"Leigh?" he whispered, stepping in.

It was so dark that he couldn't see me. I couldn't help myself. I grabbed his hand, startling him in the process, and pulled him into me. I wrapped my hands around his neck.

He smiled. "You scared me," he said softly before kissing me. Those wonderful lips, soft and hard at the same time, against mine. His hand wrapped around my hip and his thumb massaged my hip bone. I pulled him in closer, wanting his large body against mine. There's something in that feeling—raw masculinity pinned against you.

"Let's make out all night instead," I said into his mouth.

Wes laughed softly, his body responding to my words. I loved feeling that sudden change: every muscle tightening like he needed me more than he needed anything else.

He pulled me up, and I wrapped my legs around his waist. We were acting like teenagers—frantic and pawing at each other in secret—like we were going to get caught doing something we shouldn't have been doing. But unlike a teenager, Wes kissed like a man.

He pulled back eventually. "Let's go do something."

"What do you want to do?" I whispered.

He looked around until his eyes landed on the paddle boards. "Paddle boarding."

"Have you seen the waterfall in the cove?"

He shook his head at me, kissed me lightly, and put me back down on the ground. "You grab the paddles."

Wes picked up the paddle boards, one under each arm, and started out towards the dock. I picked up two paddles that were leaning on the back wall and followed him.

When he reached the edge of the dock, he lowered the first paddle board, but it slipped and slapped the water loudly. He looked at me with wide eyes and a smirk. I giggled and held my finger to my mouth. Sound traveled far across the water.

We both put our phones down and slipped off our sandals. Wes held his hand out to me, and I took it as I stepped down onto the board. He placed the second paddle board into the water quietly and lowered himself onto it. I held out a paddle for him. He smiled at me and pushed himself away from the dock.

"After you," he whispered.

I lowered my paddle into the water, and we silently made our way to the next cove over. The breeze picked up a little once we were away from the trees along the shore. Wes came up beside me, his arms flexing as he pushed the water back with his paddle. I slowed my speed so I could admire him. His calves were engaged, steadying himself on the board, and the breeze would pick up the end of his shirt slightly, so I could see his lower back. I wanted every little piece of him.

No one had made me feel like that in a long time. And it wasn't just his appearance. Everything about him turned me on. He was kind, honest, and funny. He valued life and fun and quality time. He walked around gardens for Christ's sake. He always seemed like he was listening to me when I spoke.

I could hear the waterfall as we started getting closer. We

rounded the last corner, and when it came into view, Wes looked back at me and smiled. I picked up my pace, came up beside him, and pushed him as hard as I could.

"You suck," he deadpanned before he hit the water. When he surfaced, he ran his hands through his hair, pushing it out of his face. "You can either jump in yourself, or I'll make you get in."

"Is it cold?" I asked.

"Freezing."

"Oh, then never mind. I'm not getting in."

Wes laughed and disappeared. I was a sitting duck. He popped up next to my board and pulled me in by the arm. I plunged down into the warm water.

I stuck my tongue out at him when I came up for air and treaded water. "It's not cold."

"I know."

"I'm going to have to get Charlotte to point out your eyebrow thing to me."

"You'd love that, wouldn't you?" He pulled me into him. "Come here, you tiny thing. You can't stand."

I wrapped my legs around his waist at the same time his hands came up my thighs.

He made a face at me. "Maybe that's a good thing. The bottom feels gross."

I smiled at him and let myself go, slipping underwater. He held my hand as my feet found the cool mush at the bottom. It came up between my toes like wet mud. I pulled myself back up and wrapped around Wes again. I wiped the water from my eyes. "Ew."

"I'm so glad I came on this trip," he laughed, slipping his hands around my waist and walking toward the waterfall. "I almost didn't."

He kissed me before I could respond and kept walking until the waterfall hit us on the tops of our heads. I wanted to shut my brain off and not worry about all of my nonsensical problems. I didn't want to worry about reading into everything that came out of his mouth. I wanted to be happy in the moment. I put my hands around his face, leaned back, and smiled, letting the waterfall hit me in the face. I'd seen this waterfall hundreds of times, but I'd never once stood under it. It was colder than the pool of water.

Wes slipped us behind it, into a pocket underneath the rock. He pushed my hair out of my face and kissed me below my eye. "I do wish I could take back this black eye though."

I guessed the water had washed away my makeup. I shook my head. "I wouldn't take it back for anything."

"You sure about that? It led to the mother fiasco."

I thought about it for a second. "Still no, even though that is probably now the number one most embarrassing moment of my life."

"Don't say I never gave you anything."

"What's your most embarrassing moment?"

Wes laughed. "Jesus, Leigh. I'm not sure I can trust you *that* much."

"You *said* you would tell me anything I wanted to know."

"I did say that, didn't I?" Wes squeezed my waist. "Alright. Freshman year I liked this girl in my Econ class, and I finally got the nerve to talk to her. So, we're walking across campus talking, and we cut through a parking lot. I'm about to ask her for her number, but instead, I trip over one of those parking space cement block things. I don't know what they're called, but I was looking at her instead of the ground, and I face planted. She tried not to laugh at me, which only made it worse. After that, I had to sit in class with her, wishing every week I could drop, but it was past the cutoff date, and I would have gotten a W."

"*You're* the infamous Parking Lot Face Smash Boy?"

Wes narrowed his eyes at me and placed his forehead on my

shoulder. "God, I hope you're joking."

"You'll never know." He couldn't see my smile, but I knew he could hear it. "She probably still would've gone out with you, you know. Every girl I knew in college was obsessed with you."

"Oh, yeah?" He picked his head back up.

"Yeah. I don't know how many girls used to ask me if you were single. It was annoying actually."

"Did that make you jealous?" Wes said playfully as his face came toward mine.

I nodded.

"How jealous?" he whispered, slipping his hands around my butt.

"Like... really, really jealous." There was really no other way to describe it.

Wes pulled my chin down with his thumb, kissed me, and nibbled my bottom lip, making a small sound come up from my throat. He broke away and groaned.

"Those little sounds. We have to stop before I push you up against this rock."

"You don't want to have sex with me against a rock?" I asked with a frown.

Wes bit my earlobe. "I can't do what I want to do to you against a rock. Besides, I think it would be painful."

I looked over at the rock wall, only then noticing the jagged edges. "You're such a gentleman."

"Only when I want to be."

I felt his words between my legs. The thought of him being ungentlemanly, forceful, and demanding in the bedroom, which I'd never even considered a possibility, was undulating through my body.

I looked at the rock above our heads. "It looks slimy."

Wes looked up and silently reached his hand up and rubbed the rock ceiling with his fingertips. He brought his hand back down and found my hand under the water. He tried pulling it up, but I resisted because I didn't want to touch a gross rock, so instead, he placed his lips on the bottom of my palm first and kissed me lightly while he held eye contact, the gray sucking me in. I felt his tongue softly graze my skin. Then he tried again, pulling my hand up with his. I gave in because he was staring back at me with his magically-turned-blue eyes, somehow making us touching a rock together the sexiest thing in the world. It was freezing against my warm, watered-down hand; slimy but also smooth. I could feel algae tickling the pads of my fingers. He moved my fingers with his, lacing them together in and out.

But I didn't want to look anywhere but in Wes' eyes. I tightened my legs around his waist, and I detected the faintest little smile behind his lips. His arm around my waist pulled me tighter against his abs. The thumb of my other hand found the hard line between them. I could feel his arousal against the back of my thigh. I didn't know what I wanted him to do—maybe a small part of me wanted him to ravish me right there—but I also just had an urge to be closer to him in this strangely intimate moment we were sharing.

He flattened my hand against the rock, and my palm turned cold as it laid fully against the slick surface. His fingers trailed down to my wrist. His thumb rubbed over the tendons popping up tightly against my skin. One finger came down my forearm—I wasn't sure which because I was hypnotized—before he played with the back of my elbow. Then those long, manly fingers tightened around my bicep. With his eyes still on mine, he lowered his head slightly, and instead of ravishing me, he kissed the inside of my upper arm. His full lips pressed firmly against my muscle, right below where his fingers were holding me. I felt his lips open a millimeter before he kissed me again and the end of his tongue glided against me. His hand moved back up my arm painstakingly slowly before the tips of his fingers pulled my palm away from the rock and back into his hand.

"God, Wes," I whispered as he brought our hands down together, and he placed my hand on the back of his neck.

My mind was out of control. How could this man be like this? Perfect for me in every way.

This must be what finding your soulmate feels like. As soon as I caught myself saying that in my head, I thought about checking myself into a mental institution. Most people's soulmates aren't attached to their brother, and most people don't think they've found their soulmate after one weekend.

Or could I say it had been a long nine years?

Those delicious fingers held me around my jaw again. "I know," he whispered before he brought my mouth to his.

He walked me back through the waterfall, then looked up at the sky. I followed his line of sight. The stars were intense—something we never got to enjoy in New York.

Wes looked around for a paddle board. Both had floated to the bank underneath a low-hanging tree.

"Float for a second. I'll get it."

I treaded water as I watched him swim underneath the branches. He grabbed one and pushed it toward me. I gripped the edge and slid myself up to sit in the middle. The cold air hit my skin, making my teeth chatter.

Wes pushed himself up on the board with me.

"Shit, it's cold," he remarked. He pulled his wet T-shirt off and reached for mine. His fingers peeled it off my wet skin and over my head. "Better?"

I still shivered, but it was slightly warmer without the wet fabric clinging to me. Now, my boobs were the only thing freezing underneath my bra. My nipples were as hard as rocks. "A little."

Wes ran his hand down my arm. "You're so beautiful, Leigh."

"You don't see Owen when you look at me?" I asked him hesitantly.

"No, I see you." He pulled me down with him as we lay back on the paddle board together. I put my head on his shoulder and draped my arm across his stomach, partly using him for his body heat.

We lay in silence looking at the stars for a long time.

"This is one of the best nights I've had in a really, really long time," I whispered. Maybe ever.

Wes just kissed me on the head.

—

WHEN WE APPROACHED the dock an hour later, laughing and talking, Wes held my board steady as I climbed up. I sat on the edge and held the board with my feet while Wes picked his board up out of the water before grabbing mine.

He laid both of them down on the dock and stood up. "I don't want to go upstairs," he said, slapping my butt. I started to turn around, but my toes got caught in one of my sandals that I'd left on the dock.

"Shit," I cried too loudly as I stumbled backward and fell on my ass.

Wes tried to muffle his laughter. "You're going to wake everyone up." He looked up towards the house and laughed harder. "Uh oh, too late."

My eyes went wide. I snapped my head around to see the outline of my mom standing on her bedroom deck in the dark.

"It's just us, Nancy," Wes said softly, but loud enough for his voice to carry up to her.

"Goodnight, you two." Her voice was almost a whisper when it reached us. She went back into her open doorway and slid the sliding glass door closed.

"She has bat ears," Wes exclaimed. "I'm amazed you were ever able to sneak out of the house."

"She's the lightest sleeper. So annoying."

Wes held his hand out to me. I took it, palm to palm, and he pulled me up in a swift motion. "Do you think she's watching us through the window? Because I really want to kiss you. And I don't want to do it softly."

I grinned and clutched his hand harder before turning around and dragging him up the stairs and back underneath the house.

The wooden door swung shut with a loud bang behind us, but neither of us cared. Wes pushed me up against the cold cement wall, grabbed my wrists, and pinned my hands above my head. His mouth connected with mine vigorously. If I could have kissed him forever, I would have. Just to feel like that—uninhibited, unrestrained, untamed. His tongue worked its way over my neck, my shoulders, and my chest.

"I'm going to get you alone tomorrow," he whispered right below my ear. "Inside the house."

The touch of his breath descended to my toes. "You better," I murmured into his ear as he sucked my neck.

When I finally lay back down in bed at 3:30 a.m., all I could think about was that quick and eager tensing I felt throughout his whole body that was pushed hard against mine when I said that.

CHAPTER 12

"Will you preheat the oven to three fifty for me?" I asked my mom.

"Sure, sweetie." She sidestepped to her right and turned the dial. She went back to making her chicken salad.

I had my ingredients laid out on the kitchen island. I opened two drawers before I found a whisk. I turned back around and measured three cups of flour into my large metal mixing bowl.

I kept glancing to my left at the spot where I'd been the day before with Wes. I hoped eventually I would be able to look at anything in the house and have a memory of him attached to it—without my mother. But I had to focus on my flag cake, or I'd mess it up.

I measured out the salt and the baking soda. Then I picked up the cream of tartar and started daydreaming again—feeling his breath on my ear, his large hand against my waist, his tongue gliding over my cartilage, his mouth against my eye socket, his arm around me as we lay on the paddle board, and that intense contraction of his body.

"Leigh?" My mom's voice went from low to high like she was pulling me out of a vacuum.

"Sorry, what'd you say?"

"How much butter does it call for?"

"Oh." I looked at my phone. "A stick and a half. One for the batter, a half for the icing."

She set aside a stick and cut another in half as I started whisking the ingredients together in my bowl.

"Hello, Leigh?" I heard her voice again an octave higher.

I looked up. "Yeah?"

"Do you need the electronic mixer?"

"Yeah, I do," I replied. "For the next step."

She opened the cabinet next to the oven and placed the mixer next to me. Her hands hesitated on top of the box. "Do you want to talk about it?"

I glanced out the kitchen window to the dock where Emma, Owen, Katie, Kathryn, and Nick were swimming and laying out.

"Ugh, not really, Mom."

"Alright," she said. She was going to let me come to her.

I got the mixer out of the box and snapped the pieces into it. My curiosity overwhelmed me. My words came out rushed. "Did you tell Dad?"

"No, I haven't."

I breathed a sigh of relief for Wes, who was golfing with my dad, and began beating the butter, sugar, and oil together in a separate bowl.

"Have you told Owen?" my mom asked. She already knew the answer, but she was trying to be polite.

"You know I haven't."

She opened the refrigerator. "How many eggs?"

"One."

She nodded and placed an egg from the carton down in front of me. "Are you going to?"

"I don't know. Wes wants to," I said.

LEIGH MAKES THREE

I added the water and cracked open the egg on the side of the bowl.

"How long has it been going on?" she asked.

I laughed as I plugged in the mixer. "Uh, it's complicated, I guess. One weekend? A month? Eight years?"

My mom spun around and repeated me with horror in her voice. "Eight years?"

"We kissed once in college," I elaborated before turning on the mixer. I watched the egg yolk make a spiral through my batter before slowly disappearing.

"Oh." She relaxed. "And why do you say a month?"

"Because we stopped ourselves a month ago before it escalated."

I poured my first bowl of ingredients into the second bowl and mixed them together. My mom was watching me intently while she waited for the whirring to stop.

"So, you both feel guilty?"

"Of course we do."

"What are you afraid of?"

I shrugged. "Lots of things."

I pulled the large pan out from the drawer and lined it with parchment paper before continuing. "Pissing off Owen. Stealing his best friend from him. And what if it didn't work out, and Owen has to choose sides? What happens if something goes wrong? I'd come between their friendship."

"Are y'all dating?" my mom asked as the oven beeped.

"I don't know. We haven't talked about it. I don't know what he wants." I kneaded the batter from the bowl into the pan, using my fingers to spread it out evenly into the rectangular shape.

"Maybe you should start there," she suggested. I could tell from her voice she was trying to give me advice, but not be an overbearing mother while still trying not to make it seem like she was choosing a side. She was not in the best position.

I shook my head. "I'm not ready for 'the talk' with him yet."

Ugh, the dreaded 'what are we' talk. Was it too soon? Would I scare him away?

"Well, it's no secret how much I love him. I've always, what do you kids say—shipped?—y'all. I've noticed the chemistry you two have over the years. I'd be surprised if Owen never noticed it."

I put my pan in the oven and spun around. "Where did you pick that word up?"

"I'm just with it," she said.

I laughed under my breath and turned back to the oven. I set a timer for sixteen minutes. "Do you think Owen will be mad?"

"Maybe a little at first. I think he'll be mad y'all kept it from him more than anything. But if you explain things to him and reassure him, I think he can accept it."

"Wes is a much better person than I am. I'm not ready to tell Owen."

I turned back to the island and proceeded to make the icing in silence. I got out a clean bowl and mixed the remaining ingredients together. I opened the vanilla and poured it out carefully on my teeny fourth teaspoon. The smell wafted up to my nose, reminding me of Wes' scent that followed him everywhere. I tipped it into my bowl, watching the dark liquid splatter against the white icing. I folded the mixture over with my spatula as the brownish vanilla slowly dissipated.

My timer beeped, bringing me out of my thoughts. I pulled the pan from the oven and let it cool for a few minutes.

I turned my focus out the window. Emma was laying out on the dock texting Logan, I was sure. Owen had dragged the water trampoline out of storage and flipped it upside down in the water so they could sit in it—him and Katie, Kathryn and Nick.

I imagined if Wes and I were sitting with him and Katie instead;

as two couples. Would Owen be able to handle that? Katie had seemed to change him in ways. She'd made him a better person. Maybe he could accept it if we loved each other. Maybe my mom was right. Figuring out what we were was probably the first step.

When my pan was cool enough, I spread out the icing on top. When I had a thick layer, I placed the blueberries in the top left corner, making a small rectangle. I cut my strawberries into slices on the cutting board and started placing them in stripes along the top.

"Do you like him?" my mom asked me.

I nodded my head without looking at her. I finished the rest of my flag and put it in the refrigerator to set.

I heard the side door open.

"This man is a hell of a golfer," my dad said, walking into the kitchen. "I'm going to replace Owen with you whenever you come up from now on."

I looked at my dad, then Wes (in his sexy golf polo and khaki pants), then my mom. Not the best thing to hear after the conversation we'd just had. My mom gave me a reassuring smile.

"I had fun. You're not so bad yourself. Thanks for letting me tag along," Wes said genuinely, patting my dad on the shoulder. He turned and smiled at me. "Hey!"

"I'm going to get ready for the potluck. Everyone's out on the dock," I said back.

My mom had brought on an intense feeling of shame. I didn't know why because she had all but straight out said she was elated.

He looked between me and my mom curiously, then at the counter with all of our baking crap in a floury mess. His eyes met mine again with a new look of understanding. He knew we'd been talking about him.

Wes vs. Twin Bond was a hell of a match.

I PUT MY flag cake down on the long row of tables filled with food. This was the eighteenth annual July Fourth potluck. We and our neighbors took turns hosting it each year. We'd grown so close with so many families that spent their summers there over the years. I had a ton of second families. All of the parents would get together for dinner and drinks while all of the kids would play. It had become house roulette every week from June to August. Then we got older, and a lot of the kids couldn't spend the entire summer there anymore. Now all of the parents were retired, and they spent even more time together.

I looked around at all my mountain families. I had so many memories at each of their houses: movie nights, pool tournaments, bonfires, skinny dipping, making out. It was like an escape world up there—somewhere you could go to be a crazy kid and do crazy kid things with everyone else.

Emma and I found two seats together.

"Remember when you made out with Stephen all summer?" I laughed.

"His kisses were so wet, I don't want to remember. His tongue was, like, so far down my throat that I was choking."

"He was fun though. And he was such a good wakeboarder," I reminded her.

"True. It was fun to watch him and let him teach me. He always grabbed my ass under the water." She laughed. "And he loved s'mores. We should do a bonfire after the fireworks tonight."

I smiled brightly at Emma. "For sure. We'll have to get Owen to get some firewood out from under the house. I can't remember the last time we built a fire and did s'mores."

My phone dinged in my lap.

Wes texted me: **Your mom asked me to come get something back at** the house. No one's here... we'll be alone.

My body and my heart betrayed my mind as it played tug-of-war, but it was two against one. The shame my mom had made me feel was nothing compared to the ache between my legs and the longing I felt to become closer to Wes.

I looked up at Emma. "Would you hate me if I left you for a little while?"

"It better be good," she smirked at me.

"I love you! Text me if anyone leaves."

I looked around at the party before getting up and walking up the driveway and down two houses to mine. I went in through the front door. The house was eerily quiet. I stood in the foyer listening for any creak in the house. Nothing. I waited for a minute until I heard his footsteps coming up the staircase from the basement. I saw his blond hair first, then his gray eyes. I was immediately glad I came.

"Hey," Wes said when he saw it was me.

"Hey, yourself."

He walked toward me and wrapped his hand around the back of my neck. He bent and kissed me slowly. My hands found their way under his shirt.

His tongue ran across my bottom lip as he made a low sound into my mouth which made me kiss him back harder. He pulled me in toward him, and I jumped up and straddled him. He ran his tongue down my throat before sucking my skin gently, then harder.

"God, Wes," I whispered toward the ceiling. I rubbed myself against him, craving more, wishing we were in swimsuits instead of jean shorts and pants. "How long do you think we have this time?"

He pulled back. "Now that I've finally got you alone, I told you the next time I'd be pleasing you, so as long as you want."

I wanted to give him full control again. "What have you always wanted to do to me?"

"Do you trust me?" he asked, his voice low.

I nodded. He reached behind him and pulled out one of his ties. "I want to blindfold you. Are you okay with that?"

"Yes," I whispered.

His pupils enlarged, wiping out the gray. I'm almost positive I felt my own pupils dilate. I was so intoxicated by the idea.

I grabbed hold of his neck as he tied the light blue tie over my eyes. I could just see a sliver if I looked down hard. I closed my eyes against the fabric. I wanted to be completely immersed.

He laughed softly. "I'm not going to do anything crazy, I promise. It will just make everything better. Tell me to stop at any point, and I'll stop."

I nodded.

He grabbed my ass hard, turned around, and headed up the stairs. I thought he turned to the left, but I wasn't sure. I heard him close a door we must have walked through, and a lock clicked.

"No one's going to walk in this time." He slipped off my sandals behind his back and lowered me down slightly. "Stand up."

I put my bare feet down on the carpet.

"Stay still," he instructed me, his voice gruff in my ear. His tongue darted out and flicked my earlobe. I felt his breath come down to my neck before his lips kissed me below my ear. He pulled my hair to the side and massaged his tongue down my neck. He pulled back before I felt his breath on my jawbone next. He bit me lightly before bringing his mouth up to mine and slipping his tongue between my lips.

Wes' fingertips came up underneath my shirt and lightly brushed my stomach. Static electricity bounced off my skin like his fingers were charged.

His mouth disconnected from mine as his fingers went up and down the front of my stomach. He moved to my sides, brushing lightly and creating a wave of goosebumps.

"Arms up," he said softly.

I raised my arms above my head, and he gripped the bottom of my shirt, bringing it up over my head, careful not to mess up my blindfold. He readjusted it a little bit.

I could feel him standing in front of me. I could hear him breathing softly. I wasn't sure how because my heart was pulsing loudly and rapidly, anticipating his next touch.

His voice in my ear surprised me. I didn't know his face was so close to mine. "Do you know how sexy you are?"

I shook my head slightly.

"So fucking sexy, you're all I think about."

One of his fingers touched me at the nape of my neck before running around to the front, down between my boobs, down to my belly button, and back up. He gripped my waist as his mouth touched my upper chest, kissing its way across from left to right.

I pushed my chest out for him, lost in the sensation that I could only feel him and not see him. I felt like I needed to be closer even though we were connected, like the surface area wasn't enough. His tongue licked me across the top edge of the right cup of my bra, down to the middle, and back up the left cup. His hands and mouth fell away from my body.

The guessing game of where he'd end up next was driving me wild, and I was quickly figuring out that Wes was going to drive me wilder than anyone ever had. Just like he said he would.

Suddenly, his thumb ran over my lips before he kissed me again. I let out a small moan into his mouth. He kissed me harder as his hands pulled me in by the small of my back. I could feel how hard he was. I reached down to run my hand over him.

"I want a dick pic from you later," I joked against his lips.

He laughed softly. His hand slowly caressed up my back to my bra, and he unhooked it effortlessly.

He tore his mouth and hands away. My bra was hanging loosely off my shoulders. I couldn't feel his presence at first, but his hands slipped underneath my straps, and he slowly slid them down my arms. I heard it hit the floor.

The air moved around me, and I was pretty sure Wes was standing behind me, but he didn't touch me again for a few seconds. On second number three, I felt a sudden thirst. Two seconds later, he kissed my shoulder blade, then bit my shoulder, while his hand came up the back of my neck. He gripped my hair close to my scalp and pulled my head to the side gently, then harder. He sucked his way up the side of my neck as his other hand came up my stomach and grabbed my right breast.

I pushed against him harder, grinding my butt into him. He released my hair and brought his hand to my front, grabbing both of my breasts and massaging them. He pinched my nipples and rolled them around between his fingers.

Wes licked the side of my neck, and whispered in my ear, "Are you having fun?"

"I've never been this turned on in my life," I said into the air.

"Can I take it further?"

"Please," I begged. "I'll tell you if I want to stop, remember?"

He released me, but I couldn't tell where he went until his tongue flicked my right nipple. Then he flicked my left before grabbing my breast and sucking while he played with the other between his fingers.

"God, Wes." I reached my hands up to find his head. I ran my hands across the back of it. "Don't ever stop."

He released his suction on me, and I felt him stand up. He stepped around me again with a low laugh. "We're just getting started."

A few of his fingers traced down my spine, sending a shiver from my lower back to my feet.

Another few seconds passed. Each one was deepening the

longing of having his touch back. The next three seconds were torture.

His fingers finally came around my waist and unbuttoned my jean shorts. His left hand trailed up my stomach before he wrapped his arm tightly across my upper chest, holding me firmly against him. His right hand slipped into my jean shorts over my underwear, and he grabbed me tightly like he was staking claim to me. He relaxed and rubbed over me in a small circle. He brought his hand back up before going back down below my underwear.

I gasped at his touch against my skin. I spread my legs slightly for him as he applied more pressure and increased his speed. His fingers stopped rubbing suddenly before he entered me with his middle finger. I could feel the blood rushing down to meet his touch.

I gasped again as he put repeated pressure against the front wall of me. I arched my back into him and moaned. I picked my arms up over my head and found the back of his neck, gripping it hard. I gyrated against him and his fingers.

"That feels so good, Wes," I breathed out in pleasure.

His lips and tongue played with my earlobe.

"Moan louder for me when I hit the spot you like," he said, licking the cartilage of my ear from bottom to top.

I nodded against his chest, turned on more by his willingness to figure out what I liked. He adjusted his finger, but I stayed quiet. He moved slightly higher, and he got closer. On the third time, he found it. My knees went a little weak, and I moaned loudly.

"There it is," he whispered. "Fuck, you're so hot." He grabbed the side of my face and turned my head up roughly—a rough I liked—so he could kiss me hungrily while he concentrated on that spot. I whimpered into his mouth, consumed by the feelings he was giving me.

Suddenly, he pulled both of his hands back at once and stopped kissing me. His touch was gone for a few seconds before he gripped the waistband of my shorts and tugged them down quickly. I stepped out of them when I felt them around my ankles. I didn't remember what underwear I'd put on that morning until I felt Wes' breath as he laughed against the back of my thigh.

"Your thong has your face all over them," Wes stated.

Oh, right.

"A joke gift from Emma," I explained to the room. She'd given them to me when I hit my six-month no-sex streak. He didn't need to know that.

I think he was on his knees behind me as his mouth came up the back of my thigh. He grabbed my ass, pushing his long fingers into it, taking hard handfuls. He rubbed his palms over both cheeks, gripping my hips as he planted kisses on my butt. He was an ass guy.

He slipped his thumb between my legs, making me go weak again as he rubbed over me. He moved my thong to the side and put one of his thumbs inside me, knowing right where to go, while he rubbed me with his other thumb.

I moaned louder while he kissed my left butt cheek. I rose up on the balls of my feet slightly as the pleasure built.

He slowly pulled out and replaced my underwear. He grabbed my waist as he stood up, licking my spine in the process. His arms curved around my waist, and he came back to standing in front of me. I felt his warm breath against my lips, and I tipped my head up slightly, waiting for him to kiss me.

"I've been thinking about how much I want my face between your legs all day," he whispered instead of kissing me. He ran his hands down both of my arms and pulled my hands up under his shirt. I felt every curve I couldn't see with my fingertips. Then his shirt lifted away from my arms like he took it off.

"So, I guess I'm going to have to buy you some new underwear with my face on them." I could hear the smile in his voice.

He pulled me closer to him by my ass, taking it between his hands hard. He had taken his shirt off. I caressed my hands over his abs, up his chest, and down his arms. One hand came between my legs again, rubbing slowly, before he pushed me back gently. I backed up until I felt the edge of a bed. My bed I thought.

"Lie back," Wes commanded me.

I lowered my body onto the bed, feeling my comforter beneath my hands. I scooted myself back a little and put my head down. I thought Wes was still standing because I didn't feel his weight on the bed.

His fingers grabbed my left ankle and brought it up into the air. He kissed my anklebone softly before making his way up my calf and placing my foot back down on the bed. He repeated that with my other leg before his hands roughly pushed my thighs wide apart.

"Fuck, look how wet you are," he said in a low masculine voice. "Tell me how much you like this."

"I don't know a word for it," I said, arching my back almost involuntarily just from the words he was saying.

"Leigh, you always have words." His hand rubbed over the wet area of my thong. "Tell me."

I let out a breath and rocked my hips against his hand. "You're the only one who can make me this wet, and I want more."

"You like giving up your control to me," he said more as a statement than a question.

I nodded my head as my hands clenched around my comforter at the gratification his voice was giving me.

His fingers caught the edge of my thong, and he pulled them off slowly. My legs went high in the air before dropping back to the bed. I opened my legs wide for him, begging silently for him to make contact again.

I heard him laugh softly. "Aren't you full of surprises?"

I didn't know what he was referring to until he kissed me lightly over my tattoo and licked it.

"Touch yourself for me," he said.

Heat pierced me at the bottom of my stomach. The thought of him watching me sent another wave of blood rushing down. I started with my boobs, grabbing them between my hands, and playing with my nipples. I brought my right hand down and rubbed myself slowly before picking up speed. It didn't feel as good as when he did it, but I knew it was turning him on. I wished I could see his face. I inserted a finger bringing it in and out a few times until his fingers grasped my wrist and pulled me out.

"Does that feel as good as when I do it?" he asked me.

"God, no," I breathed out hard.

His tongue and lips gripped the finger I'd just used and sucked it.

His dominance was turning me on more than I knew was possible. I'd never been with someone who told me what to do in bed like that.

He pulled my finger out of his mouth slowly, and a second later, I felt his weight on the bed. He was hovering above me, then he kissed me. His tongue was soft and forceful at the same time. I reached down and found his erection, rubbing him over his pants. He brought my arms above my head and took both my wrists into his hand, pinning them down. His mouth came down to my neck, sucking gently. He grinded himself against me.

"Wes," I moaned.

He let go of my wrists and brought his mouth down to my breasts, gripping them hard, taking my nipples in his mouth. My fingers ran through his hair as he brought wave after wave of bliss with each flick of his tongue. He brought his mouth down to my ribs, kissing the bottom of my rib cage. He circled his tongue around my bellybutton.

Suddenly, he wasn't touching me anymore.

"Where'd you go?" I whimpered and arched my back. I waited.

And waited.

And waited.

I felt his hot breath between my legs. It sent one firework up through my stomach, exploding into my heart, as it pumped faster and faster. He kissed me on the inside of my right thigh, then my left. He nibbled closer toward me. His fingers rubbed over me as he nibbled his way even closer. He slowly entered me with one finger. His other hand was caressing my inner thigh.

"Wes," I moaned louder.

"I love hearing you moan my name," he said against my thigh as he curled his finger up. I rocked my hips. It felt good, but it wasn't *the* spot. He knew. He adjusted his fingers until he found it, and my legs tensed by themselves.

He kissed my inner thigh. "I can feel it in your legs when I find it, but I want to hear it too."

His voice had some sort of hold over my body, and maybe mine did over his. He liked to hear my pleasure. His fingers exited before I finally felt his wet tongue on me, flat at first as he ran up me.

My arms reached down to his head, my fingers wrapping around the back. His hands came up to my tits and he squeezed them. He used the end of his tongue to flick me quickly again and again, sending shockwaves between my legs.

"Holy shit, Wes."

His tongue entered me all of a sudden, the tip running over that spot just once. I'd never had a guy do that, and the sensation was different, but I got the feeling it was something Wes was doing for his own enjoyment. When he exited, he applied suction, then pulled back. He breathed out on me as two of his fingers entered me very slowly. He hooked them up into the correct spot that time. God, he was a quick learner. I arched my hips hard and moaned for him.

"Good girl," he breathed against my inner thigh and lightly bit me as he focused there with his fingers. "Are you ready to come?"

I nodded and whispered, "Yes, please."

He pushed my legs back wider. He brought his tongue back down on me and used two fingers to stimulate my own personal G-spot. W-Spot? He was perfectly rhythmic with his tongue and finger, bringing me to the edge.

I moaned loudly. If someone was in the house, they were going to hear me, but I didn't give a flying fuck. I wanted to scream his name. Wes wrapped his arm around my stomach, holding me down as I rocked my hips against his mouth and my thighs clenched around his head.

"Fuck, Wes, I'm coming," I moaned as I felt the wave of my orgasm start. I rode it for over thirty seconds to maybe a minute. I didn't really know how long, but it was definitely the longest orgasm I'd ever had (thanks partly to my extended time without one and partly to Wes, who quickly figured out how to drive me fucking nuts). Wes used his strength to hold me in position until I became so sensitive that I pulled him up by his hair.

He kissed me softly and lay beside me as I rapidly breathed in and out. He pushed the tie up off my eyes, but I kept my eyes closed, not wanting to come down from the high.

He kissed me harder and chuckled. "That was fun. Want to do that again?"

"God, you are so hot," I said, opening my eyes. I rolled on top of him, straddling him. "What about you?"

He shook his head. "I think people will start wondering where we are."

He sat up and kissed me. His hands snaked into my hair before he tugged it close to my scalp, bringing my head to the side.

"We have lots of time when we get back to New York," he whispered in my ear.

I kissed his neck before he stood up and gently placed me on the ground. He picked up my clothes and handed them to me. I dressed quickly before we headed back to the potluck.

Spaced out, of course. But not so spaced out that it was obvious.

CHAPTER 13

I stared at the open refrigerator like my next snack would decide my life—cheese, strawberries, yogurt, olives? Why when you want a snack, nothing seems appealing? And even after all the food I'd eaten at the potluck, I was still hungry.

"Hey!" Wes' voice said loudly in my ear.

I jumped out of my skin and turned around. "You scared the shit out of me."

"That's payback," he said.

"Man, you hold a grudge."

"Is everyone still napping?"

"Yeah, the potluck really wipes you out the older you get. Gotta recharge for the fireworks."

"I've got a surprise for you."

I raised my eyebrows at him. He kissed me.

"Not like that." He reached into his pocket and pulled out a vaporizer.

"I don't smoke those things," I told him.

"It's a weed vape pen," he clarified.

I cracked a wide smile. "That changes things. Dock?"

Wes nodded and followed me out of the house.

"Where'd you get that?" I asked him as we went down the steps. "I feel so old now."

"Nick knew someone. I figured you'd like it for the fireworks."

"Why's that?"

"Because of what you told me about the carousel."

I smiled at the thought of him remembering that and contemplated bringing up the 'what are we' talk. Maybe if I knew, I could figure out how to proceed.

When we reached the dock, we both slipped off our sandals and sat on the edge. I dangled my feet down into the cool water. Little minnows came up, curious about what I was, before swimming away at my movement.

Wes handed me the pen first, and I took a hit.

"Do you ever miss being a stupid kid?" I handed it back to him.

"Yes and no," he said before taking a hit and putting it down between us. "I like being an adult. Having my own place, being independent. But yeah, I wish sometimes we'd get a break from the weight of it all."

I nodded and laughed. "Adulthood equals anxiety."

"What do you get anxious about?" Wes asked me.

"Work. Family. Friends. My apartment. It's all the small things on top of each other, I guess." I thought for a second. "Like, am I going to lose my job because that client hated my ideas? Is my apartment rent going to go up? I feel much more sucked into my own shit. And then I wonder, do I call everyone enough and check in with them? Am I being a good friend? A good sister? A good daughter? Sometimes I look back and wonder how long it's been since I called any of them. At least I work with Emma. You don't get anxious?"

"Yeah, of course I do," Wes said. "All of that stuff is definitely important. I try to remind myself that if I got sick tomorrow, none of that shit would matter. My job doesn't come first. The people I love do, and the people that love me would matter the most in the end. They'd be there with me, no matter what. And you have a ton of people that love you, no matter what. Screw wasting time. Time is one of the few things you can never get back."

"Yeah," I whispered to my feet as they swirled in the water. Of course, he was right, and he would know that just as much as anyone. Certainly more than me. "I need to be better about that."

"Would you go back to high school or college if you could?" he asked me.

"No, I wouldn't. I'm ready for some of those adult things eventually. I want to get married and have children. Watch my kids grow up and be stupid kids."

Wes' phone dinged in his pocket, but he ignored it.

"You gonna get that?" I asked curiously. It was the third time I thought that had happened.

"Nah." He shook his head. "Have you thought about telling Owen? I really want to, and you know I can't lie."

"Noooo," I drawled and hit him in the arm. "Don't make me anxious. You'll ruin my buzz."

He grabbed the top of my thigh and squeezed. He brought his foot over to mine, and we sat for a minute playing footsie in the water.

"I can't stop thinking about today," he said, breaking the silence.

"Me either," I confessed. The thought of it brought heat between my legs. I didn't even really nap because first, I had to tell Emma everything, and then I kept tossing thinking about it.

Wes leaned into my ear. The vibrations of his voice traveled throughout my body. "Are you getting turned on thinking about it like I am?"

I nodded and whispered, "That was the best orgasm I've ever had."

"Seriously?" He pinched my side. "Don't lie to me if it wasn't. I won't learn what you like if you lie."

I let out a short laugh. Wes definitely took the time to learn what I liked, but I felt a hollow pit in my stomach that time, wondering if this was about sex for him. "I'm not lying!"

"What's the story behind that tattoo?"

I smirked at him and shrugged. "I was drunk."

"Is it supposed to symbolize this place?"

"Duh." I rolled my eyes at him. "It's my favorite place. I actually got it right before the trip up here when we kissed."

"Ah," he laughed. "I wish I would have seen it back then."

"It's probably better that you didn't. We were young and dumb."

"We're still young and dumb. Forever," he pointed out. "Want another hit?"

I nodded, and he picked it up and handed it to me.

"You're right. I don't think I'll ever grow up. Or maybe I mean, I will in some ways, but I won't in others."

He smiled and leaned in to kiss me. "I like you just the way you are."

Okay, good segue. "Wes—"

Emma's voice interrupted me. "Don't think you two can come out here and make out while everyone's napping *and* smoke weed without me."

Wes and I turned our waists toward her. She was eyeing the pen in my hand.

"I know you're not smoking an e-cigarette," she stated.

I laughed and handed it to her. "I wasn't holding out. Wes was."

She sat down behind us and took the pen from me. Wes and I turned, so we made a little circle, as she took a hit.

"Wes, Leigh and I are a package deal. Don't forget it."

"You think I don't know that?"

"Just checking." She handed the pen back to me. "But we won't fulfill any threesome fantasies you have."

I took another hit and handed it to Wes. "Yeah, we already tried that. Not pretty."

Wes eyed me, trying to decipher if I was joking or not, as he took a second hit.

"We got so into it we ignored the guy," Emma added.

Wes' eyes slid to Emma.

"Joking," Emma remarked and shook her head. "Men."

Wes laughed. "I'm not into threesomes. I would hope that I'm enough, and so is she."

"Good answer," Emma replied. "Almost *too* good."

Emma motioned to Wes to give her back the vape. She took a long hit from it and placed it in the middle of our circle.

"Never Have I Ever?" She glanced at me before looking at Wes, challenging him. "Hands up."

Wes chuckled and lifted his ten fingers. I loved how he didn't care. He'd put up with Emma's games, trying to squeeze information out of him.

Emma stared at my hands.

"Ugh, fine," I relented, bringing my hands up. "You're a child."

"Circle of trust," Emma said before starting with a surprise question out of nowhere. "Never have I ever had a threesome."

Wes kept his fingers up as he glanced at mine and Emma's. One of Emma's fingers went down. Mine stayed up. Her threesome was not with me.

"Aren't you supposed to say things you've never actually done?" Wes joked.

Emma shrugged. "My rules."

"So, who was your threesome with?" Wes asked her.

"Blake and Tori from college."

"Wow!" Wes laughed. "He wasn't lying."

Emma rolled her eyes. "Of course, he told people. Is nothing sacred anymore?"

"Don't worry," Wes reassured her. "Literally, no one believed him."

"That's the beauty of being Emma," I said and went next. "Never have I ever gotten a lap dance."

Wes' finger was the only one to go down. He continued, "Never have I ever been to a strip club."

Wes didn't move, but both Emma and I put our fingers down.

"Where'd you get a lap dance?" I asked curiously.

"A frat party in college," he explained.

"Never have I ever slept with someone whose name I didn't know or couldn't remember," Emma said.

No one put a finger down.

My turn. "Never have I ever had a friend with benefits."

Emma and Wes both put their fingers down. Shit. I regretted it as soon as I saw him move. Was he talking about me? And did he put any thought into me not putting my finger down? Did I out myself?

Wes' turn. "Never have I ever sent a nude photo."

Emma and I put a finger down while Wes stayed still.

"No dick pics?" Emma smirked at Wes. "I approve. Never have I ever kissed more than one person in a day."

My finger was the only one to go down.

"Never have I ever had a one-night stand," I said.

Emma's finger went down, and she was left with one hand. Emma and I knew too much about each other. We could play this game one for one if we wanted, the winner being whoever went first.

"Never have I ever flirted with someone to get a free drink," Wes said.

Emma put her finger down and snorted. "Unfair question that doesn't apply to you. Never have I ever hid something from my best friend or brother."

Wes and I looked at each other and put our fingers down.

"Unfair question that doesn't apply to you," I parroted Emma. "Never have I ever hooked up with an ex."

Emma and Wes put their fingers down. He wouldn't have hooked up with Rachel post-breakup, would he?

Wes' turn. "Never have I ever filmed myself having sex."

No one's finger went down.

Emma's turn. "Never have I ever had phone sex."

We all put our fingers down. Wes and I both lost a hand. Emma only had two fingers left.

"Never have I ever cheated," I continued.

No fingers down.

"Never have I ever faked an orgasm," Wes said.

Emma and I put our fingers down. I hoped he didn't think that was with him. It was Vanill-Dyl.

"Never have I ever had sex in a pool," Emma said.

Wes and I put a finger down.

My turn. "Never have I ever lied about how many people I've slept with."

No one put their finger down.

"Never have I ever gotten a tattoo that can't be seen," Wes said, looking at me.

I put my finger down.

"Never have I ever had a sex dream about someone sitting on this dock," Emma laughed.

I narrowed my eyes at her and quickly glanced at Wes. He was smirking at me. I didn't move until I saw his finger twitch. We put our fingers down together.

"Never have I ever gone on a blind date," I said.

Emma and Wes put their fingers down.

Emma was out, partly due to her own questions testing Wes. I only had one finger left.

"Never have I ever gone skinny dipping aside from sex in a pool," Wes continued.

I was out.

Wes laughed and wiggled his two fingers. "I'm the innocent one of this group?"

I nudged him with my arm. "So wholesome."

Emma raised her eyebrows at Wes. "Maybe I should have said 'never have I ever lied in this game' as one."

Wes smirked at her. "Wouldn't have made a difference."

I didn't get the feeling he was lying. Wes seemed genuine in everything he said and did. He smiled at me when he caught me staring at him.

Emma picked up the vape pen and took a third hit. "One more?" Emma asked, holding it out to both of us.

"Why not?" I shrugged. "I probably won't do this again for another few years."

It was starting to get dark. Wes looked at his watch. "They should be coming down soon."

Fifteen minutes later everyone joined us on the dock.

"It's going to be a tight squeeze," my dad said as we stepped onto the boat.

Emma, Wes, and I squeezed into the row to the right in the front. Owen, Katie, and my mom squeezed in the row across from us, and Nick and Kathryn sat in the back behind my dad who drove. He slowly pulled away from the dock as Emma started laughing under her breath, who knows about what, which set me off, which set Wes off. We were stoned and probably shouldn't have taken that third hit.

Owen looked between the three of us and put his arm around

Katie as my dad increased his speed. If Owen had something to say, it was too loud now.

The wind was rushing through my hair and face, making the inside of my ears hurt a bit. When we emerged into the wider part of the lake, my dad slowed down to maneuver around all the boats and find a spot. My face tingled when the wind stopped, making me smile. The motion of my surroundings was intensified.

My dad positioned us toward the shoreline, a large lot with a sloping hill and no trees. They'd been shooting fireworks from there for the last fifteen years. It'd become so big that our boat almost looked like it was parked in a huge marina. My dad waved at two families he knew in neighboring boats.

Wes put his arm around the back of my seat, leaned in, and pulled up one side of his lips into a smile near my face. "I haven't been high in such a long time. Since college."

I looked up into his red and heavy eyes, which made me giggle. I wished he would just bring his face down and kiss me. To hell with everyone around us.

The first firework streaked up into the sky, popping and lighting everything green. The color felt magnetic and more vivid than I remembered. I leaned back against Wes' arm, completely relaxed, giving in to the magnet that was pulling me, and feeling his arm against my back. My head was slightly looking up and turned in his direction. Our boat silently watched the sky and everything around us being coated in reds, blues, greens, purples, golds, whites, and yellows. They all seemed neon as they broke open across the sky.

I felt Wes' phone buzz in his pocket against my leg, but of course, he didn't move to get it. I watched Wes' face as the lights bounced off of his features. I was happy in the moment. Happy we were co-workers. Happy we made such a good team. Happy he had shared a piece of himself with me. Happy we were at least friends if nothing more. That was probably the weed talking.

He looked down at me and smiled. My heart dropped and bounced back up off the trampoline of my diaphragm. I was in too deep with him.

I focused back on the fireworks and the vibrations it was setting off like my body was a tuning fork.

"I NEED THIS s'more in my life so bad right now," I said, staring at the marshmallow on the end of my metal spike. The fire was crackling, sending sparks up, and browning my marshmallow just right. I hated them burnt—they were best with a golden coat.

Emma, on my right, and Wes, across the fire sitting next to Owen, nodded in agreement.

Owen looked at me from across the fire pit. "You got something you want to tell me?"

Wes' head sprang up from his phone, where he was texting, to look at Owen.

I looked up at Owen through the orange haze of the fire. Was it too quickly or was the THC just affecting my brain? "What?"

"How stoned are you three right now?" he guessed.

I relaxed. "Very."

Emma and Wes nodded again which made me giggle.

"Emma, why are you only sharing with them two?" Owen accused her.

"It's not mine. Wes brought it," she shot back.

"Dude." Owen turned to Wes who already had the vape pen in his hand, holding it out to him.

Owen snatched it out of his hand.

Wes went back to burying his face in his phone. I tried not to watch him as I laid my marshmallow on the graham cracker and topped it with chocolate and another graham cracker. It was the most delicious thing I'd ever eaten. I grabbed another marshmallow from the bag and sat down on a log to roast it.

I hadn't seen Wes so engaged with his phone since... ever. I wondered if it had to do with all those text messages he'd been ignoring. His face looked serious with his brow furrowed. His fingers would fly over the keyboard, then hover for a minute while he'd read, then go back to typing frantically. Occasionally a small smile would break through, then his mouth would fall back to serious or sad.

I turned to Emma, trying to distract myself. "What do you have going on this week at work?"

"Ugh, I don't want to talk about work. We're on vacation, Leigh. Don't be a buzzkill."

"Fine. What's Logan doing for the Fourth tomorrow?"

"He's going to some friend's rooftop party," she replied.

"That sounds fun!" I said. "Jack's is always so fun at New Year's. I miss him. I wish he could have come up here this year."

"The whole office would have been out," Emma laughed. She suddenly swatted the air, then brushed her leg.

"Are you hallucinating?" I joked.

"There are bugs everywhere. I'm going to go get some bug spray or a citronella candle." She rose from the log and made her way to the stairs.

I watched the fire swirl into gray smoke for a while until it drew my gaze upward, and I watched the tops of the tall trees sway. After a minute I felt too dizzy staring up like that. I looked across the lake and watched the fireflies dance in the darkness.

Everything about the lake and the mountains was special. It embodied the essence of simplicity. The essence of disconnecting and living in the moment. Those few and far between days we experience where you realize you haven't looked at your phone the entire day. And it feels good.

Wes sat down beside me, phone in hand.

I frowned at him. "I don't want to go back to work on Monday."

"Me either. But I don't go back until Friday."

"You're staying here that long?" I asked him, confused. I was pretty sure my parents were going back to Birmingham on Tuesday.

"No, I'm leaving tomorrow to go to Nashville for a few days," he explained.

"Oh. On the Fourth?"

"Yeah," he said vaguely. "I have things I need to do on Sunday."

Don't pry. Don't pry. Don't pry.

"Like what?" I pried.

"Just important stuff I need to take care of."

I stayed silent for a few seconds.

"You don't want to tell me?" I pried further with a laugh. It sounded so fake to my ears.

He avoided the question completely and nudged me with his shoulder. "I definitely don't want to leave this place though."

An uneasy feeling washed over me, but I tried to ignore it.

I nodded. "I hope I can retire here one day."

"Fishing and golfing and staring at a lake all day. You couldn't dream of a better retirement," Wes agreed.

"And old women."

"Woman," he corrected me.

"One old woman?"

"Isn't that the goal?" he asked me. "To share your life with someone?"

"Yeah, I guess it is." Another perfect segue, but we were high, and Owen was around. I talked myself out of bringing it up.

"Wes, will you help me get some more firewood from under the house?" Owen called from behind us.

"Sure." Wes stood up.

I looked into the dimmed fire. The embers were red hot at the bottom. Nick started poking it with a stick, which caused them to puff up in a cloud.

Something buzzed beside me, and I looked down to see Wes' phone that I hadn't realized he put down.

Rachel Cooper.

1 Message.

I couldn't help but read it. It could have said Rcehal Coeopr, and I'd have been able to decode it in the nanosecond of time I'd glanced at it. Even in my weed haze.

It buzzed again.

Rachel Cooper.

2 Messages.

My heart went through a shredder—the slivers piling up at my feet. I wanted to throw them all in the fire and watch them burn.

This was about sex. He befriended me with benefits. He wanted to finish what he started in college while he was texting his semi-ex-girlfriend the whole time. And he was going to see her in Nashville.

CHAPTER 14

There were two short knocks on my open door. Emma and I looked toward the sound from where we were sitting on my bed.

Wes was standing slightly inside my room. "I'm about to head out. I wanted to come say goodbye."

"This early?" Emma asked, getting up off the bed.

"I have to drive to Asheville, and you know I like to be early to the airport," Wes said.

"Happy Fourth! See you at work." Emma hugged him and left the room.

"Have a safe drive and flight," I smiled at him.

He studied my face. "Are you okay?"

"Yeah, I'm fine," I lied.

He let out a low laugh that sounded like I'd said the most unfunny thing ever. "The three words a man dreads most."

"Really, I'm fine!"

He looked at me skeptically and crossed the room to the edge of my bed. I didn't like that he could read me so well.

"You've been acting differently since last night. Did something happen?" he asked me.

I smiled at him. "Nope, just tired. I probably smoked too much of that vape pen."

He leaned down and kissed me on the lips softly. I kissed him back—just a little.

He pulled back and studied my eyes for a few seconds. He could feel that the kiss wasn't one hundred percent, but I didn't want to give it to him. I know I said I wasn't going to let him go that time, but that was before I knew Rachel was in the picture. I wasn't going to participate in some love triangle just because we hadn't discussed our relationship status.

All right, it's obvious we were already in some kind of strange love triangle with Owen, who was unaware that he was in one. So, was I in a love rhombus?

I smiled again. Wes could sense I wasn't going to tell him.

"I'll see you back in New York, okay? My flight comes in on Thursday," he told me.

"Okay," I said brightly.

He furrowed his brow for a second, grappling with the change of air between us. "Leigh..."

"What?"

My voice sounded flat. I watched him decide not to press it.

"Happy Fourth of July!" he said instead of whatever he was thinking. Probably: *Women. Always so talkative until they shut down, wanting me to read their mind instead of just telling me what's wrong.*

Guilty.

"Happy Fourth of July," I echoed.

He pivoted, and I looked down, refusing to watch him walk out of the room.

I heard his footsteps go down the stairs.

Emma came back a few seconds later. "What'd—"

I widened my eyes and shushed her. I got up off the bed, shut the door, and whispered, "He'll hear you."

"What'd you say?" she said in an exaggerated whisper.

"Nothing," I whispered back. "I'm not going to say anything. I have to work with him. I have to see him with Owen. I have to see him at the wedding. Ugh, I'm walking down the aisle with him."

I threw myself onto the bed.

"So, what are you going to do? Continue sleeping with him?"

"We haven't *technically* had sex, Em. And no, I'm not going to continue doing anything. He'll get the hint. But I'm definitely not telling him I fell for him."

"It's not embarrassing that you fell for him. He's a great guy. He's good-looking. You shouldn't have to apologize for that," Emma said. "Plus, you don't even *technically* know how he feels. Maybe he likes both of you."

"I think the serious girlfriend of seven—sorry, six—years overrides his weekend fling," I grumbled.

"She cheated on him. You don't know that."

I rolled my eyes at her. "God, I am so happy we didn't tell Owen. Now, he never has to know, and things can just go back to the way they were."

Emma snorted, which made me angrier. "You're just going to magically go back to not being aroused by every move he makes?"

"Yes!" I glared at her. "I am."

"Yeah, okay," she said skeptically.

I picked up a pillow and screamed, "Fuck!" into it. I breathed in against the pillowcase, squeezing my eyes shut. I breathed in again deeper.

Emma grabbed it. "Don't smother yourself."

"Want to go lay out on the dock in silence?" I asked, composing myself.

Once we made it out to the dock in our swimsuits, we fanned two towels out next to each other. I lay down on my back, sunglasses on and eyes closed, and essentially relived the last nine years of my life.

—

FRESHMAN YEAR, OWEN texted me to ask if I wanted to get pizza. I think it was around Thanksgiving because I remember decorations in the windows. When I walked in, I saw Owen sitting in a booth with his girlfriend of the month and a guy I'd never met.

"Leigh, this is Wes," he said when I sat down. "Wes, this is my sister, Leigh."

Wes looked up at me and my stomach ballooned. His gray eyes beneath his long eyelashes, his genuine smile, and the way he stuck his hand out to shake mine, made me feel light. I could tell he was tall even though he was sitting.

"Hey, Leigh. It's nice to meet you," he said. It was the first time in a long time that I'd been tongue-tied.

"Hou too," I managed to say, combining hey and you because my brain wasn't computing. But Owen had lots of hot friends. I knew he wouldn't be any different once he opened his mouth—they were mostly assholes.

"You want to split a pizza?" Wes asked me. "I'll compromise unless you're into nasty buffalo chicken pizzas too."

"Not all twins are alike," I replied. "I hate buffalo chicken, but I won't be able to help you either. I'm a Hawaiian girl. Only special people like pineapple on pizza."

Wes smiled wide, surprised. He opened his mouth to say something, but Owen beat him to it.

"Oh, I forgot to tell you that, Wes. Leigh loves pineapple pizza," he said before looking at me. "I brought him specifically for you. He loves pineapple pizza too. You can eat that crap together."

And there began my crush and the first line item on my Wes List.

Sophomore year, Emma and I went to a Halloween party as a surgeon and a patient. Emma had found a slightly sexy doctor costume. I found a sleeveless nude bodysuit and these tight pink shorts, and I hand-made small body part stickers to stick all over my body. It was tight and hugged my curves. We were slutty, but not too slutty. Slutty with a funny edge.

Emma and I danced for the majority of the night. Wes had been dancing with some girl right next to us.

After the song ended, I heard Wes' voice in my ear. "You dropped this."

I turned around to see him holding up one of my stickers.

"Where does it go?" he asked me. I got excited at the thought of him touching my skin to stick it back on me.

I looked at the little sticker in his hand. "It's my Adam's apple," I said, lifting my chin and pointing to my neck.

He chuckled and eyed my throat. "So does it belong to me or you?"

It was okay to flirt with him a little. He certainly sounded flirty. "Well, that—" I started.

Someone bumped into Wes, hard, and his drink spilled all over the front of my chest.

"Shit," he muttered. "Leigh, I'm so sorry."

I laughed. "It's fine. Sticky, but fine."

"Come with me." His hand slid down my arm, and he grabbed my hand. He led me into the kitchen and set me against the counter next to the sink. He tore off a few paper towels from the holder under the cabinet and ran them under the water. He started to come toward my upper chest but changed his mind.

"Here," he said, handing me the towels. "Did I ruin your costume?"

I shook my head and smiled at him, wondering if it was see-through. "No, and it will dry super quick. It's really thin."

He shifted away from me after I said that.

"You win best costume though." His eyes glossed over my body like he couldn't help it. I knew I looked good, and I got a rush for a minute thinking I made him forget who I was to him.

These moments between us were rare. We never hung out unless it was a coincidence or because Owen invited me. We'd share a casual hello and a hug. We'd have group conversations, but even when we were in the same place at the same time, we didn't have many conversations between just the two of us.

"And you are Stan Smith?" I hesitated, looking at his suit and American flag pin. "Oh, I guess you could be the president. I love *American Dad!*"

Wes looked at me with wide eyes, making his irises look like full moons. "You're the first person to get it right. That show is hilarious."

"Right! Who knew you were smart too?" I harmlessly flirted a little. He always said things that surprised me—caught me off guard in a good way—when I learned a new scrap of information about him.

I watched him as I wiped my chest off. He purposely looked away. Even when he was drunk, he was a guy who didn't watch girls wipe their wet boobs off with a paper towel.

"You didn't have to be so nice and help me," I said when I was finished.

"Of course, I did," he remarked. "What kind of guy would I be if I didn't help my best friend's sister after I poured my drink on her? Any girl, really."

His words hit me in the head like a wrecking ball, slamming me back to the ground.

The summer after that, we kissed.

The fall after that, he met Rachel Cooper at a party. She was a beautiful, petite, blonde cheerleader. I watched them dance and talk out of the corner of my eye. I couldn't help it. Wes dated or hung out with different girls over the two years I'd known him. He wasn't a saint. He was definitely still a guy. But of course, he was a catch, and girls knew it. I wasn't lying when I told Wes girls were obsessed with him. I really could count on all my fingers and toes and all of your fingers and toes the number of times girls asked me if Owen or Wes were single. It was like I was their weird gatekeeper. A gatekeeper who couldn't open the gate myself and lock it behind me. But she seemed different. I also knew it didn't really matter what happened with them because what happened between us was a fluke. Within a few weeks, they were inseparable.

I didn't see Wes much junior year, except when we happened to be working at the same time with his dad or our one class together. But he always sat with his guy friends, and I'd started my year-long relationship with Nate anyway. I was definitely wilder than Nate, but he could be fun. I never thought it would go beyond college though.

The summer between junior and senior year, Owen brought a few friends home with their girlfriends to Birmingham after finals were over—including Wes and Rachel.

Emma was on a family cruise with no cell service until she got Wi-Fi, so I was all alone at home. I wasn't friends with any of Owen's friends' girlfriends, and it was just weird, me being the odd wheel out. I mostly stayed to myself.

I couldn't sleep one night, so I was down in the living room, stuffing my face with ice cream around one in the morning and watching TV.

Wes walked in from the foyer shirtless, his shoulders jumping when he saw me. "Sorry, I didn't know anyone was awake."

"I couldn't sleep," I told him. "Want some ice cream?"

He looked at the ice cream in my lap and hesitated. "Sure."

I smiled at him and put it on the coffee table. He went into the kitchen and came back with a spoon. He sat down beside me, picked up the ice cream, and put his feet up on the table.

"Where's Emma?"

"The Bahamas," I replied.

"Oh, nice! And that guy? Nate?" he asked me. It surprised me that he knew his name. I didn't think he'd ever met him.

"We broke up," I told him.

"I'm sorry. That sucks."

"Not really," I laughed. "Besides, I want to move to New York after graduation."

"How does your mom feel about that?"

I reached into the ice cream with my spoon. "She doesn't know yet. Don't say anything."

"I don't want to see what you'd do to someone who revealed your secrets," he said.

Our secret popped into my head. Wes and I had the one shared unspoken secret that was always sort of looming. Was he thinking about it too? I wondered why neither of us ever brought it up. Maybe we liked to hold on to it. Like it was only ours, the only thing we shared together, and we would ruin it if we tried to find closure. Maybe we didn't want to find closure at all, so we could cling to the thought that if something were to be different, we'd find our way back. I probably should have been saying 'I' instead of 'we' in my head as I was thinking these things because all of those feelings were probably one-sided.

I eyed Wes thinking about being in that same situation if we were both single—alone together on a couch in the middle of the night—and what I would've done. He caught me staring. He looked quickly down at my lips and back up. I knew then he was thinking about it. I couldn't read his eyes, but I begged him with mine not to bring it up.

He picked up the remote. "Want to watch *American Dad!?*"

"Is Steve still a virgin?" I said, relieved that he deflected. If you don't know, don't ask—you're on the outside.

I got up and grabbed a blanket from the basket next to our couch while Wes laughed at my back. I hadn't heard his real laugh in so long. A feather circled around my stomach, tickling my insides.

I offered him part of the blanket, but he shook his head. I draped the blanket over myself, and we ate ice cream together for an episode until I lay down next to him and fell asleep in the middle of the second episode.

I woke up alone to darkness a couple of hours later. My head was on my pillow from my bed. Wes must have gotten it from my room and put it under me. I turned over and went back to sleep.

Senior year, I saw him mostly in passing at work, classes, and parties. He was in love. I figured they'd be a couple that would get engaged right out of college. I didn't know that his mom was battling cancer.

When we graduated, I moved to New York and met Dylan. It's funny how Wes didn't really cross my mind for five years unless he was standing in front of me. I saw him once or twice when he happened to be with Owen. But I was happy—or so I thought—and my crush had faded.

And then he was standing in front of me in my office. All of a sudden, I couldn't get him out of my head, thanks to circumstance, and it all came rushing back. I know technically that's probably an insult, but I didn't want to be thinking about him all the time. Hard to do when I saw him all the time though.

I turned over on my stomach on the dock and fell asleep.

—

IT WAS MUCH easier when I didn't have to see him.

On Sunday morning, I got one text from him: an *American Dad!* gif of Stan jumping out of bed.

I held down on the picture and clicked the 'haha' response without saying anything else.

He didn't text me back.

Emma and I flew back to New York later that day. Emma had plans with Logan, so I let my couch comfort me once again and binge-watched more rom-coms. I was right back to where I'd been seven months earlier.

Monday felt like the old days of me, Emma, and Jack.

"I'm coming next year," Jack exclaimed as we were eating lunch. "To hell with my family. I miss out on everything. Wes must look good in a swimsuit."

Emma slid her eyes to mine.

"What was that look?" Jack questioned us.

We were both silent. Too silent.

"Oh my God, did y'all break the tension?" he guessed.

"It's over as quick as it began," I said.

"Bummer," Jack said. "All those late nights you spend together could have been fun. Was that the consensus? It was a one-and-done thing?"

I shrugged. "He's in Nashville visiting his ex-girlfriend, so he made it a one-and-done thing. I'm good, but *you* will not be setting me up on any more dates."

"Leigh, I didn't know that guy that well," Jack huffed. "At least you finally broke your streak."

"Well..." Emma trailed off. "Never mind, I guess technically you did."

"Can we not talk about my sex life at lunch, please?"

Jack furrowed his brow. "What is that supposed to mean, *technically?*"

"We didn't *technically* have sex. He did something else."

"A man who gave for nothing in return?" Jack laughed. "That's a friends-with-benefits situation I've never heard of."

"Whatever. We didn't have much alone time up there. How many different ways can I say 'end of story'? The end. That's it."

"That's all folks," Emma said.

"Epilogue?" Jack said.

"No epilogue," I replied.

"When all is said and done," Jack tried again.

"At long last," Emma added.

"Climax!" Jack laughed.

Emma kept going. "Cease and desist! She's going to sue him for giving her the best orgasm she's ever had."

Jack smirked. "No surprise there."

"Y'all know too much about me. Game over! Ha, in more ways than one," I ended it.

After lunch, I collected my thoughts in my office before taking a deep breath and marching over to Daniel's office.

I knocked softly on the door, and he looked up at me from his desk.

"Hey, Daniel," I said, shutting the door behind me.

He looked at me curiously. I wasn't one to come over to his office and close the door ominously. He knew I had something to say. I always wonder how men feel when we do that. Foreboding? Uneasy? Exasperated? What now?

"How can I help you, Leigh?"

I took a deep breath and told myself to act like any man would. "I want to talk with you about a raise."

I sat down across from his desk and straightened my back high, trying not to look like a nervous wreck of a petite woman.

Daniel seemed to relax a little. "I'd be happy to discuss it with you."

"I've been working hard over the last month. I've helped bring in a lot of new accounts. I've put in long hours. Wes and I have made a great team, and I deserve it."

"I agree," he replied. Of course, he agreed. He would have never brought it up if I hadn't though. "I think we have it in the budget to compensate you for the hard work you've put in here."

"Thank you," I said, trying not to sound relieved. "I appreciate the recognition."

"What percent increase are you looking for?" Daniel asked. He wasn't going to throw out a number until he heard mine.

Here's where I took a gamble. "I want you to match Wes' salary."

I raised an eyebrow at Daniel. I wasn't going to let on that I had no clue what Wes made. Whatever it was, I was confident it was more than me. I didn't care if I got a one percent raise, but I wanted to make sure we were on a level playing field. I wanted the satisfaction of knowing he wasn't making more than me because he was a man. We had the same years of experience. I worked just as hard, and I was just as good as Wes. And we worked even better together. I didn't care if he thought Wes told me.

"That's fair," Daniel replied.

He turned to his computer and started typing for a minute while I smiled excitedly in my head. "I'll put in the request to HR now. I'm very proud of the work you've done. You two make an incredible team."

"Thank you, Daniel. I appreciate it."

"They should email you your new salary if it's approved, which I'm sure it will be. It shouldn't take long. Thank you again."

I stood and made my way back to my desk.

Two hours later, I received my new salary from the HR director. Wes made nineteen thousand fucking more dollars than me.

Wes didn't text me again the rest of the week, and I certainly didn't text him. I guess I could have thanked him for closing one very tiny part of the very large and real gender pay gap.

So, thank you, Wes.

Tuesday, Wednesday, and Thursday were uneventful.

CHAPTER 15

"Morning, Leigh." Wes' voice cut through my office.

I knew this moment was coming. I'd tried preparing myself all day the day before.

I'd done yoga in my office but pulled my hamstring.

I tried meditating, but I kept wondering how people brought themselves to orgasm through meditation because that was going to be my life from then on.

So, I switched to listening to rain sounds, but I kept nodding off at my desk.

Then I tried to get a thirty-minute massage on my lunch break at the spa down the street, but every time I closed my eyes, I imagined it was Wes' hands. Getting a massage with your eyes wide open is an awkward experience, to say the least.

I gave up after that.

"Good morning," I said, looking up at him. Bright, cheery, happy-go-lucky. I wasn't going to let him rattle me.

He hesitated in my doorway, trying to decide if he should bring it up at work. I just smiled at him.

He looked at me for a few seconds with hardened eyebrows. He cupped his hand around the doorframe, patted it twice, and walked into his office. I watched him through the glass, but he didn't look at me.

At 9:43 a.m. I went into his office to give him a packet for our next project.

"Here you go," I said, dropping it on his desk. "If you want to look over it before we start."

"Thanks! I'll start as soon as I catch up on the hundreds of emails I have waiting."

I tried to keep my tone even. "Yeah, of course. How was Nashville?"

His face flashed something I couldn't read across it like a hologram. "Good. Not good. Great. Not great."

If that wasn't the most cryptic, complex answer I'd ever gotten in my life.

"That sounds like a lot to unpack. I'm sorry about whatever happened." I turned and walked back to my office while he sat there watching me and rubbing his hand over his mouth.

At 11:46, he came and gave me the file back with only a smile. He left to get lunch after that.

At 1:12 p.m. I went back into his office. I was playing a game of Don't Let the Bomb Explode.

"When do you want to start?" I asked him.

I would never let it, and Wes knew it. He was just trying to be professional and not detonate it at work.

He swiveled in his chair, unable to resist any longer. "Did Owen say something to you?"

"About what?" I questioned him.

"Seriously?" Wes scoffed. "You know what."

"About us?"

"What else would I be talking about?" he said angrily.

Well, Owen was his best friend. I was sure he knew about Nashville and Rachel, but I knew he didn't know about us because he hadn't called me freaking out. And I was confident that Wes knew Owen would never tell me anything about Wes' dating life, so Wes didn't have to worry about me finding out about Rachel.

"He hasn't said anything to me out of the ordinary, no."

He studied me like he was trying to decide if I was lying or not.

"Did he say something to you?" I asked.

He shrugged. "He made a comment about our friendship when we were getting firewood. I want to tell him something happened between us, Leigh."

I widened my eyes at him and turned around to shut his office door. I twirled back around. "He doesn't need to know."

"I can't keep lying to him regardless."

"You don't have to worry about it," I laughed, unsure if he was implying that we would be having more secret sex romps.

"What's that supposed to mean?" he shot back with an edge in his voice, maybe hurt. "You just want me to forget it happened?"

"It's probably for the best."

"Then tell me what happened."

"What do you mean?" I asked innocently.

"I can take a hint from you, Leigh. Tell me why you're sending me only a 'haha' text."

"I don't want to talk about this at work." I turned around and walked out the door as he called my name behind me.

I think I stared at the clock in the bottom right of my computer screen from 1:18 to 5:00. I bolted out the door as soon as work was over.

T. Fucking. G. I. F.

Wes texted me later that night: **I'm not going to forget about it.**

I didn't respond.

Instead, I screenshot it and sent it to Emma.

You should at least talk to him. Don't leave him hanging like that, she replied.

Don't be a voice of reason now, Em.

I know you. You are not just going to get over it without talking about it. You're not like Owen.

Can you not know me so well? I texted back.

Too late for that.

Of course, she was right, but I still texted: Ugh.

You also have to work with him every day and see him all through the wedding weekend coming up. Might as well get it over with.

No thanks. I'll live in denial for now. Bye!

Saturday I went shopping to pick myself up. I got a new work dress, sunglasses, and a new purse. I settled in on my couch when I got home and pulled up my delivery app. I was going to stuff my face with Rawesome Sushi. They were closing soon for their remodel. I ordered a seaweed salad, miso soup, tuna nigiri, and four huge rolls. I loved seeing how many chopsticks they'd give me when I ordered like that. How many people did they think I was ordering for? It was a game of guessing a number between two and five.

They buzzed at the door downstairs thirty minutes later, and I pressed the button to let them in. I opened my door when they knocked to see Wes standing in my hallway instead. My heart punched me in the throat.

"*This* definitely qualifies as stalking," I accused him. "I don't recall ever telling you where I live."

"Emma told me," he replied.

Traitor.

I stared at him, telling myself he did not look good.

"Can I come in?" he asked me.

"I'm waiting on my sushi," I said like that was an appropriate response to his question. Of course, he couldn't come in when I had food being delivered. If I'd known it was him, I wouldn't have buzzed him up.

"Can your apartment only fit one or the other?"

I rolled my eyes and stepped to the side. "You got lucky I thought you were the delivery guy," I muttered.

He brushed past me, ignoring what I said, and turned around. "Leigh, did Owen say something to you?"

"Nope," I said.

"Then what did I do?"

"You didn't do anything. I'm just not ready for this."

He looked away and sat down on my couch. The look on his face made it seem like he was going to need it to comfort him. I saw pain, maybe self-doubt. He sat in silence, staring at the coffee table. "Like it's too soon?" he asked eventually.

"No, emotionally. I just don't think I can handle it."

My words didn't help. He fidgeted with his fingernails. "Because of Owen?"

"No," I said flatly.

"Then what?" he said, trying to sound calm but not succeeding. "Did I scare you? Come on too strong?"

"No, you're perfect," I grumbled. "As always."

"I'm too perfect?" He looked up at me confused. "Now I've heard everything. What the hell does that mean? Is this some new 'it's not you, it's me' brush off?"

"I'm just not like Owen," I explained.

That made total sense, right?

"What?" He leaned back against the couch briskly. "And?"

"You know how Owen is. Or was, I guess. I can't handle things like that."

Again, so clear, right?

"Leigh, I wish I could read your mind, but you're going to have to clarify what 'things like that' means. Can you please talk to me?"

"You know." I waved my hand. "Friends with benefits. A relationship based on sex."

He laughed.

"I can't do that, Wes," I said angrily, annoyed by the sound of his laugh for the first time in my life.

His voice rose but gave off an air of amusement. "You thought I just wanted to fuck you? My best friend's sister? I'm just in this to get some ass? I could get ass anywhere I wanted."

That was the first and only time I'd heard him sound conceited. He surely could—even girls who cheated on him still wanted him. I scrunched up my face in irritation.

He called himself out with a softened voice. "Okay, that sounded... whatever. But I'm not just trying to have sex with you, Leigh. If that's what I wanted, I wouldn't be rooting around in Owen's family. His twin sister of all people."

I crossed my arms, and he laughed again. Exasperated sounding.

"Stop laughing at me!"

He threw his head back and rubbed his hands over his face.

"Leigh, I have liked you ever since you opened your mouth and told me you were a Hawaiian type of girl. What the hell is a guy supposed to do when the girl he so desperately wants to ask out is his best friend's sister?"

"I don't know," I shot back.

"I don't either," he muttered. "This isn't about sex. I'm not going to piss off Owen just so I can hook up with you, and I know you don't really hook up. You forget I spent four years going to school with you. Watching you date. Listening to guys ask Owen about you. Listening to guys talk about you. I like you. I've always liked you. I want a serious relationship with you."

"Well, I thought you might be talking about me when we played Never Have I Ever," I explained.

"God!" he huffed. "I've had one friend with benefits in my life. Freshman year of college. And it was explicitly agreed upon by both of us before we started. I would never do that without talking with the person first. Give me more credit than that."

My heart softened, but I had to stay mad. "That still doesn't explain Rachel."

"What the hell does she have to do with this?" he said angrily. His eyes got dark as he stared at me.

"You were texting her all night when we had that bonfire. You kept ignoring her texts whenever I was with you," I said back angrier.

His face came to a sudden understanding. "That girl just continues to fuck up my life," he muttered under his breath before speaking louder. "Is that what happened for you to all of a sudden hate me? You saw my phone? Leigh," he said, staring at me intensely, "is this what this is really all about?"

I just stared at him.

Wes stood and pulled out his phone. He swiped it open and took three long strides to me where I was still standing close to the door.

"I have nothing to hide from you, Leigh. I meant it when I told you I would tell you whatever you want. Here." He turned his phone around and stepped a little to the side of it so he could also see it.

"She texts me all the damn time about how much she still loves me and misses me. How she made a mistake."

I glanced at it and read, **Please answer me** below **Are you in Nashville?** before he started scrolling up through the never-ending gray texts.

"And I engaged with her craziness one time since I've been working with you. I guess I was feeling reckless or hopeless or whatever after you told me we should stop what we were doing. But as soon as I texted her, I regretted it."

He scrolled until I saw blue texts and stopped. He held it up to my face.

Blue: I don't know what you want me to say.

Gray: I want you to say how you feel. I still love you. You are the best person I know, and I would never do that again to you. Can I come to New York, or you come to Nashville, and we can talk?

Blue: I don't think that's a good idea. I don't have anything to say.

Gray: I have a lot to say. Please let me show you I still love you.

Blue: I don't love you, Rachel. That's all I have to say.

"There you go. That's everything." He shoved his phone toward me in the air. "Do you want to read it all? You can go back through our entire relationship."

I shook my head. I didn't want that.

"Yes, I loved Rachel at one point in my life, but I didn't want to rush into a marriage I wasn't ready for just so my mom could see me get married before she died. And I'm so happy I made that decision because I don't want anything to do with Rachel now. I would thank her for cheating on me if she was here right now because, if she hadn't, I wouldn't be here with you. You have no idea how happy I was to see you that first day at work. I thought about asking Owen for your number when I moved here, but I knew you were dating that guy. I wasn't interested in being just friends with you. If I'd known you broke up, maybe I would have. I didn't even know you had until you wrapped me around your finger on that Goddamn plane. I was stupid in college, and I should have just talked to Owen and told him what happened; that I liked you. Which is what I was *trying* to do last weekend. I thought you knew that, but obviously, I should have made that clearer. I should've known better with that brain of yours."

"Why'd you tell me you just wanted to be friends then? Why did you walk out of your office that night? You were practically telling me at the park *and* on the subway that whatever we were doing was over. And I didn't see your eyebrow twitching or whatever."

Wes sat back down on the couch, withdrawing. "Leigh, it was obvious you were struggling with the guilt. I don't feel guilty for liking you. I only feel guilty for not talking to Owen. I didn't want to push you. I was scared you'd retreat further, that I'd lose you. But you are like a boomerang. One day you're flirting with me and sending me texts in the middle of the night, you're complimenting my eyes, the next you're ignoring me at work, the next you're telling me how I make you feel and you want my hands on you; making me think I have a shot, but then you're telling me you can't come between me and Owen, and the next you're putting your hand on my thigh and leaving infuriatingly thoughtful birthday gifts on my desk.

"For my own sake, I had to try to put a stop to it because if you can't be with me completely, I don't see any point in continuing. This isn't a casual thing for me. I couldn't do that to myself mentally. I'm *not* interested in hooking up with you in secret. North Carolina was my fault. I had to sit there and listen to you talk about your dates like it didn't bother me. Like it didn't bother me how close I had gotten; how resistant you were to me. It all slipped through my fingers. But then you gave me that damn *look*, and I couldn't fight it anymore. I was hoping you'd be ready, so I took a chance."

Wes made a damn good case.

"Okay, I admit I was... *am* a basket case," I conceded. One thing was still nagging at me though. "But why'd you go to Nashville then?"

His eyebrows furrowed in dismay. "You thought I went to see Rachel, didn't you?"

"What else was I supposed to think? You wouldn't answer the question when I asked you." I threw my hands up. "Multiple times."

He put his head in his hands and sighed. When he spoke again his voice was soft and light like it was being carried by the air blowing out of the AC around my apartment.

"Tuesday was the anniversary of my mom's death. I went to celebrate her life with my family. And I didn't tell you because it was depressing and sad and we were high and it was the Fourth of July," he breathed out all at once. "It was Charlotte I was texting at the bonfire. Not Rachel. I wasn't trying to hide anything from you. I just didn't want to bring everything down by talking about it."

"God, you really know how to make a girl feel terrible," I whispered.

My door buzzed.

I walked over to the intercom and pressed the button. We stared at each other in silence.

"I'm sorry," I said softly.

He scrunched his eyebrows up and shook his head like he was saying it was okay, but his face looked worried. "Sorry for what…?"

He had no idea if I was apologizing because he was right and I couldn't be with him completely, or if I was apologizing for the way I acted. But by the time I figured out what he was asking, there was a knock on my door.

I put the sushi down on the coffee table and sat down beside him. I pulled it out of the bags.

"Jesus, how much sushi did you order?"

I fanned out the chopsticks. "If I count the chopsticks, enough for four people."

I laid them down next to the sushi and paused. I didn't want to turn to look at him.

"Wes," I started, "I've always had a crush on you, but I never let myself think about it too much in reality because of Owen. I tortured myself all through college. Then you walked into my office during a… weird? time in my life. I thought it was about sex at first myself because I haven't had sex in over seven months now."

I cringed and laughed. I turned to look at his face. "God, I hate saying that out loud. Those underwear with my face on them were a gift from Emma because I was the only one pleasing myself. Anyway, I was so… turned on by everything you did. Hell, I still am. I don't blame you for anything. I am a crazy person. I couldn't deal with my own inner tug-of-war between wanting you and not wanting to hurt Owen. Choosing to be happy for yourself is a lot harder than you'd think. But I fell for you, then freaked out, and then I screwed it all up *again* by assuming things, instead of just talking to you. I want you, and all I want from you is to want me back."

When I finished, Wes just stared at me intensely, bouncing his eyes back and forth between mine.

I opened my mouth to start to tell him I was sorry again, but his mouth covered mine before I could. He brought his hand up to the side of my face, his tongue ran across my top lip before he took it into his mouth. He plunged his tongue back into my mouth against mine.

"Wes," I said breathlessly into his mouth as I climbed on top of his lap. "I'm sorry."

His hands wrapped around my butt as his mouth trailed down my neck. "Don't be."

His warm breath was starting a fire in each place it touched. He slipped his hands under my shirt and grabbed me over my bra. I wished he would rip it off.

I pulled back and brought my shirt over my head, throwing it to the side. I reached behind me and unhooked my bra with urgency.

"I need your tongue on me," I groaned as I slipped out of my straps.

This was like life or death. Fast motion. Not his usual slow-motion torment. We needed each other desperately, and it had to happen as quickly as possible.

He grabbed my tits in his hands and circled me with his tongue and flicked. I ran my hands through his hair as I looked up to the ceiling and arched my back.

My nerves were popping off one by one. I moaned and grinded myself against him. His fingers brushed their way up to my wrists and he gripped them hard. He pulled my arms away from his head and brought them around my back. He put my wrists together in one hand, pinning my arms behind my back and pulling down, making me push my chest out further for him. He brought one hand back to the front and switched to my right breast, licking and sucking before taking my nipple between his teeth.

I moaned louder.

"I want you to be mine," Wes said gruffly between my chest, but he suddenly pulled back. "Fuck, I can't believe I'm about to say this."

I snapped my head down at him.

He released my arms. "Leigh, we have to talk to Owen first."

"God, noooo," I dragged out. "Don't be the good guy right now."

I wrapped my hands around the back of his head and kissed him hard. I wasn't going to make it easy on him.

"Fuck me, please," I whispered into his ear as I rubbed myself over his lap.

His hands came up and down my thighs slowly, and I pulled back to look at him.

"I will," he said, slipping his hand between my legs and rubbing me over my pajama shorts. I rocked against his fingers. "But not until I talk to Owen."

"I don't want to wait that long," I pouted.

"What's another two weeks?" he asked, continuing to rub me, stoking my fire.

"You're not going to tell him next weekend?"

"On his wedding weekend?" Wes shook his head. "Hell no. I'll wait until he comes back from Hawaii."

"Ugh," I sighed and wrapped my fingers around him, rubbing softly. "Why are you doing this to me?"

His hand came up to my stomach, brushing his fingers over my abs. His eyes trailed his fingers as they played with my left nipple.

"Because it's the right thing to do, and you're worth it," he whispered. He gripped my waist and pulled me down against him. "Trust me, it's killing me."

"But I want to feel your cock slide into me right now," I whined in humor, but also trying to tempt him.

He slipped his index finger into my mouth, and I sucked it, caressing it with my tongue.

"When did you get such a dirty mouth?" he asked me as he watched my lips around his finger.

"Since you turned me into a sex-crazed animal," I said, releasing his finger, then biting the tip.

He chuckled. He brought his wet finger down my chin, across my neck, around my right nipple, over my belly button, and hooked the edge of my shorts. He ran his finger to the right and left under the seam.

"You like tempting me, don't you?" he said in a low voice. He slipped his hand into my underwear, running over me.

I gasped under my breath and nodded. "Is it working?"

"A little."

I kissed him hard, pushing my tongue against his. His hands traced their way up my sides before settling around my rib cage. His thumbs ran over the sides of my boobs. A groan came up from his throat and rattled down into my lungs. He brought one hand down and rubbed his thumb over me in small circles. I moaned softly into his mouth, returning the favor.

"I'm going to make you moan louder than that, Leigh." He brought his hand back out. "Just let me talk to Owen first."

"Fine," I breathed out.

He sat up and kissed me lightly. "It will be easier this way."

It wasn't going to be easy either way.

CHAPTER 16

I should invent a crazy-ass word for not being able to have sex after seven months of abstinence, even though it's right in front of you. Waiting. Torturing you. Dangling in front of you every damn day. And he's just so damn good. And he's just so damn attractive. And his voice makes you feel like you're sitting on a sparkler. And the gray smoke in his eyes makes your stomach feel like a yo-yo. And the touch of his fingers leaves a prickle behind. And you both want it like you've never wanted anything so badly in your life. But he's so damn adamant that this will make it easier for another person to accept.

Nonexxxistent.

Stubbporness.

Erotillicit.

Absofuckinghornievable.

That's what the next week was like.

We worked together every day. We only went out in public. We did not go to either of our apartments. We couldn't be alone together.

Monday, I wore my new dress to work, and Wes couldn't take his eyes off me. Monday night, we went to a bar with Emma and

Logan, who was perfect for her by the way. I gave him the third degree, but like the lawyer he actually was, he survived my avalanche of questions. Wes was convinced that even Owen would like him.

Tuesday, I told Wes to stop rolling up his sleeves. Tuesday night, we went out to dinner. We met each other there and left separately.

Wednesday, Wes and I had to leave the conference room to go back to our offices because we couldn't be trusted if we weren't in someone's line of sight. Wednesday night, we packed separately in the comfort of our own apartments. Wes insisted we get to the airport early, so I made him promise me he would never book us another flight that was before ten in the morning again. I was on time though because somehow Wes made me a better person.

When Emma, Logan, Wes, and I touched down in Nashville, we had to hurry to the hotel because the limo buses would be there to pick everyone up in an hour.

I looked over the itinerary I'd emailed out the prior week as we walked into our hotel.

2 p.m. - Guys Topgolf, Girls mani/pedis

5 p.m. - River cruise with dinner

8 p.m. - Drinks at the hotel bar

After drinks 'til - Guys and girls split for the night

It was pretty much just one long day of drinking.

Emma and Logan got out on the fifth floor to go to their room.

"I'll text you when I'm heading down," I told Emma as she got off the elevator.

Wes nodded at Logan in some unspoken man conversation they were having.

The natural differences between men and women have always fascinated me. In a very generalized way, we're like night and day, even though there are many shades of masculinity and femininity.

We're talkative, emotional, and intuitive which contrasts with their inwardness, straightforwardness, and rationality. And the funny thing is, that those differences simultaneously drive us crazy and excite us.

He turned back to me when the doors closed and pulled me into him against the wall. "Are the next twenty seconds the only alone time we're going to get this weekend?"

"Better make it count." I tipped my head up towards him, and he kissed me softly.

I furrowed my eyebrows at him. "Nuh uh, not enough."

He smiled at me with closed lips and kissed me deeper. The elevator dinged.

"Ugh," he groaned. He grabbed my ass as I turned around to exit. "See you on the boat."

An hour and a half later, I was seated between Katie and Emma, and all the girls from the wedding party were situated on massage chairs, champagne in hand, and feet soaking in pedicure tubs.

"I'm actually looking forward to all of this being over," Katie exclaimed. "I just want to sit on the beach and not think about it anymore."

I laughed. "Completely understandable. Are you stressing?"

"Not anymore. If it's not done or fixed or set up by now, then oh well. Time to party!"

We clinked our champagne glasses. Katie was much more fun than I originally gave her credit for. When we'd first met, she was quiet and stuck close to Owen, but as she came around more, she'd come out of her shell.

Katie leaned forward to look at Emma. "I can't wait to meet Logan. I'm so glad he came."

"He's all right." Emma shrugged.

"He's more than all right," I countered. "He and Emma

whispered together the whole flight like middle schoolers. Flirting, kissing, laughing. I've never seen her act like this. Just wait."

"What's he do?" Katie asked.

"He's a lawyer," Emma replied. "He's got a grown-up side and a wild side. Just the way I like them."

"He's hot and has a dirty sense of humor too," I laughed. "I can't believe you found someone so perfect for you on a dating app."

"Are you still on any dating apps?" Katie asked me.

I scoffed. "No, that was hopeless."

"Are you dating at all?"

"Not really," I said, shifting my weight in the chair a little, uncomfortable with my lie. That was only a little white lie, right?

The nail tech saved me (or so I thought) by sitting down in front of Katie. She put a towel down and patted for her to put her foot up.

Katie didn't let it go though. "Weddings are a great place to meet people. I have a ton of single guy friends. And a few of the groomsmen are single. But I guess that's weird for you?"

Her tone of voice made me think she felt like she was in some type of know. She just didn't know the complete know.

"Yeah," I laughed trying to sound vague like I had no idea what she was talking about.

"What's your type?" she pressed.

"Uh," I stammered. "I don't think I have one."

Another nail tech sat down in front of me. I hoped she'd engage me in a conversation about my toes. If she had, toes would have turned into the most interesting topic in the world. I'd have suddenly developed a foot fetish. But no such luck.

"Please! Everyone has a type."

Emma interjected. "What's the male equivalent of a lady in the street, but a whore in the bedroom? That's her type."

I glared at her.

"A gentleman in the street, but a whore in the bedroom?" Katie looked at Emma puzzled.

"Nice try, but no," Emma said, shaking her head. "You have to come up with something better than that. Like… polite around town, savage going down."

The nail techs giggled. I was going to stop telling Emma about my life.

"Oh," Katie thought for a second before getting excited. "Refined in the streets, ravishing in the sheets!"

"Yes! Katie, you're going to fit right in. Docile in public, dominant in bed."

Katie was having a blast. "Mild in the open, wild in the sack."

"Emma isn't as funny as she thinks she is," I told Katie, trying to stop them, even though I was amused.

Katie laughed. "Well, I haven't slept with any of the guys coming to the wedding, so I wouldn't know. Who's the nicest? Wes? He's hot. I bet he could secretly be fun in bed."

Emma smirked beside me.

"He's Owen's best friend," I said, trying to stop the conversation before we headed down that road. To me, my voice sounded like I was screaming *STOP!*

Katie gave me a sidelong glance like she could hear me screeching. "So what? Didn't Owen sleep with all of your friends?"

Was she testing me about Wes or Owen?

I laughed awkwardly. "Yes, he did. But he's a one-woman guy now."

She ignored my second comment. "Y'all also work together now. Why do guys think that's okay for them to do, but not us? My brother was always telling his friends to stay away from me. I flirted with them all the time though."

"And they resisted you?" I said, shocked. "Who could resist you with that spin class body?"

"Some did, some didn't," she said with a sly smile. "We went to the same high school. What did he expect?"

"I know the feeling," I said.

"What? Did you actually listen to Owen?"

"Yeah, pretty much. He was telling his friends to stay away from me too."

Katie laughed a laugh like she was bringing back old memories. "Shove yourself in their face and most of them will temporarily forget about guy code."

Dammit, I glanced down at her cleavage. She probably got whatever she wanted with those boobs, but I didn't have that.

"But you're not in high school anymore anyway. Aren't you looking for a serious relationship?" she continued, ignoring my temporary downward eye line.

I nodded.

"It's not like you're trying to have an immature relationship or just hook up."

"He'd still probably be pissed," I laughed. "Anyway, not an issue."

"Yeah…" Katie replied with a curious look—like she was going to say something else but decided against it.

"He's the best brother I could ask for. I'm just sorry you have to marry him," I joked.

Katie sighed. "Ugh, I know. Too bad I love him."

I smiled at her. They really were in love. She did something to Owen I'd never seen before. "Owen is a lucky guy. He is really happy. He's changed in such a great way, thanks to you."

"You're going to make me cry!" She playfully wiped fake tears from her cheeks. "Thanks, Leigh. I know I was kind of stand-offish when I first met y'all. I wanted y'all to love me, and I was so nervous about saying the wrong thing. Your family is so close, and

Owen thinks the world of you. He'd do anything for you. I can't wait to be a part of your family."

"Now you're going to make me cry!"

Katie reached her hand out and squeezed my arm. "But really, I love your brother so much. When you know, you know."

It doesn't matter if you meet the love of your life on a plane or at the gym or at a strip club. It doesn't matter if you've known them your entire life or five years or six months.

You can date someone for five years and never be sure you want to spend the rest of your life with them (e.g. Dylan with me).

You can date someone for five years and think you want to be with them forever but realize you were wrong (e.g. Me with Dylan).

You can meet someone and go on five dates and know you never want to leave their side again (e.g. Emma and how I suspected she felt about Logan).

You can meet someone and know six months later that they're different (e.g. Owen with Katie).

But the thing that sets *the* person apart is that when you do have that sudden understanding of who they have become to you, that feeling is now a fact—without question, without a doubt. It's an impossible feeling to describe. But once you do feel it for the first time, you only realize then, that you've never felt it before.

And the feeling can hit you at any point—on the first date or the thousandth date. And you can feel it anywhere—while you're texting or driving or having sex or sitting in a massage chair while your back is being kneaded and your toes are being painted a soft pink.

—

"DOES LETTIE'S CHICKEN franchise?" I asked Wes. "We should open one up in New York!"

"And leave the exciting world of advertising?" Wes replied. "Do you think we'd make as good of a team deep frying chicken?"

"I want this chicken in my life every day though. I miss it."

Water lapped against the side of the boat as we went over a small wake from a passing boat, making me tilt. Wes laughed and wiped sauce from the side of my mouth.

"Thanks. How was Topgolf?"

"Fun! We let Owen win all the games we played. Don't mention it to him though. He sucks," Wes said with a smirk. "I'm going to have to give him some lessons."

"He always resisted when he was young and never wanted to play," I explained. "I know my dad regrets it. I think Owen regrets it now. Of course, I'll have to learn in preparation for retirement."

"We can arrange that," Wes smiled at me. "There's a great driving range at Chelsea Piers."

"You're going to teach me to golf?" I smiled back. "Do you have enough patience for that?"

"For you—of course, I do," he said, not responding to the humor in my voice.

"Is that another New York favorite thing to do?"

"Yeah. I've spent a lot of time by myself this past year," Wes laughed. "You want another drink?"

I nodded with my mouth full of chicken and smiled at Wes as he got up from the padded bench.

I caught my mom's eye and glanced away quickly. She was sitting in the shade with my dad and Katie's parents at a high table. I wondered if she had some sort of mother-daughter connection I didn't know about because I wasn't a mother—the ability to read me without me realizing it. Could she sense the shift in my feelings? The look on her face seemed to be all-knowing.

The breeze picked up over the water as I watched the buildings pass, feeling the distant familiarity of when that city was my home.

Wes came back with two beers and opened mine for me. He handed me some napkins.

"Do you miss Nashville?" I asked him.

"Sometimes."

I gave him time to follow up, but he stuck by his man-response in silence.

"Sometimes… and? Sometimes… but?" I continued.

His lip twitched up on one side. "I miss Lettie's Chicken. I miss working with my dad. I miss Owen. I miss the familiarity. I miss the hills. I miss the orange leaves in the fall. But I don't miss all the places that remind me of my mom."

"Will you bring me there tomorrow?" I asked him hesitantly.

He turned his head from where he was studying the skyline to study my eyes. "Where she's buried?"

"Yes," I said softly.

"Sure," he replied. "If you'd like to."

"I would love to."

"I would love to, too."

We took a few sips of our beers together in silence.

"You don't miss Birmingham?" he asked me.

"Sometimes," I said with finality.

Wes smiled and took a sip of his beer, waiting for me to continue because he knew I would.

"I miss the milder winters. I miss good barbecue. I miss my parents. I miss the room I slept in for eighteen years." I glanced at my mom. "And I know my mom misses me."

"She does. She tells me all the time."

"Does she have you on speed dial?"

"Is that still a thing in the twenty-first century? In her favorites, maybe."

"She probably calls you more than me," I guessed. "But I love New York too. I love that I can get pineapple pizza at three a.m., I love the diversity—how I can walk down the street and hear five different languages, I love standing in Grand Central Station and wondering where everyone is going and coming from, and I love sitting on the sun chairs in High Line Park."

"I love that park," Wes agreed. "My favorite is the tenth avenue overlook."

"This skyline is pretty great too." I pointed my beer out over the water. "And that sunset."

We watched the sunset together, romantic but in a way where no one could know we were romanticizing it.

"Would you ever move back?" Wes asked me when the sun disappeared.

"To Nashville or Birmingham?"

"Either."

"Maybe," I confessed. "I've considered it before. Sometimes I wonder if I'll want to if and when I have kids."

A sudden fear overwhelmed me as I contemplated his words.

"Do you want to?" I wasn't sure if Wes could hear the panic in my voice.

"I don't know." Wes shrugged. "Sometimes I don't want to step foot here ever again, but other times I want to get out of New York. Who knows? That was before…"

I was seventy-five percent positive when he trailed off that he was going to say *you,* but he didn't leave me any room to doubt.

"That was before you," he said again confidently.

Maybe during-me got a say. Maybe during-me was important enough to be included in the conversation, to be a factor in any decision of whether he stayed or went. And if the decision was to go, maybe during-us went together.

I opened my mouth to reply, but suddenly the music blasted through the sound system. My open mouth closed into a smile.

Emma came over from where she'd been talking with Logan.

"Let's dance!" she yelled over the music and dragged me up.

Logan took my seat when I got up, and Katie dragged my mom over to where Emma and I were. I danced and watched Owen bring beers to Wes and Logan. They were laughing and talking. Obviously, Owen and Wes didn't get to spend as much time together as they used to, and I knew they missed each other. They did almost everything together in college and until Wes moved.

As I watched them, I realized how much they reminded me of myself and Emma. I couldn't imagine keeping something so big from Emma. She didn't have a brother, but if she did… fuck. The feeling of what we were doing consumed me. I wondered if Wes felt the nimbus cloud hovering over his head like I felt over mine—sitting there, following our every move, waiting to break open and pour buckets of rain on both of us.

I pushed all of that out of my mind as the alcohol started to kick in. The four of us danced until the rap music started, and my mom went to sit down. Of course, that only made me, Emma, and Katie take our dancing up a notch. I swore Katie was some sort of siren. Every pair of eyes watched her while she danced. I looked over at the guys, and Owen was staring at Katie with a look of puppy love I'd never seen before. But when I looked at Wes, he was just staring back at me.

CHAPTER 17

I woke up with a splitting headache.
God, I drank way too much and mixed every type of alcohol under the sun: champagne, beer, vodka, and probably a lot more I didn't remember. After we got off the river cruise, we started at the hotel's rooftop bar. I remembered having a lemon drop. I remembered stealing secret kisses with Wes near the bathroom. I remembered feeling his hand against my back pulling me into him. I remembered his breath tickling my ear as he whispered all those dirty words I loved to hear that were just for me. Then we split up, and the girls bar-hopped all night, drinking and dancing.

I tumbled out of bed and rooted around in my suitcase for Advil. I took three and drank two glasses of water before lying back down.

I picked my phone up off the nightstand to text Wes but found our drunken conversation that came flooding back into my memory instead. I read through it laughing. You could see the two of us getting drunker as the night went on because the texts were so spread out.

Me: hey I like you

Wes: hey I like you

Wes: hey I miss you

Me: hey I miss you

Wes: even though I saw you four hours ago

Me: am I going to be able to tlk you into coming to my room tonight

Wes: lets see………

Me: ill get on my knees all night and let you contorl the speed by my hair

Wes: fuck

Wes: I want to see your eyes looking up at me through your eyelaashes right now

Wes: and in the words of Leigh Sullivan, finally slide my cock into you

Wes: but we needd to stopp bc I'm getting too hard thinking about it

Me: :(

Me: I don't want to

Me: I like mkingg you hard

Me: ugh pleaseeee

Wes: one more week

Me: as mchh as its annoyng me right now, I wouldnt lik you so muchh if you werent so goddamn decent

Wes: and I wouldn't liike you so much if you weren't so godddamn fiery

That was the point in our conversation where Katie dragged me away from the bar and onto the dance floor, so I never responded. I'm sure autocorrect helped out for a ton of the words that were actually spelled correctly.

I texted him: The only thing I have in bed with me right now is a headache, but my Advil is kicking in.

He replied: I'm the only one who woke up with a strange man in my bed? Doesn't sound like you had a fun bachelorette party!

Then he added: Coffee? And then I can take you to see my mom.

I loved his text and said: Meet you downstairs in forty-five minutes? Sounds good.

I showered and blew my hair dry before I threw it in a ponytail and put on some light makeup. I stared at my suitcase wondering what to wear. I chose a casual denim sundress after agonizing about what one wears to visit someone's grave. She'd never met me. She didn't know me. I wanted her to like me.

When I met Wes downstairs, he got us a cab to Starbucks first, then another to the cemetery. I made the driver stop so I could get some flowers, even though Wes insisted it wasn't necessary.

Wes took my hand and laced his fingers through mine when we got out of the car.

"You look beautiful, by the way," he said, kissing me on the shoulder.

"I didn't know what to wear."

He chuckled and started to lead me through a maze of headstones. "She can't see you, Leigh."

"She might be able to," I whispered.

He squeezed my hand.

You never know. Those that have passed could be watching us from the sky or they could be standing right next to us, invisible to the living world, and watching the remainder of their loved ones' lives play out.

I liked to think that about my grandmother who I was close with. She died when I was in college. She missed my college graduation, and I thought all the time about how she'd miss my future wedding and her future great-grandchildren. But it comforted me to think she was there with me in some way still getting to experience it.

After another minute, he stopped in front of a large headstone covered in flowers that read:

ELEANOR MILLER ADAMS
BELOVED WIFE AND MOTHER OF THREE

I tucked my flowers into the ones they'd left a week ago, which were drying out.

"See! She needed new ones." I smiled at Wes and put my head against his upper arm. We were both silent for a few minutes until I said, "I wish I could have met her."

"Me too. She would have loved you," Wes said before laughing. "She never liked Rachel very much. She thought she was 'stuffy.'"

"Hopefully, your mom sees how unstuffy I am."

Wes kissed the top of my head. "You're the unstuffiest."

"Your dad used to talk about her all the time at work. What's your favorite memory you have with her?" I asked. "Your mom. Not Rachel."

Wes laughed into my hair.

"So many. But I have three that I always think about," he said. "She loved college football and brought me to my first Vanderbilt football game when I was five. It's actually one of my very earliest memories. I was so excited. I loved the loud noises, the fireworks, and the halftime show. She danced all crazy with me because I wanted to get up on the big screen so badly. We finally did in the third quarter, and in the fourth quarter, I ended up falling asleep on her lap."

I squeezed his hand. "That's a great memory."

"I hope I can bring my son to his first Vanderbilt game one day," he said, staring at the ground.

Wes was lost in thought for a minute, so I let him relive the memory by himself until he spoke again.

"The second is from when I was sixteen. I was sneaking out of my house, but I fell from the lower roof and broke my arm. My mom heard me and came out of the house screaming at me until she saw how fucked up my arm was—it was almost at a ninety-degree angle. She passed out. Then my dad came out screaming at me about why my mom was on the ground. My mom woke up and yelled at me the whole way to the ER."

Wes and I laughed together.

"She laughed about it later though."

"What color was your cast?" I asked.

"That's such a personal question," Wes joked. "Black, of course. And my third is from when I was taking care of her. She loved the movie *Singin' in the Rain*, so I used to watch it with her all the time when she didn't feel good enough to get up that day. We used to sing all the songs together even though I felt like an idiot."

Tears were streaming down my face at that point. "That's such a good movie."

He nodded. "One of my favorites now."

We stood in silence again for a couple of minutes before Wes spoke again.

"She loved Owen too. You know how sometimes you treat people who aren't family better than your own." He laughed a little under his breath. "It's so shitty, but I think everyone does it because your family has to love you no matter what. It's easier to be a dick to them or take your bad moods out on them. At least, I know I was like that, and I think Owen can be like that too. He doesn't show y'all his best self *all the time*, and he was always flying through girls. But he's deeper than he allows you to think he is."

I laughed through my tears. "I see that now. He needed the right girl to bring it out of him."

I knew Owen could be deeper than he let on, but I didn't realize how deep. It's not like he told me all of his secrets. We were twins but we were opposite gender twins. I didn't want to hear about certain things, and he certainly didn't want to hear about specific aspects of my life. We knew enough going to the same schools together.

"I was just worried he would never meet her," Wes exclaimed. "Anyway, he was really sweet to my mom, and she loved him. She always used to joke and ask him why he was such good friends with me."

"What would Owen say?"

"He'd say it was because I was a better person than him," he laughed. "My mom never believed him, or she pretended not to. She used to complain about all the gray hairs I gave her as a teenager. My sisters were angels. That's why I'm so happy I got to show her the best version of myself before she died."

"She already knew your best version. Moms just know." I wasn't a mom, but I knew what I was saying was the truth.

Wes put his arm around my shoulders and pulled me into him, kissing me on the top of my head. He brought the bottom of his shirt up to wipe my tears off my face.

"How are you not crying right now?" I laughed and more tears spilled out of my eyes.

He wiped them away again. "This isn't a sad moment. I'm happy."

"Happy tea—," I started to argue, but Wes kissed me mid-word.

I wrapped my arms around his neck and his arms wrapped around my waist as the kiss became deeper. There wasn't anything sexy or hot about it. It was loving, and my brain was only screaming that I loved him. That this man was the man for me. All five hundred sides I'd seen of him and all five hundred sides I hadn't seen yet. I wanted them all.

It was way too soon to tell him that though.

"Do you want to get a Hawaiian pizza on the way back to the hotel?" he asked me when we broke apart.

I placed my chin on his chest and looked up at him. "Yessss, that will cure my hangover."

We weaved our way back to the front, holding hands, careful not to step any place where someone was lying.

LEIGH MAKES THREE

—

"WE SHOULD HAVE sat and eaten it in the booth where we met," I said as we stepped off the elevator onto Wes' floor. "I can't believe that was almost a decade ago."

I looked up at him, and Wes grabbed my hand, pulling me into his side as we started to walk down the hall. He kissed me on the forehead. "I like making new memories with you."

"Me too," I said before we both turned our heads forward and saw Owen standing in the middle of the hallway, staring at us. Wes and I abruptly stopped walking.

"Shit," Wes muttered barely audibly.

Owen was already briskly making his way toward us, his face turning red with anger.

"I knew it!" he said loudly. "I fucking knew something was going on between you two!"

I looked up at Wes, who was staring at Owen. I didn't know if he wanted me to start trying to explain or him. Was one of us more responsible over the situation than the other? But Owen kept talking.

"You two always sitting by each other, getting high together, smiling at each other, your damn inside jokes. I assumed you'd just become friends." Owen's voice was too loud for a hotel hallway. "But then, Wes, your fucking face is always in your phone smiling. I wondered why you wouldn't tell me if you were seeing someone. When the thought crossed my mind, I thought there was no way either of you would do that without telling me. Without talking to me. Clearly, I was wrong."

Owen let out a depressing sort of laugh as he stared at Wes. "How long have you been fucking my twin sister behind my back?"

"Owen!" I cried.

"Don't talk, Leigh," he shot back, still staring at Wes. It was clear his anger was directed at Wes. It was something they needed to work out between the two of them, but I'm me, and I wasn't going to stay quiet. I opened my mouth, but Wes spoke first.

"It's not like that," Wes said.

"Like hell it's not. You've been staring at her since y'all got here," Owen countered and said again slowly, "Tell me how long my best friend has been fucking my sister."

"Stop talking about me like I'm not standing right here," I said firmly. He couldn't just tell me not to talk, and he was pissing me off. We could both be pissed off about different things at the same time. He didn't just get to be pissed at us.

Owen didn't take his eyes off of Wes. "For once in your life, Leigh, stop talking."

"We haven't had sex," Wes responded before I could retort.

Owen looked at me like he was expecting a different answer. Ah, the age-old debate of whether oral sex is sex. I was going to go with no in this situation.

Owen kept staring at me and raised his eyebrows. Oh, *now* he wanted me to talk. Brothers can be so annoying.

"We haven't had sex," I confirmed. Now I could see why Wes was so adamant that we didn't because that's all Owen could focus on. Or was he more mad about us lying like my mom thought he would be?

"You expect me to believe that?" he spat out back at Wes. "I come up here to hang out with you before I get married tomorrow. You know, my best friend, who I never get to see since you moved to New York. Instead, I find you walking down the hall to your room with a disgusting pineapple pizza and kissing Leigh on the forehead like you've been doing it all your life."

"I promise you we haven't slept together," Wes assured him.

Owen narrowed his eyes at him.

"I promise," Wes said again softer.

"Fucking hell, Wes!" he said loudly.

Someone was going to open one of their room doors soon. I was sure at least one person behind one of the doors to our sides was looking at us through their peephole because when I looked to my right, I saw the light through it vanish. If the people across were in, they were watching too.

"Let's say I believe you. And both of you have been lying to me for… how long?"

I looked back up at Wes, almost terrified of what the answer was when you really thought about it.

Don't get technical, I tried to scream at him in my brain. *Push down the good guy.*

Wes is a *much* better person than I am, obviously.

"There isn't an easy answer to that," Wes tried to explain.

Owen looked like his head was about to erupt. "What the fuck is that supposed to mean?"

Wes was intensely focused on Owen. "It's complicated."

"Explain to me how this is complicated," Owen yelled, taking a small step toward Wes. "You're either hooking up or you're not! You're either dating or you're not! You're either lying about everything or you're not!"

Wes got caught up in the high emotions swirling between the three of us and his anger started to get the better of him. I could feel the tension in his body suddenly, his jaw clenching. But Owen was practically screaming in his face, so how could you blame him?

"Because I lov—" Wes started to yell before he abruptly cut himself off when he realized what he was about to say and that he hadn't said it to me.

I snapped my head up at him with wide eyes. I already knew I loved him. Without question. Without a doubt. I wanted to spend the rest of my life with him. I wanted to grow old with him. I wanted to remain a child with him. I just didn't know he loved me back. My eyes softened, and the corners of my mouth slowly slid into a smile when he looked down at me from the top of his six-foot-four-inch tall body.

He turned and stepped in front of me, his back to Owen. He shifted the pizza box to his side. His voice was soft and low. "I love you, Leigh."

I glanced to Owen, whose eyes were as wide as mine had been the second before. His jaw dropped when his brain registered I was about to say it back. I looked back at Wes.

"I love you," I whispered.

Wes smiled and leaned in to kiss me.

"I love you, Wesley," I said again against his lips because I wanted to say it a thousand times. I wrapped my hands around the sides of his head as he kissed me.

He straightened and turned back to Owen.

"It's complicated because I love her, and there's more to it than a straightforward answer to your question."

Owen's jaw closed and his face warped as he stared menacingly at Wes. His voice was filled with more fury. It had a low and ominous tone. "Leigh, get out of here."

"What?" I stammered. "No!"

Wes' hand ran down to my elbow. "It's okay. I'll meet you back in your room."

"Listen to him if you're not going to listen to me," Owen sneered at me.

I shook my head. "I'm not going anywhere. We were going to tell you when you got back from your honeymoon."

He laughed at me. "How considerate of you."

I narrowed my eyes at him. "Stop being an asshole."

"Leigh, I'm serious." Owen glared back at me. "Turn the fuck around and walk away."

"Owen, don't talk to her like that," Wes defended me.

LEIGH MAKES THREE

"Is this how it's going to be from now on?" Owen laughed. "You two become a team? You won't be my best friend anymore. You'll be Leigh's boyfriend."

"No, I don't want that to happen. I don't want it to be us versus you. I just don't want you to talk to her like that. You can take it out on me."

"Why the fuck do you think I want her to leave?" Owen yelled again.

Wes held the pizza box out to me. I looked down at it and scrunched my eyebrows up. He nudged it at me, telling me to take it and leave. I took it from him but didn't move.

"My mom is going to love this." Owen laughed under his breath. He'd flipped from anger to dark humor.

"I'll tell you everything back in my room," Wes offered.

Wes knew better than to bring up that she already knew, right? My mom tried to stay out of it as much as she could and minded her own business. She likely had a side, but Owen didn't need to know that.

"By all means, Wes. What the hell do you think I've been asking for?"

Wes dug into his back pocket and pulled out his wallet. He fished his hotel key out of one of the slits and extended it towards Owen.

Owen snatched it out of Wes' hand. "Your girlfriend is saving you from being punched in the fucking jaw for now."

Wes smirked at Owen. "I'll be there in a minute."

"I'll be happy to give you a black eye like you gave her." Owen backed up a few steps, staring at me, before he turned on his heels and made his way down the hall. It was almost completely gone, so I narrowed my eyes at him for bringing that up. I was terrified he might actually punch him.

Wes turned back to look at my concerned face as I watched

Owen retreat further away.

"He's not being serious," Wes said softly.

"Are you sure?" I whispered. "He punched someone once in high school over me."

Granted, he was my ex-boyfriend who got mad at me for breaking up with him and showed a personal picture of me to his friends.

One of their football teammates told Owen the guy was showing it to some people in the locker room that morning. So after class, Owen confronted him in the hallway and told him to delete it. My ex refused, so Owen tried prying the phone out of his hand, but he wouldn't give it up. It escalated so quickly that Owen punched him and broke his nose. Then Owen grabbed the phone from his hand and deleted his entire photo roll and our text history. When he explained to the principal why he punched him, Owen got an in-school suspension that wouldn't go on his record, and my ex-boyfriend got suspended for two days.

"Hey, look at me."

I brought my gaze up to meet Wes'.

"I'm sure. He's not going to punch me. He's trying to piss me off and simultaneously make you worry."

I nodded as Wes brought his hands up to my cheeks. He kissed me softly at first, then a little harder, parting my lips gently with his tongue.

He pulled back. "I love you. Don't worry."

Owen's voice cut through the hallway. "Get a fucking room, you two. Oh, wait—I'm standing in front of it."

Wes' lips twitched up in a brief smile like he was trying not to laugh.

"This isn't funny," I said, scrunching up my nose.

Wes laughed again under his breath. "I know. I'm only laughing because he knows how to push my buttons. We know each other too well. Like you and Emma. And obviously, he knows you way too well."

"Okay," I whispered. "I trust you."

He smiled at me, close to my face, reminding me of that first day when he sat down in my office. A long time ago. Or so it felt. I'd fallen in love with him over two very long months.

"I'll come by your room when we're done. It will probably be a while though."

I brought my hand up to rest it on his forearm and nodded. "I love you."

He kissed me again, brushed my cheeks with his fingers as he pulled them back, and headed down the hallway. When Owen saw Wes coming, he finally put the key in the lock and disappeared through the door.

When Wes reached the door, I heard Owen say, "I really should fucking punch you."

"Go the fuck ahead if it will make you feel better," Wes replied as he stepped into the room, and I heard the door close.

Is there a universal exponent that guys use for the word fuck when they get out of earshot of a woman because they think our ears are too delicate? Like fuck[3]. I swear that's a thing. Of course, Owen forgot about the rule in his moment of rage.

I contemplated seeing if I could hear through the door but decided against it and headed back toward the elevator. There were things that I was better off not hearing.

At least I had pizza.

CHAPTER 18

Hell has broken loose, I texted Emma.
I know you're off with Logan, so I'm going to sit here, eat my pizza, and text you all of the different ways I can think of to say it until you see your phone and respond. I know it will probably be a while. No rush.

I opened the pizza box on my bed, pulled off a piece, and took a bite.

Shit hit the fan.

I leaned back on my pillows. Was Wes really going to tell him *everything*? I didn't think Owen really needed to know everything. Bits and pieces maybe. But where did my Wes stop and Owen's Wes start?

Everything went sideways.

Eventually, I was going to have to talk to Owen myself.

Things went south.

I didn't want to. I didn't want to face what we'd done. What I'd done.

It all turned to shit.

I finished my piece of pizza and picked up another one.

Out the frying pan into the fire.

I wished I could crawl under a rock and never come out. I

could fly to North Carolina and find a nice, beautiful rock to live under. Become the petrichor.
>Got rekt.

I ruined my brother's wedding weekend.
>This sucks.

I am the worst twin sister anyone could ask for.
>Worst case scenario.

I picked up my third piece of pizza. I was going to eat the entire thing and probably not be able to fit in my bridesmaid dress.
>I fucked up.

My phone finally dinged after thirty minutes.
>Be there soon!

I now knew one thing to be completely true. I should have let Wes talk to Owen during the Fourth of July. There wasn't anything worse than him finding out the way he did. Actually, it would have been worse if he walked in on us having sex, but you get the idea.

My heart started warming like I put it in an Easy-Bake Oven. Wes loved me. I sat there on the bed and just thought that one thought over and over for over a minute.

And Owen had a soft spot for me. He was always my protector. If he knew that this wasn't just us having some fun behind his back, maybe he could be happy for us. Happy that we'd found what he had with Katie. Wes was everything he told me to hold out for.

If he could just get past the fact that we lied.

An hour and a whole pizza later a knock came at my door. Emma or Wes or Owen? I got off the bed and pushed my eye up against the peephole. Emma.

I opened the door for her. "How many pieces of pizza is too many?"

"One piece more than a pizza and a half," Emma replied, hugging me. "What happened?"

"Owen saw Wes kiss my forehead when we got off the elevator.

My forehead," I repeated. "And he flipped his shit just like I said he would."

Emma sat on my bed. "Are they talking right now?"

I nodded and sat down beside her. "It was obvious he was angrier at Wes. I guess it's more of a best friend issue. Or he just wanted to be able to scream fuck as many times as he wanted. Who knows?"

"I'm sure he's worried he's going to lose his best friend."

"Are you trying to make me feel better or worse?"

"Just saying," Emma remarked. "It's two-fold. One side: things are great, but now Wes is your boyfriend, not just Owen's best friend."

Owen's words echoed in my head; *you two become a team.*

Emma continued to make me feel bad. "Think about vacations and parties and holidays. Who gets Wes' attention? Owen definitely knows he's going to get the short end of the stick."

"I'm such a bitch," I said under my breath.

Emma didn't stop. "And if things go terribly wrong, Owen's stuck with you, and Wes is out. Out with you, out with Owen, out with your family. Plus, it would be super awkward at work. Wes is risking a lot for you. And Owen knows it."

"God, Emma!" I snapped at her. "Couldn't you have told me all of this before?"

Emma laughed. "No, because then I would have scared you into not going for it. None of that means you don't try. Especially if he means what I think he means to you."

"He told me he loves me," I whispered like it was some kind of secret. It was all out now. No sense in hiding anything anymore.

"Y'all aren't that stealth," Emma laughed. "I'm so happy for y'all. Of course, he loves you. Like I said, he's risking a lot. Guys like Wes aren't going to do that for just anyone. And I can just tell you're in love. Why do you think I was so pushy? Y'all are perfect for each other. Y'all can make it a happy coincidence that he's Owen's best friend and make the best of it."

I forced a sad smile. "I guess so."

Emma eyed me with a look. She could tell I was withholding something. "What is it?"

"I'm scared Wes is going to change his mind," I whispered. I didn't want to put those words out into the world. I felt like if I did, the existence of the sound waves would materialize it into reality.

But there. I said it. It had been one of the biggest things pricking at my brain the whole time as if it was getting acupuncture: Wes was going to talk to Owen and Owen was going to talk him out of it. Out of me.

Emma took my hand in both of hers. "Leigh. He loves you. I don't think you can talk a heart out of anything."

Maybe she was right. Feelings of the heart are cemented—only able to change by itself—but sometimes the brain wins anyway.

I nodded. I didn't want to let more words increase the chance of it happening.

"So have you completed all three stages yet?"

"What?" I asked her.

"What was it I said a long time ago? Depression, realization, happiness? Depression, check! Realization, check! Happiness?"

I shook my head and laughed, trying to sound happier. Revert back to my unserious self. "Maybe after I find out what happens with Owen!"

"He'll come around."

"Probably with a list of demands," I joked.

"Oh, definitely," Emma stated. "A long list. But he loves you and Wes."

"I know."

"Oh, and I forgot about Katie! She's totally on your side. That girl could talk Owen into anything. I think she could sense y'all liked each other."

"Maybe so," I said, though I wasn't convinced.

Emma looked at her phone. "We're going to have to start getting ready for the rehearsal soon. Is your speech ready?"

"Ugh," I groaned. "You think I should just change it to 'I'm sorry I love your best friend?'"

Emma laughed.

"How can I stand up there and say any of it now?" I asked her seriously. "I ruined what is supposed to be the best weekend of his life."

"Don't be so hard on yourself. And I'd really love to see Owen cry," Emma smirked.

"I think he's more likely to scream at me and punch a wall."

"I'll have my camera ready for both," Emma assured me. "But Owen loves you, Leigh. He's going to give you a chance. Just give him time."

I nodded silently.

"You want me to stay with you a little longer?" Emma asked me.

"Please?" I replied. "I need to start getting ready."

"Sure." Emma picked up the remote and started flipping through channels as I got up to take a shower.

I checked my phone in the bathroom. I didn't have any calls or texts. It'd been over two hours since Wes went into his room with Owen. I didn't know Owen was capable of having a two-hour conversation. Maybe there was a lot of silence.

I cried in the shower, letting the hot water mix with my tears. I cried sad tears for the way I treated Owen and how unfair I was to him. I cried happy and sad tears because Wes loved me, but I was also unfair to him by making him withhold a secret like that from Owen. I was a melting pot of emotions.

When I came out with wet hair and in a T-shirt, Wes was sitting on my bed instead of Emma. My heart rumbled like a train pulling away from a station.

"That wasn't ideal."

My shoulders dropped. "What happened?"

He motioned for me to come sit beside him. I shuffled over and lay back beside him.

"Don't hate me," Wes started.

I didn't like his tone. His face. Hesitant. Serious.

I knew if I said it, it would come to life. I wanted to kick myself. Suck back the air my words were carried out on.

"What!" I cried. "Don't scare me."

"He wants to talk with you first," Wes continued. "I promised I wouldn't say anything."

I sighed. "Seriously?"

"I promised." Wes finally smiled, but when he spoke again, I wasn't sure why. "After all, he is my best friend."

—

I FELT LIKE a dark shadow was following me down the hallway, up the elevator, back down the hallway, and to the door to Wes' room, where Owen was waiting. Owen was going to eat me alive, and there was nothing I could do about it. I was going to be dropped into a shark-infested fishbowl.

I used Wes' key to let myself in. Owen was sitting on the little couch in the far back corner leaning back and looking at me. I couldn't read his expression or lack of expression. His face looked blank, his head in his hand with his elbow resting on the armrest.

There was only one thing I could say. "I'm so sorry, Owen."

"Leigh—"

I cut him off. "This is all my fault. Wes wanted to tell you so many times, and I begged him not to."

He opened his mouth again, but I just needed to get it all out there. "I should have told you I liked him. I did try to stay away from him at first. I promise. But I was too selfish. I told Wes I could never live with myself if I came between y'all, and now I have. I don't know how you can ever forgive me."

I paused.

"I'm—" he tried again.

I hurried my words over his. "And we never wanted you to find out that way. Wes was going to come to Nashville to talk to you after you got back from Hawaii. We didn't want to say anything on your wedding weekend. And now I've ruined it. I'm a selfish bitch of a twin sister."

I took a deep breath. He smirked at me, seeing if I was going to continue talking.

"Can I talk now?" Owen asked me sarcastically.

Did I have anything more to say? "I'm sorry, Owen. I love you. Okay, now you can talk."

"First things first. Don't interrupt me," he said with humor in his tone. My mind ticked up at the thought that that might be a good sign.

I nodded silently.

"I love you too. And I'm happy for you if you are in love. I just never thought it would be with Wes, of all people. New York is a city of almost ten million people, and you pick *my* best friend. And you don't even tell me. What am I supposed to do if something happens?"

Ugh, I opened my mouth, but he held up his hand.

"Rhetorical question. If Wes breaks your heart, can I not be friends with him anymore? If you break his heart, is he going to want to be friends with me anymore? I may not be in your relationship, but it involves me more than you realize. Or maybe you did realize, I don't know. But if anything goes wrong, I am in the middle of something I never asked for. That sucks."

"I kno—" I started. I can't ever keep my mouth shut.

"Nope, still me," Owen shushed me. "I can't choose Wes over you, Leigh. You're family. My twin. So if it comes to that, I lose my best friend. Not to mention how protective I am of you. Probably too much. Are you going to come to me when y'all get in a fight? Am I going to have to hear about some shitty thing one of y'all did to the other and choose a side? When we hang out, I don't want to be the third wheel with my own best friend. Honestly, a lot of this just sucks for me. I'm not trying to sound selfish. I'm scared."

I shook my head but kept my mouth shut. I hadn't thought about a lot of that. This was way more complicated than I let myself think it was. Ha, no, I knew. I said I wouldn't lie. Who am I kidding?

"I know I always went after your friends, so what say do I have now? Well, what say did I ever have, I guess. You're adults. I can't tell you who to date. I don't really have any say, but I was an asshole back then. I know I always told my friends to stay away from you and for you to stay away from them. Honestly, I only did that because all my friends were assholes. I didn't want them treating you the way we treated girls.

"I know I told you you need someone who appreciates you. Someone loyal. And Wes fits that description. He's my best friend for a reason. He's one of the best people I know. Wes is the *only* friend of mine I would approve of you dating, so at least there's that.

"I'll admit when I heard you were working together, I got worried. I figured this could be a possibility. Maybe that's why I never told you he moved to New York. I wasn't blind in college—you two fit together. Hell, maybe that's why I like him so much. I guess I'm the selfish one. I know he loves you. And I'm not going to stand between you two and tell you that you can't be together. I love you both too much. I want you to be happy. I want you to be with the person you love. And if that's Wes, then I can accept that and be truly happy for you. I promise. I just wish you would have talked to me—let me know that this was a possibility. I wouldn't have been so blindsided, and I probably wouldn't have freaked the fuck out. I'm sorry I acted like that."

"It's okay," I whispered.

"I know that was all your fault," Owen smirked at me.

"It really was," I promised. "I told him not to so many times. Owen, I can try really, really hard to not let this get in the middle of your friendship. I know things are going to be a little different, but things can be the same in so many ways."

Owen nodded. "It could also be really fun. Holidays, birthdays, vacations. Maybe he will be my brother in the future if y'all actually feel that way about each other. But let me ease into it, please."

I nodded in agreement.

"I established two ground rules with Wes that he agrees with," Owen continued.

"All right…" I said hesitantly. At least there were only two.

"One: Wes doesn't tell me anything about you he wouldn't say in front of Mom or Dad unless he wants to get punched in the throat."

I laughed under my breath. "Fair."

"Two: he doesn't get to just flip to being your boyfriend. He still has to stay my best friend, which means sometimes you get left out."

"I can handle that."

"Good. And I'm happy you're not compromising, Leigh. You deserve him, and he deserves you."

"I really love him," I said softly.

"I know." Owen stood up.

"And I love you."

Owen bear hugged me. "I know."

I hugged him hard back.

"And who knew Emma could keep a secret for eight years?" he added. "I sure didn't. Actually, I'm impressed."

I buried my face in his chest. "Ugh, Owen. We're not talking about it."

"I've done worse on that pool table, so don't think about trying that again."

"Ew!" I exclaimed. "You're so gross."

"What are brothers for?"

CHAPTER 19

I folded the piece of paper with my speech on it into the smallest square possible—seven folds—or is that a myth? I sat there trying to fold it an eighth time using all my strength before it was my turn in the toast rotation. I held the tiny square tight in my fist as I stood up. I had memorized it anyway. My palms were so sweaty I was nervous I would drop my champagne glass. I took a deep breath.

"As you all know, Owen has lived exactly eleven minutes of his life without me. They were probably the worst eleven minutes of his life; so traumatizing that he's blocked it from his memory. But they also had to have been the worst eleven minutes of my life too because when we lived in different cities for the first time in twenty-two years, I had déjà vu. I left a piece of my heart in Nashville with him, and I brought a piece of his heart with me to New York. He's the best big brother I could ask for.

"But then he found Katie, who made him even better. She has completely changed him into someone who shows unconditional love openly, who cherishes things I've never seen him express, and who smiles bigger than ever before. You two are truly in love, and I am so happy to see Owen so happy.

"Katie, I can't wait to welcome you into our family as my sister tomorrow. I couldn't have wished for a better person for my brother to spend the rest of his life with. You love him in a way I aspire to love someone, and I know your life together will be filled with happiness, patience, and love.

"I also want to thank our parents, who showed me and Owen how to stay young with someone, even as we grow older, and for showing us how to be a truly amazing partner. I love you both.

"Everyone raise your glass to Owen and Katie!"

Short and sweet. I didn't want to talk for longer than that, standing up in front of our family and close friends, rambling my innermost thoughts. I didn't want to make jokes, and I didn't want to recount childhood memories.

But Owen and Katie still beamed at me. He didn't cry (it would take a lot more for Owen's bottled-up manly emotions to fizzle up into tears), but he didn't punch a wall either.

"You didn't want to take all those loving sister of the groom swipes at him?" Wes laughed in my ear as I sat back down. "That was perfect."

Wes put his arm around me and kissed the side of my head. In public. Out in the open. I smiled up at him but glanced back at Owen and Katie, as Owen's request of easing him into it popped into my mind.

Owen and Katie were still looking at me. But Owen smiled at me and mouthed, *I love you,* and Katie winked at me before they both turned their attention to my dad as he stood up.

My dad's toast was sap city.

Nancy story.

Birth story.

Twin story.

Father-son story.

Katie story.

Future grandchildren story.

He checked all the boxes, but Owen still didn't cry. I hadn't seen him cry since before the age of twelve. My mom, Katie, and I bawled though, thoroughly messing up our makeup.

When I came back from the bathroom, Wes had pulled my chair closer to his. Whew, that made me feel things. I sat and ordered a medium-rare filet mignon. There are few things as good as a good steak.

Wes is my filet mignon, I joked to myself as I put my head against his shoulder. *Emma was right.* I looked at her across the table and smiled. *She's always right.*

"I wish y'all weren't doing boys' night tonight," I sighed to Wes. "I knowww, I have to get left out. Hey, how'd you make Owen so agreeable?"

"I explained everything to him, of course."

"That's a broad answer. How much silence was there?"

Wes looked at me sideways when I picked my head up. "Twenty-five percent?"

"I would've guessed at least fifty."

"I'm in this for the long haul, Leigh. I just needed him to see that."

I ran my hand down his tie and pulled him closer, breathing in his scent. "Why don't you haul me out of here and up to your hotel room? Wait a second," I paused, looking down at the light blue fabric I was clutching. I lowered my voice. "Is this *the* tie?" Oh, it was. It definitely was. "Is this one of your kinks?"

Wes' lips slowly started to form a smile in the corners, but I pressed my index finger against them before he could open his mouth to respond. I could feel the tornado of lust starting inside me like a horny Tasmanian devil, and my body pinched below my belly button.

I whispered in his ear, "Never mind, it's *my* new kink. I want you to tie me up with your ties and then wear them to work the next day."

Wes chuckled, and I could see his body responding when I looked down at his lap. "I like that idea very much. Let's go get another drink from the bar."

He stood and took my hand. I started to walk toward the bar in the front foyer, but Wes tugged me gently toward the outside bar and garden where we'd started the rehearsal dinner. I looked at him confused, but he just jerked his head toward the empty patio with a side smile.

He led me outside, down the stone patio steps, past the bar where the bartender greeted us (I got it then), and turned the corner. We were in the walkway nestled in the back garden.

He spun me around by my hand and pulled me in close. His lips met mine, soft and warm. Whenever he drank, he always tasted like strawberry beer. I pushed apart his lips with my tongue so I could feel it on my taste buds.

His hand came up to my throat as he kissed me back harder. He rubbed his thumb over my collarbone, playing with the hill it created under my skin. He ran his hands down my arms and laced his fingers through mine as he pulled back.

"I love you so much," Wes said.

"We haven't even had sex yet," I teased him. "What if we aren't sexually compatible? You'll hate me."

Wes laughed and leaned in close to my ear. "I don't think that's going to be a problem. Besides, I thought I gave you the best orgasm you've ever had?"

I nodded against his cheek. "I renamed my G-spot the W-spot."

"All for me?" Wes' voice hummed. "So, you want to change that right now?"

He pushed me back against the wall at the same time I grabbed his suit and pulled him into me. He kissed me hard, and I made a small noise into his mouth.

"Why are you wearing this long dress?" Wes said into my mouth as his hand gripped the floral fabric, his fingers taking more and more into his palm.

His tongue came down to my neck as his fingers finally found the bottom of my dress and slipped underneath. I knew he was joking when he said it, but I really would have had sex with him against that wall.

The gate to my left creaked open slowly.

"God," Wes breathed out in frustration before laughing against my neck and letting my dress fall back to the ground.

I put my foot back down from where my leg had found its way around Wes. We both turned our heads to look down the breezeway.

Jesus H. Christ.

"What the fuck?" Wes muttered under his breath.

I could see Wes turn his head to look at me, but Rachel and I just kept staring at each other.

Wes spoke first. "Seriously, Rachel? What are you doing here?"

Rachel's head turned slightly toward Wes while her eyes stayed on mine. It felt like the next day when her eyes finally followed her head.

"You won't return any of my calls or texts," she said. "I wanted to talk to you."

"How did you know where I was?" Wes questioned her, but I knew it was from social media.

"Not that hard to find out." She let out a small laugh. "Apparently, it's harder to find out that you're seeing someone."

Wes shook his head and looked down. I thought he was partly pissed and partly didn't want to look at her anymore. I mean, she was right. Everyone was tagging the restaurant and using wedding hashtags in their posts, and there was nothing on the internet even close to hinting at the fact that Wes and I were together.

Her eyes glossed back over to me. "Leigh? Your best friend's sister? Is it a secret, you two back here alone?"

Her voice didn't have malice in it. Curiosity maybe? Confusion? She definitely didn't know Wes had a girl in his life. But I did get a little catty girl satisfaction from knowing she remembered my name.

His head cranked back up. "No, Leigh is my girlfriend."

That was the first time he'd ever said that. I didn't even have to bring up those three small words—what are we—and just like that, I had a boyfriend.

Rachel's eyes followed my hand as I reached out and squeezed Wes' arm. "I'm going to let y'all talk."

"No," Wes said quietly to me.

"I think you should." I gave Rachel a small smile. "It's good to see you again, Rachel."

"You too, Leigh," she said.

I turned around, walked around the corner, but stopped. I wasn't *that* sweet, and I could be a little nosy in this situation. I'd earned the right as a now-girlfriend, and I'd never dealt with ex-girlfriend drama before.

"Wes, I'm sorry," Rachel started. "I didn't know what else to do."

"You can't take a hint that I'm not interested? There's not much more I can do besides straight up ignoring you."

"I can," Rachel laughed. "I thought you were still pissed, still heartbroken, but if I was persistent enough, I could show you that I wanted to make us work more than anything. I thought you'd allow me back in your life a little at a time because I was serious. What I did to you, to us, was indefensible, but I know you're capable of forgiveness. Then you dangled that carrot of hope in front of me..." she trailed off.

"That's my fault, and I'm sorry. I wasn't with Leigh at the time. I'd had a bad day, and as soon as I texted you, I knew I shouldn't have."

"It's okay. I thought you were still single though, I promise. I wouldn't have kept calling you and texting you if I knew you were dating her."

"I forgive you, Rachel. I'm not heartbroken anymore," Wes said. "Actually, I'm thankful."

"I'm happy for you," Rachel said genuinely. "You deserve it, Wes. I'm sorry for everything." She paused. "I ruined the one good thing in my life."

There was silence for a second.

"You'll thank me one day for ignoring you," he said softly.

I'd heard enough. They had clearly been through a lot together. Six years is a long time to share your life with someone, and there was probably hurt on both sides.

What would I say to Dylan if I saw him again? More than likely, it would be the same thing—a lot of thank yous, and that I was genuinely happy for him if he'd found what he was looking for. That's all I'd want for anyone.

—

ARMS WRAPPED AROUND my shoulders as I took the last bite of my steak. I'd recognize those hands and jewelry anywhere.

She squeezed me tight. "I love you, Leigh."

"I love you too, Mom," I said, wrapping my hands around her arms.

She sat down in the chair next to me. "I didn't know you were listening to me whenever I would give you the key to long-lasting happiness," she joked.

"I never really knew what you meant until recently."

"Until you fell in love." She wasn't guessing.

"Until I fell in love," I repeated. "Do you have some sixth mom-sense?"

She shrugged. "Moms just know. It makes me happy to see you so happy."

"You got any more old-lady wisdom for me?"

"Hey!" my mom scoffed. "I'm still young."

"Figure of speech. My own figure of speech?" I wasn't purposely trying to call her old.

She laughed. "What about your wisdom? You still surprise me all the time. I wonder where you got your spark from every once in a while."

"The mailman?"

"If you got it from me, I'd have a great response to that up my sleeve. Anyway, my only other wisdom is to not complicate the fact that you want to be with each other. It's really straightforward when you think about it."

I mulled over my mom's words. It's funny that we can take a simple concept such as wanting to be with someone and make it hard, make it messy, and convolute it into so much sadness and heartache. But I guess that's just one of the many downfalls of the human psyche.

Wes and I made it hard on each other—on ourselves—for four years. So hard that we almost lived completely separate lives. We would have, if it hadn't been for the exes in our lives who pushed us forward to something happier, unbeknownst to us. It went without saying—I also made it hard the last few months.

"People suck," I laughed. Those two words can sum up most of life.

"I don't suck *that* much," Wes said, slipping his hands around my shoulders.

I placed my hand on one of his.

My mom rose and gave him a huge Nancy smile and hug. "You two have fun," she said before standing on her tiptoes and saying something into Wes' ear that I couldn't hear.

"Jesus, what creepy son-in-law comment did she just make?" I asked when Wes sat beside me. "I'm going to have to talk to her."

Wes smiled against his beer bottle as he took a sip. "I'll never tell. And I did finally get to apologize to her earlier about the Fourth."

"Wes," I said with my most intense stare, "we are going to have to have a talk about you being *too* good sometimes. No one needs to dredge up that moment ever again."

"Would you rather your mom or Rachel walk in on us having sex?" Wes joked.

"Rachel, definitely. With some luck, I'll never have to see her again."

"I don't think we will," Wes said. He leaned into me and kissed me on the cheek before whispering, "Thank you."

"Of course," I whispered back. "Did she get what she needed?"

I already knew what Rachel needed—closure—but the kind where you know you aren't responsible for ruining someone's life forever. The kind where you know you devastated them, and you wish it could have gone differently, but ultimately it was for the best. She'd probably hung on to a lot of guilt over the last few years, and I hoped she'd be released from it. Wes and I both wanted her to move on in peace.

"Yeah," he said. "I think she just needed to know I was happy."

Even when you want to be with someone, you still hurt them occasionally. I looked at Wes and thought about how many times in the future we would hurt each other. It's not like you ever really want to, but it's inevitable.

"What?" Wes said, studying me studying him.

I shook my head and smiled. "I just love you."

"I love you."

"And I really want to be with you. I don't want to convolute it, you know? Not anymore at least."

Wes looked at me confused, his smile turning up slowly in surprise. "What are you trying to say underneath that?"

"You don't have to know everything about me," I said slyly.

Wes put his arm around me. "I'm sure you will always continue to surprise me, but I have no doubt that whatever you are saying came from your mother."

What did she actually whisper in his ear?

CHAPTER 20

I looked down at my phone, but Wes hadn't texted me back. It was already almost 1 a.m. Owen and the groomsmen were spending Owen's last night of singleness together in Owen's hotel room.

Of course, I couldn't sleep. I kept rolling over and kicking my legs. I kept readjusting my pillow and throwing my comforter on and off. I didn't know why I was anxious. I wasn't the one getting married.

I sat up and turned the TV on. I flipped through the channels trying to find anything decent to watch until I heard bbbeeehhh.

Ah, how fitting!

The top four answers are on the board. Name an emotion I was feeling.

1. Anxious (because my twin brother was getting married the next day).

2.. Absofuckinghornievable (because I was on an I-have-no-idea-how-many-days streak).

3. Vexed (because despite having a boyfriend, I still couldn't seem to get laid).

4. Salty (because television game shows would never let me

forget it).

There was the softest of knocks on my door as I was watching a second episode and laughing. I wasn't even one hundred percent sure if I'd imagined it or not.

I crept to the door and stood on my tiptoes to look through the peephole. Wes was looking back at me as he ran his hand through his hair.

"I figured you'd still be awake," he said, grinning at me when I opened the door. "Can't sleep?"

I shook my head. "No, I can't stop thinking."

Wes strode past me and turned around as I shut the door. There was no way I was going to ask if he ditched the guys to come see me. I was hoping he was there to stay.

"I couldn't stop thinking about you all alone in this hotel room," he said huskily as he reached out and grabbed my oversized T-shirt, pulling me toward him.

I went from a AAA battery to a struck lightning rod.

"You came to keep me company?" I whispered.

He shook his head.

"You came to watch TV with me? I whispered as his lips hovered over mine.

He shook his head again but didn't come closer.

"You want to play a board game with me?"

He smiled close to my lips. I wanted to reach out and grab his bottom lip with my teeth.

"What about knitting?"

He shook his head. He wasn't going to come closer until I said it, until I was begging him to put his lips on mine.

"What do you really want to do?" he questioned me, tightening the grip he had on my shirt and pulling my body against his. I knew it.

"I want you to fuck me," I whispered eagerly, placing my hands against his abs.

His lips brushed mine too softly, making me want it all, but he didn't give it to me. "How badly?"

"I've never wanted anything as badly in my life," I whined.

"Because you know how good I can make you feel."

I looked up into his eyes and nodded, my lips going up and down softly over his.

His lips met mine roughly, and his tongue pushed its way into my mouth. His hands came around my waist as I found the hem of his shirt and slipped my hands underneath it.

"I want you to let go," Wes told me after he pulled away.

I nodded as he pulled me back towards my bed. When we reached the side, he twisted our arms together over my head, spinning me to face away from him and pulling me into him with his arms around my waist. He slipped off his shoes and sat down on the bed, directing me with the force of his arms, and sitting me in between his legs, my back against his chest.

I tipped my head to the side to look at him, and he kissed me again. His tongue hit all those little spots in my mouth that made me feel a rush in my stomach.

His hands came up to my breasts over my shirt. He squeezed them before massaging with his fingers. He played with my nipples that he had made hard seconds earlier, poking out against my thin T-shirt. I didn't have a bra on because who the hell sleeps in a bra?

I moaned into his mouth as he brought his hands up under my shirt, pinching my nipples harder. I arched my back at the sensation that shot down from my boobs to my lower stomach.

Wes' fingers snaked into my hair and pulled me away from his mouth. He tugged it to the left as his mouth and wet tongue sucked on the side of my neck. His hands came down and gripped both of my legs by my inner thighs before he pulled them wide apart roughly. My fingers dug into the tops of his thighs in anticipation of his touch between my legs. His fingers lightly brushed my inner thighs, not giving me what I wanted, but sending sparks up like he was crushing bang snaps against my skin.

He made a deep 'yum' noise in his throat as his right hand settled over my pajama shorts. He rubbed me back and forth with all of his fingers while his warm tongue was pushing against my throat. I reached behind my back and found his erection. I gripped it over his pants, and he made another throaty noise against my neck.

His hand came up my front and found the hem of my shorts. Wes lifted it with one finger at a time, before all five found their way under my underwear. His mouth came up to my ear and he bit my earlobe, rubbing over me with one finger. I gasped under my breath. He increased his speed slightly with two fingers, then went faster with three.

"Put your fingers inside me," I begged.

He shook his lips against my ear and licked it as he slowed his fingers. "Let go, Leigh."

I nodded and rested my head back. I closed my eyes, taking in every sensation. The heat searing between my legs, his warm breath on my ear, his body underneath mine, his hard-on pressing into the top of my butt. I was lost in it. I rocked my hips against his fingers as he increased his speed again.

"There you go," he whispered into my ear, making me wetter. I could feel it as his fingers found it and brought it back up, circling around me with more lubrication.

He brought his hand up to my lips, gliding over them, before slipping two of his fingers into my mouth. I sucked them, running my tongue along the bottom of them, tasting the sweetness of myself.

"You taste good, don't you?" Wes said low into my ear.

I opened my eyes and looked up at him, his fingers still in my mouth. I nodded my head slightly.

"You make me so fucking hard," he whispered.

I gripped my hand around him harder with my fingers and rubbed as he pulled his fingers out of my mouth slowly and placed them around my chin. His tongue plunged into my mouth as his kiss became deeper and rougher. His hand went back below my underwear, where he rubbed over me for a few seconds before finally slipping a finger inside me.

I begged him with a moan into his mouth to find my G-spot—sorry W-spot—but he was going to take his damn time as his finger came in and out slowly. I arched my back and Wes increased the speed. Then he slipped a second finger inside and slowed his speed again. He stayed there for a minute.

His fingers explored inside me before finally making their way to his spot. He applied pressure and held it there without moving for a few seconds, claiming it, while he nibbled and sucked on my bottom lip. Then he stroked me with his finger, gradually going a little faster before he changed to a circular motion and applied more pressure.

I broke away from his mouth as my hips gyrated by themselves. "Oh my God, Wes."

He exited me and rubbed his hands up and down my inner thighs as I rubbed him over his pants.

His fingers came down to rub me under my shorts in a quick circular motion. The pressure he was building was hitting against the wall of my lower abdomen. He was already going to make me come if he wasn't careful.

"Wes," I moaned under my breath.

"Moan my name louder," he said gruffly in my ear as he slipped a finger back inside to stimulate me in both areas.

"Mm, Wes," I moaned again, louder.

"Who else can make you feel like this?"

"No one," I whimpered. "You're going to make me come already."

He slowed down his speed and took the pressure off with his fingers, pulling me back from the ledge he had me dangling from.

"You can have multiple orgasms, right?" Wes whispered.

I could by myself—no guy had ever achieved it. I was almost sure he could achieve it, but he could feel my hesitation.

"Is that a no?" he said as his fingers got even slower, torturing me.

"Sort of," I whispered. "Only by myself."

"Are you challenging me?" Wes bit my ear playfully and went back to rubbing me. His voice turned seductive. "I love a good challenge, but no faking it. I'll make you come more than twice if you're good for me. But you have to give in to it."

I nodded as his mouth licked the side of my neck, my nerves firing off as he sucked gently.

He inserted two fingers super slowly. He picked up his speed again, going back to his pattern: strokes and circular motion, all while increasing the pressure. His other hand just gripped the inside of my thigh. My heart was racing, my chest expanding like a hot air balloon. I reached my hand up and gripped the back of Wes' neck. My fingers dug into his skin as my hips rocked against his fingers.

"That's it." His voice was deep but lower than a whisper. He brought his other hand up my thigh to stimulate me in both areas. "It feels good, doesn't it?"

If I could record Wes' voice in these moments and walk around with headphones listening to it, I would. But of course, walking around having orgasms while doing everyday things would be frowned upon. His voice, not just his touch, was bringing me to a place in my mind I'd never been, and I was completely consumed by the pleasure like Wes told me. I was getting out of my head—

not thinking of any other thought—focused only on the pleasure Wes was surging between my legs and up to my brain. I'm going to say pleasure again—pleasure. It was like I had only one synapse firing, and the only communication it could relay was pleasure, pleasure, pleasure.

"Come on my fingers," Wes demanded. "I want to feel it."

"God, yes," I let out breathily as my body listened. I tightened around his fingers, my legs tensing and shaking. The heat between my legs was exploding like dynamite. And his fingers kept going, stretching it out longer, as I rocked against him, moaning, and letting myself go for as long as my body would allow.

"Fuck, Leigh, those moans are so sexy," he said against my neck as my body started to slow. My breath staggered as I recovered. He removed his fingers and glided over me slowly, stimulating me differently, creating heat again in a different way. I could feel my body already revving back up. Shit, he had no idea just how horny he made me. I really had no idea how he could do that to me, but I realized then that maybe it wasn't that my exes couldn't bring me to orgasm twice, it was that they never took the time.

I flipped myself around on all fours to face him and kissed him hard, pushing my tongue against his. I kissed his neck softly and reached down to pull his shirt over his head. He reciprocated, slowly pulling my shirt off by the bottom hem. He gripped me around the ribs, pushing me up to kneel straight, as he buried his face between my breasts. His mouth licked and sucked my nipples with force as he hummed against my skin. I dropped my head back when he planted kisses down my rib cage.

My hands ran through his hair as I looked to my left at the full-length mirror next to the bed and got an idea when I remembered my drunken words.

I pulled back and slid off the bed. Wes smiled at me as I grabbed his hands and pulled him to stand. I kissed and licked my way down his abs to his happy trail before I kneeled in front of him. I looked up at his toned body, reveling that it was mine. I unbuttoned his pants and yanked them down, running my hand over him still in his boxers. He stepped out of his pants, and I gripped the elastic waistband, pulling his boxers down quicker.

It's true taller guys are bigger. Maybe that's another primal reason why we love tall men.

I looked up into Wes' eyes as I finally took him into my hand. He sucked in a breath as his hand ran through my hair. I licked him along the bottom before taking him into my mouth, and he moaned. I increased my speed slightly while I gripped his thighs. His fingers entangled themselves in my hair at the back of my scalp and held me there as he pushed himself deeper, making my stomach flip at how much I liked having him in my mouth, so I told him.

"Fuck, Leigh," Wes said in a gruff voice, but he surprised me when he started to tell me a story. "You remember that Halloween when we were at the same party? God, you looked so hot that night in those tight little pink shorts. I watched you dance all night. Your ass was driving me nuts. All I could think about was stripping you naked and seeing your mouth around me, those lips gripping me."

His other hand came around the back of my head, and he pulled my hair harder, controlling the speed, as he watched himself move in and out. My body was buzzing at his words.

I *knew* he was flirting with me that night, caught between a rock and a hard place—oh, the glorious puns—like we both had always been.

"Mmm," I said in the back of my throat, telling him he was driving me nuts as I looked up at him.

"I wanted to see your eyes looking up at me like they are right now. It's even better than I pictured it," Wes continued. "And then

I spilled that drink on you. I felt bad, but shit, I could see your perfect little nipples poking through that thin fabric. All I wanted was to suck on them."

He brought his fingers down to play with one of them. "And now, I finally can whenever I want."

He paused and made a low sound. "You look so fucking sexy with my dick in your mouth."

He pulled my head back and removed himself from me. I ran my hand up and down him. I bit my bottom lip and gave him a seductive smile.

"Do you like sucking my cock?" he asked, his voice gravelly and assertive.

I nodded and licked the end of him. "Give it to me."

"Good girl," he said, playing with himself against my lips before pushing himself back into my mouth.

His words were turning me on, lighting fire after fire. He knew how to stroke my brain, not just my body. Make me think of nothing else but the experience we were sharing together. Who hasn't thought some weird thought during sex that completely turns you off? Or maybe that was just me and my neurotic mind.

I could be guilty of it with Dylan: Did I turn off the oven? What is my neighbor watching so loud on TV? Did they like that idea at work today?

But this was different. Wes kept me in my head space, tickling parts of my brain that kept me engaged and focused only on me and him. He kept me turned on even when I wasn't receiving the physical pleasure.

Wes reached down and slid his hand down and up my back. "God, you're amazing at it."

I moaned as he reached under my shorts and grabbed my ass, shaking it a little in his hand. His fingers came down between my legs and played with me. I widened my legs for him before he slipped a finger inside me.

His hand came out and pulled my hair back into a ponytail as he watched us in the mirror. He stepped to his side, repositioning us so we could see a side profile of both of us.

"Take it deeper," he instructed me.

I opened my throat and took him in as deep as I could, and his knees shook slightly. One thing I'd now learned that drove him wild—he wanted to feel himself hit the back of my throat.

"Look how hot you look on your knees in front of me," Wes directed me.

I looked to my side. I looked at myself first before making eye contact with Wes in the mirror. God, I felt hot.

He pulled me up by my hair and kissed me hard. His tongue circled mine and he bit my bottom lip. He sat on the edge of the bed and pulled my shorts and underwear down at once. I stepped out of them as he pulled me in closer by my ass.

He leaned back, his head near the headboard, as he said, "Get up here."

I wasn't exactly sure what he wanted me to do, but I climbed onto the bed on my knees. Wes placed his hands under my butt and leaned back completely, pulling me towards his face.

Oh, yes.

I scooted up around him and positioned myself above his mouth. He licked me from back to front, and I moaned his name.

The end of his tongue flicked me a few times before he pushed his tongue into me.

"You taste so good," he hummed against me when he took it back. That little tongue move was for him, I was sure of it, which only exhilarated me, finding out another little piece about him, something he liked—it made me feel like he couldn't get enough of me. He certainly seemed to be into the giving, not just the receiving, and of course, that just made everything better.

My hips rocked against his tongue as it circled me. I gripped his hair as he grabbed my ass hard, his hands focusing there for a minute until he brought his hands up to my boobs, squeezing. He brought one of his hands down to pleasure himself as I circled my hips over his tongue, and he held it out flat for me to work myself over. I held the headboard tight as I rocked myself against his tongue, controlling the position and speed as Wes pinched my nipples. He was going to make me come for a second time, and I was in complete awe of him. All of his sexual sides were amazing.

I looked down at him, and I knew he could sense it. His eyes seemed to smile, telling me to let go. I could hear his voice even though he wasn't saying anything.

"Wes," I breathed out.

"Mm hmm," he hummed back and sucked. Then he used the top end of his tongue to rub over me quickly.

I wasn't sure if Wes was just that in tune with my body, or if I had some mental leap that I only had with him because he was camping out inside my brain. He just did everything right to turn on every light switch in my body.

"Just like that. Don't. Stop," I told him between heavy breaths. And he didn't. Wes knew that meant not to change a thing—unlike half the guys I'd been with who'd change it up all of a sudden and ruin it when I said that. Wes stuck to it exactly like that, never changing pressure or speed, as the earthquake started and measured an eight on the Richter scale by the time I was finished. I moaned loudly when I reached the peak and relaxed when my body stopped rumbling. I fell back beside Wes as he rubbed my legs, massaging my inner thighs, and kissed me softly on the neck, still sending goosebumps across the nape of my neck.

I rolled to my side and stroked him with my hand. His teeth skimmed my throat while he pulled my head back by my hair.

"I've waited nine long years for this," he said as he bit my neck.

"I want to be inside you." His mouth trailed down my chest as he released his grip. "You're so gorgeous."

"I love you, Wes," I whispered into his hair.

Wes picked his head up to look into my eyes. "I love you back."

We kissed each other deeply, finding a perfect rhythm as we lay next to each other naked, our chests touching. Wes' hand caressed my hip and butt before he broke his mouth apart from mine.

"You ready to break that streak?" His gray eyes twinkled with blue when he smiled at me.

Wes rolled over and grabbed his pants off the floor, dug in his pocket, and pulled out a condom. He rolled back toward me, and his mouth kissed my breasts as he slipped a hand between my legs gently.

I breathed out and laughed under my breath. He had no idea. I heard the condom wrapper tear before Wes stood. He grabbed my ankles and pulled me to the edge of the bed in a swift motion. I grinned at him, thinking about how two months ago I hadn't given this man a second thought, and now he was sexily pulling me toward him to slide his cock into me.

He wrapped one hand around my ass which was slightly off the bed as he played with himself, rubbing over me a few times.

Then he entered me slowly, pushing into me deeper, and coming back slightly.

Day 0.

"Fuck," we both whispered at the same time.

Then Wes filled me completely, rubbing all those extra places that aren't as reachable with fingers. His hands came up the sides of my thighs, pulling them around his waist, as he increased his tempo.

Sex was better than I remembered it.

I picked my neck up to meet Wes' gaze. Then I looked down to watch him sliding into me. I'd do that forever. I threw my head back to get lost in it and reached my arms behind my head, taking a handful of the sheets between my fingers hard. I arched my back and moaned as he hit all those spots again and again.

Wes' hands caressed my stomach and chest before he pulled out and flipped me over. He got on the bed on his knees, pulled me up to all fours by my waist, and entered me from behind. The way he took charge, moving me the way he wanted, was refreshing. I didn't have to think about it. I dug my fingernails into the skin of his thighs. I was going to leave scratches, but it excited me. I looked back at him craving his eye contact. His eyes came up from my ass to look at me and he spanked me with a flat hand. Everything about it just turned me on more: the sound, his face, the slight sting.

His hands snaked around my waist, but I pulled them up to my breasts, telling him to play with them. Hearing earlier how he loved my nipples was just like dumping a cup of sugar on something already sweet. He pinched my nipples and flicked them with his fingers. He started to get a little rougher before he twisted his fingers through my hair, pulled my head back, and kissed the side of my neck.

Suddenly, he slowed down like he was savoring it. "You feel so good," he huffed in my ear. He brought his fingers down to rub me. I made a soft sound from my throat at his touch. I was aching for him to go faster.

"Fuck me harder, Wes," I begged him.

Wes made a sexy man grunt as he straightened his back and went faster and deeper. His fingers tightened in my hair and his other hand glossed up my back before wrapping around the base of my neck and shoulder. It made me feel like I was his, animalistic, stirring fierce passion within him. And I loved being submissive to him. Maybe that's what it was about—thinking I was the only woman who could make him feel that way, and he needed me so badly he just had to act on his animal instincts.

He pushed my upper body down onto the bed and pulled my arms behind my back. One hand's fingers tight around my wrists and his other hand's fingers grabbing my ass hard.

"I love when you pin me down," I breathed out against the bed.

Wes was lost in it himself as he picked up his force. He leaned down into my ear and said in the hottest voice I'd ever heard, "That's because you know you belong to me."

I nodded against the bed. "I'm yours," I whispered. I didn't want to be anyone else's ever again, and I wanted to please him in whatever way he wanted.

What was it that made this so fucking hot? If Wes barked orders at me or claimed he could do with me as he pleased in everyday life (which he never would), I'd run for the hills. But in bed? God.

He kissed my shoulder and moaned into my hair, hitting all the deep spots before exiting me and turning me over onto my back. He pushed my legs open and brought his mouth down on me, stimulating me with his tongue.

"God, Wes," I said, writhing against his mouth as he kept going, faster and faster. He started to slow and pulled away.

"You're going to come for me a third time," he stated, his voice matter of fact, as he looked up at me.

I nodded as he ran a finger over me slowly, taking his time as he went up and down and in repeatedly. Our eyes were back to superglue as Wes watched the ecstasy on my face.

He slid off the bed and pulled me close to him. "On your knees."

I obeyed his command, and he grabbed my hips, pulling me against his body. He wrapped his hands around both of my thighs, directing my legs to straddle him.

I wrapped my legs around him and brought myself off of the

bed, holding on to his neck. Wes grabbed my ass and turned around, sitting on the edge of the bed.

Wes was giving me back control to do it how I liked. I lifted myself slightly as Wes positioned himself to enter me, and I lowered myself back down, our faces only inches apart. It was hot and intimate.

"Fuck," he said roughly. "I won't ever get used to that."

Wes wrapped his hand around the back of my neck and kissed me as I rocked against him. My hands were running over every back muscle, tracing his spine and shoulder blades. I adjusted my angle so that he hit my W-spot again and again.

Wes brought his hand down, rubbing over me with his thumb and giving me additional pleasure.

"You're so fucking good," Wes said in a low voice like he was going to devour me.

My fingernails scraped across his upper back at his words. He went back and forth between my nipples, increasing my sensations threefold.

I wanted to get lost in every feeling. I closed my eyes and put my head back. Wes' wet tongue glided over me, zapping my nerves like water in an electrical outlet. His thumb created a buzz in my lower abdomen like he'd turned on a neon sign. And his dick was just perfectly perfect. I was giving in to it. The key, apparently, for me to shut off every non-sexual part of my brain.

My thoughts were bringing me to the base of a mountain, and I moaned softly, completely immersed. Wes recognized I was about to hike up. He increased his speed slightly and stayed in perfect rhythm.

"God, how do you do that?" I asked rhetorically, looking into his eyes and getting lost in the silver.

"Come on me, Leigh," he said, holding my gaze. "I want to come with you."

I rocked harder against him as I started to climb. "I'm coming," I whispered into his face.

Wes kissed me hard when I hit the summit, and we moaned into each other's mouths. Wes' body tensed, and he gripped me hard, pushing me down on him, and coming right behind me.

CHAPTER 21

I woke suddenly thinking I had slept through the wedding. Which was ridiculous because it was at six that evening, and when I looked at the clock on my nightstand, it was 6:33 in the morning. We didn't have to meet in Katie's hotel suite until ten.

I rolled over to see Wes sleeping next to me, his bare chest rising and falling slowly. We'd gone to bed after three that morning. I scooted in close to him, wrapped an arm and a leg around him, and fell back asleep.

Around nine, I felt Wes' body shift underneath me, and I opened my eyes slowly.

He smiled at me. "I'm sorry I woke you up. I need to pee."

I shook my head at him and smiled back sleepily as he got out of bed. When he came back, he snuggled in next to me.

"You're so warm," I said, nuzzling against him.

Wes kissed me on the head and stroked my hair as we lay in silence. My mind couldn't focus on anything else but the night before—every word Wes spoke, every breath, every moan. And how he made me feel—special, alive, out of my own head—all while he got into my head. Being submissive was empowering. Maybe that's how Wes felt. He could take on a different role from his everyday life. And why was he so chick-flicky-good at pleasing me? That's *not* normal.

"Why are you so good at that?" I asked, breaking the silence.

"At what?" he asked genuinely. He had to know how good he was in bed. There was just no way.

"Sex, dummy. It's like you know exactly what to do."

He laughed into my hair. "You really want me to answer that?"

Oh, God. Did I? My mind started going to dark places thinking about Wes as a male escort, pleasing every type of woman, learning every trick in the book with each additional woman. Whatever it was, it couldn't be that bad.

"Yes...?" I said hesitantly.

"Remember my friend with benefits? Not you, the other one," he joked, and my mind instantly relaxed. "I was an inexperienced freshman, and I wanted to be better at sex. I got drunk with my friend one night and confessed to her that I thought my last girlfriend had been faking it. So, then we agreed to help each other out. Our sex relationship was all based on teaching the other what the opposite sex likes and how to do things right. Well, mostly. It's not one size fits all obviously. I still had to figure stuff out on my own." Wes tapped me on the forehead. "But also, a lot of it is just getting in here."

I could only guess this was another reason why girls loved Wes in college. There's a long list of pros to being a woman, but some of the cons include being paid less than our male counterparts, not being able to stand up to pee, and orgasms can be just as much mental as they are physical. Wes must have figured that last one out earlier than most men.

But maybe it took a lot more to get inside my head than most. Who knows?

"You should publish a self-help book: *Get In There, and You'll Get Her*. Also, if I ever meet her, please let me know, so I can thank her."

Wes chuckled.

I looked up at him. "Shit, do I know her?"

"No, I don't think so." Wes picked up a piece of my hair and played with it.

"Some guy out there is probably thanking you too."

"If I ever meet her husband, I'm sure he'd be thrilled to hear she learned all those tricks from me," Wes laughed and kissed me.

"You gonna teach me those tricks?" I joked, rubbing over his abs.

Wes put his mouth into my hair. "Not anything I don't like. I don't plan on ever giving another man the opportunity to be with you."

He couldn't see the smile on my face.

Wes had insisted we talk about everything before we went to sleep and made sure I was okay with everything he said and did. He was so thoughtful, asking me what I liked the most, what I liked the least. He was surprised when I told him I'd never tried being submissive. He'd just assumed by the things I'd said and did that I was already into it, but I was only feeding off of him. And I confirmed his little tongue thing—it didn't do anything for me physically, but mentally, damn, that only made me like it even more.

I wondered how Rachel could have ever strayed from him, looking for something different. I told myself not to bring her up, but of course, I did anyway.

"I didn't know what I was missing out on. If we'd gone further ten years ago, I'd have been like Rachel," I laughed.

"What?!" he exclaimed, grabbing my waist.

"No wonder she wouldn't leave you alone. Do you have a trail of sex slaves following you around like a mother duck and her ducklings?"

"No, you're my only little concubine." Wes pinched my butt and laughed under his breath. "Rachel and I weren't compatible in that way. She wasn't into all that. Not every girl is, of course, so we never explored it after I brought it up. I guess you just quickly figured out I was into it and explored it on your own."

That made my stomach feel like I'd swallowed a bag of Pop Rocks. He wasn't like that with all the girls. Maybe it was a happy accident that I discovered what turned him on, and I was freaking into it.

"Hey, do you remember that night we ate ice cream together at your house?" Wes asked me.

"Yeah, of course," I laughed. Honestly, I probably remembered almost every interaction I had with Wes in college.

"When I brought up your secrets, and we were both just staring at each other—I know we were both thinking about that kiss. In that moment, I couldn't help but wish I was single. Maybe that should have told me something. I knew I would have kissed you again if I was, and I didn't trust myself being close to you under a blanket. Then you fell asleep, and when I went to put your pillow under your head, you said something."

I looked at him with wide eyes. I didn't remember saying anything.

Wes smiled at me. "I knew you were talking in your sleep, but you reached out and grabbed my hand, snuggled it against you, and mumbled my name with this cute smile. God, hearing you say my name like that. You sounded happy. I wanted to lie down next to you and just be with you. Fall asleep next to you." He laughed. "That sounds creepy, but it's the truth. I wished you would say something else, so I stood there for a few seconds and to my surprise you did, but you sounded sad. You said, 'Why, Wes?'

"I used to think about that night all the time senior year and wonder what you were dreaming about. Were you asking me why I kissed you? Why I walked away? Why we never talked about it? Why was I with Rachel? Why I never asked you for your phone number? Why I never asked you out? Anything you could think of I asked myself. The one that scared me the most was if you were asking why I didn't like you. Sometimes I would catch myself repeating those questions over and over to myself wondering what you meant out of those two little words while I stared at the back of your head in class." He paused and smiled again. "I don't know why, but I just wanted to tell you that."

"I don't remember, but I'm sure it was 'why aren't you into me?'" I teased him.

"I *am* into you," Wes said, grabbing my ass and pulling me on top of him. He pulled my shirt trying to bring my lips down to his. "Come here."

I pouted. "I haven't brushed my teeth, and I have to be upstairs in ten minutes."

"I don't care." Wes brought his head up instead and kissed me, running his tongue along my upper lip before he rolled over on top of me and pinned my arms down by my side playfully. "And I can make you come in less than five."

He should have said less than three.

—

KATIE WAS ON the verge of hyperventilation, but she still looked beautiful.

Her strapless wedding dress had gorgeous, beaded lace above her waist that spread out into her full tulle skirt and long train. Her veil was hooked right above her low bun that draped over her bare back.

That morning she'd been calm and collected. We'd eaten breakfast catered by the hotel. We took turns getting our airbrushed makeup and hair done. There are not many things that will make you feel prettier than getting your hair and makeup done by a professional. I looked like a real-life Photoshopped version of myself.

Katie's chest rose and fell at an astronomical pace, but she seemed more nervous about having all of the attention on her. "I don't want to walk down the aisle and have everyone looking at me," she wheezed.

Kathryn and I were trying to calm her down at the back of the church.

"I'm going to trip," she said with wide eyes.

"No, you won't," I reassured her. "Your dad will have you. If you do, he'll keep you upright, and no one would know."

Katie nodded, but her eyes started to well with tears. "We should have eloped," she whispered.

"Don't look at them," Kathryn told her.

"Katie," I followed up after I couldn't help but glance at her amazing cleavage in that white dress, "look at Owen and breathe. Once you get down the aisle, it's just you and him. Forget everyone behind you. Twenty minutes later, you're a married woman and you can drink."

She nodded slowly as the violin and harp started to play. It was now or never.

I squeezed her hand in understanding. "You got this, sis."

Her bright white teeth showed two by two as she broke into a slow smile and squeezed my hand back. "I'm happy for you, by the way. I didn't know if you knew Wes was so hung up on you. He was so obvious! Don't worry about Owen. I got your back."

I laughed and threw my arms around her. "Let's go make you my sister."

She stood and we went to the back of the line hand in hand.

The officiant, Owen, and the groomsmen should have been

walking in from the side door and positioning themselves at the altar at that moment.

The wedding planner, standing on the opposite end of the foyer, across the open doorway, motioned for the grandparents at the front of our line to start down the aisle, followed by the parents. My mom looked absolutely stunning in a gray beaded dress. She was a totally hot woman in her sixties. You could never blame my dad for all of those years of PDA we had to put up with.

I didn't want anyone looking at me either, but they weren't there to see me, so what did I care? I watched as each bridesmaid turned the corner and disappeared before it was my turn. I was the last of the bridesmaids to walk down the aisle.

I looked down at my dress and ran my hand over the front like I was brushing something off it, even though there was nothing there. I ran my hand down my butt, making sure my dress was still covering it, even though it was full length. Nervous tics. I spun my bouquet in my hand until the wedding planner motioned that it was my turn.

I turned to look at Katie one last time and mouthed, *Love you.*

She mouthed it back with a huge smile.

I walked forward, looking down at my feet clacking against the wooden floor until I turned the corner for the aisle.

When I looked up, my eyes found Owen immediately. I smiled at him, so handsome in his tux, and tried to forget about everyone around me. My brother was getting married, and he looked incredibly happy. His eyes glossed, his short hair laying perfectly, and his hands clasped in front of him. I wished I could hug him one more time before he officially became a husband.

My eyes slid to Wes standing next to him, and I did forget about everyone around me.

Wesley in a tux was captivating. I looked him up and down as his eyes did the same to me in my blush pink bridesmaid dress. The chiffon hugged my torso and came up around my boobs tightly before wrapping around one shoulder. His mouth was turned up then down like he was trying to suppress his smile from getting too big. Owen glanced at Wes, wanting to see his expression at my entrance, and smiled, happy for us. Maybe Owen could read my expression.

All I could think about was how I'd marry Wes right after Owen and Katie if it was socially acceptable to piggyback off of someone else's wedding. That maybe one day I'd be hyperventilating in a wedding dress, waiting to see Wes with a look on his face like the one Owen had now.

Wes watched me the entire time as I neared the end of the aisle and stood in my spot across from him. I didn't want to look away, but I forced myself to when the ring bearer was finished and went to sit with Katie's family. He didn't have the actual rings, just little fake silver ones. The real rings were in Wes' pocket.

Katie's niece, the flower girl, came next. She left little pink petals in her wake as she rushed nervously down the aisle. When she was finished, everyone stood, and the music got louder as it hit its crescendo.

Katie and her father turned the corner, and as soon as Katie's eyes found Owen, she relaxed into a trance. Her beautiful light pink and white bouquet kept bobbing slightly as she walked.

I looked at Owen who was actually tearing up for the first time in, I dunno, fifteen years. I couldn't believe it. Wes laughed under his breath at me staring at my brother.

We turned toward Katie and Owen when she reached him, but Wes and I kept looking at each other. I couldn't help but wonder if he was thinking all the same thoughts. Probably not though, right? Guys don't imagine all the crazy wedding stuff like girls do.

When I looked out at the pews of people and the women tearing up, I realized that people don't cry at weddings for the bride and groom. The tears are formed from their own memories.

The officiant welcomed everyone and recounted the love story of Owen and Katie. When he was through, Katie's brother read an excerpt from a poem I'd never heard. Second, Wes took his position on the altar and read another poem. I thought I'd heard it before, but when he was finished, it registered that I hadn't heard a single word he said.

Next came their vows, to which Owen insisted they not write their own. He was still the old Owen in some ways. They smiled and cried as they repeated the same words spoken by millions of people. The only difference was that there was one Owen Sullivan and one Katie Hart in the world committing themselves to the other. I looked at Wes as he handed them the rings, and the two of them slid their rings on the other's fingers.

There was only one man I would commit myself to—I was already committed to—Wesley Miller Adams. No matter how many other Wes Adamses existed in the world, they weren't my Wes. I looked down at his bare ring finger, imagining that one day he could have a similar ring.

The physical ring doesn't really mean anything different when you think about it. You can commit yourself to someone without one. You can commit yourself before marriage. You can commit yourself without marriage at all. Nothing magically changes when that metal circle reaches its resting place above your knuckle—each day you wake up, you still have to choose your husband or wife. It's merely a symbol to the outside world that the person wearing it has vowed themselves to someone and in return, that someone has vowed themselves to the wearer.

In that moment, I would probably have told you I would be happy if Wes and I never married, as long as we committed ourselves to each other day after day. It was truly how I felt in that little splice of time. But later—who the hell would I be kidding? I wanted every man and woman in every corner of the world to know that that man was mine.

And at the end of that extremely fast twenty minutes—where I daydreamed through half of it—we all clapped and hollered as Mr. and Mrs. Sullivan kissed before they turned and headed down the aisle in excitement. Wes and I stepped up together, and Wes offered his arm to me. I slipped my hand into the nook of his elbow.

"Don't let me trip," I told him between my teeth.

"You sure you don't want to try for a world record?" Wes whispered. "I can just give you black eyes wherever we go."

"How romantic!"

He leaned down slightly as we started walking. "You'd still be the most beautiful woman I've ever seen, even with two black eyes."

"Is this how I find out you have some kind of raccoon fetish?"

"They're my weakness. Clever, mischievous, nocturnal," he said before pausing and smiling down at me. "Huh, it's almost as if I'm describing you."

I smiled at Wes like him comparing me to a raccoon was the most swoon-inducing thing I'd ever heard. To me, it kind of was.

"Huh, it's almost as if I love you, Wesley Adams."

Maybe one day I'd be saying that as Mrs. Wesley Adams.

√ Happiness.

Just like I'd want for you and anyone else.

Hell, I don't have any words of wisdom.

Just choose to be happy.

EPILOGUE
YES, THERE'S AN EPILOGUE

We'd missed Thanksgiving at my parents' house because I had a serious boyfriend—the kind who wanted me to go home with him for a family holiday.

You don't know him—his name was Ethan.

Kidding. Sure, Wes and I fought every once in a while, and there were days we didn't give one hundred percent. We were a normal couple, of course. Some things he did that completely annoyed me: not closing drawers he'd open in the kitchen, leaving multiple water glasses on his nightstand, the sound his foot would make when he bounced his leg up and down for a long time. *I* never did a single thing to annoy him though. He'd definitely tell you I was a model girlfriend.

But we chose each other every day, and we made each other happier than we realized we could ever be. And on top of that, we made our weird sort of love triangle with Owen work. They say good things come in threes.

Wes and Owen had their first annual boys' trip together two months before, which, of course, Katie and I would always be left out of. They golfed together on family vacations, and they fished

LEIGH MAKES THREE

together on family holidays. Some things I just had to concede.

Anyway, Wes wanted me to meet his little sister Abigail, and I hadn't seen his dad since college. I tried to be on my best behavior in Nashville and not freak them out like I had with Charlotte. No jokes. It was intimidating to be around the two most important women in Wes' life. Now I knew how Katie had felt around us.

Of course, my mom was bummed, so she made me promise we would both come to the mountains for at least a week for Christmas. It was predicted to snow, so we'd made a fire in the fireplace on the porch, and everyone was sitting under a blanket, hoping it would.

Emma wanted to make s'mores, so she went inside to gather everything with Logan, Jack, and my mom. My dad went to use the bathroom. Katie kept looking at me. Owen wouldn't look at me.

Everyone was being weird. The thought popped into my head, but I didn't think Wes would propose that soon. It had been five months since Owen's wedding.

I took Wes' hand under the blanket and cozied up against him, inconspicuously feeling his pocket for a ring box. Nothing. I wrapped my other arm around his waist and felt his other pocket. Nothing.

I relaxed. He kissed me on the head, placed his chin on top of it, and put his feet up on the table as we watched the fire and listened to it crackle.

"Too bad we don't have any weed to go with the s'mores," I commented.

His chin dug into my head a little as he laughed. His mouth came close to my ear. "You want to go out on the dock and make out?"

"Is snow white?" I replied.

"Not when you pee on it."

"You know I want to."

I grabbed our jackets from the chair, of course, inconspicuously checking his pockets. Nothing.

I laughed to myself in my head. Owen would never let me live it down if I got engaged in less time than he did, so at least I was happy he wouldn't have that to hold over my head. Maybe Katie and Owen would announce she was pregnant.

I zipped my jacket all the way to my neck when we stepped out of the warmth of the fire, trying to remember if Katie had had a drink that day. I watched Wes' ass as we stepped down the stairs carefully in the dark. No ring box in his back pockets. He definitely wasn't going to propose. I was being so ridiculous, but don't we all get a little suspicious of everything our significant other does when we think it could be coming? I'd never even told him what kind of ring I liked, and he'd never asked. He definitely wouldn't propose without us discussing those very important details.

He reached for my hand when he stepped off the last step, and we walked out onto the dock with our fingers laced.

The moon was an icy blue, and the dark silver clouds were moving quickly across the sky. I wanted it to snow super badly, even better if it happened when we were fondling each other.

"How awesome—" I started to tell him my thoughts—because I told Wes when an ant crawled in front of me—when he abruptly stopped and whirled me around by my hand to face him.

I looked up at his face in confusion. "What's wrong?"

"Leigh, you are the only woman in the world who could make me this happy. From the first moment I met you, I wished I could be the lucky man to know what you were thinking inside that brain, to get to take your hand in mine, to be the one who gets to kiss you. And you would make me even happier and luckier if you chose me to be yours forever."

I was looking at Wes through so many tears welling in my eyes that it felt like I was underwater.

He knelt down on one knee and held out the most perfect and beautiful vintage ring. I had no idea where from his body he had pulled it from or how he could pick a ring so perfect for me without asking.

"This ring was my grandmother's and my mom's, which she left for me," he continued as I made a grotesque snorting sound because I was trying to hold back my sobs at the thought that I got to be the one he wanted to give it to, "and I've never been so sure that you are the only woman in the world meant to wear it now. Will you marry me, Leigh?"

"Yes, Wesley!" The tears kept falling. I bent over to kiss him as they splattered on the dock in front of my feet. "A million yeses. I will choose you again and again forever."

He smiled at me as he slipped the ring on my finger, which he must have sneakily resized because it fit me perfectly, before standing and kissing me.

"I love you," he said against my lips.

"I love you more."

Wes wrapped his hands around my face and kissed me again.

"I don't think so," he said, gliding his hand down my arm and taking my hand. "Now, come on, your mom has been dying all day. I'm sure they're all watching us through the window."

When we went back into the house, everyone erupted with yays and congratulations and smiles and clapping. My mom gave me a huge hug and took my hand for her and Katie to look at the ring.

She hugged Wes for a long time. I wondered if this had been her dream since the moment Wes came charming himself into her life. Of course, she whispered something in his ear that I couldn't hear. Wes laughed and caught my eye. Probably something about babies and moving to Birmingham. She'd never let it go, but one day she'd probably get her wish.

Owen gave me a big hug. His eyes looked happily devious. "Do you want to play Things That Are Longer Than Leigh and Wes' Relationship?"

He would never let me live that down.

"Not particularly," I said, as our conversation from the prior year came flooding back.

He continued anyway.

"The water filter in my refrigerator."

True. I knew they lasted for six months, but I wasn't going to say it out loud. "Maybe."

"The black eye Wes gave you when he punched you."

Wes chuckled. I let him live it down. It was Owen who hadn't. He didn't let anything go. Clearly.

"Do you want me to keep going?" Owen asked me.

"Not really," I huffed.

"Oh!" Owen laughed sarcastically. "*My* relationship before *I* proposed.*"

Wes laughed harder. "I had to one-up you."

"But I couldn't be happier for both of you." Owen smiled at us and hugged Wes.

Jack hugged me hard until Emma bounded around the corner holding a big box.

"Congratulations!" she yelled with a huge smile. "I got you a gift."

She placed it down on the counter and gave me a big hug.

"Should I open that in front of everyone?" I questioned her. Emma didn't give normal gifts. With my luck, it would be sex toys or lingerie or something equally embarrassing. Wes had given me underwear with his face on them already because he didn't want to be left out. Of course, Emma knew that.

She nodded and smiled. "Go ahead."

I looked at Logan to confirm, but he raised his hands like he was saying, *Don't look at me.* He hugged me and said,

"Congratulations!"

I pulled it hesitantly toward myself and ripped off the wrapping paper. I opened the edges of the cardboard box and peered inside. It looked like she had put together a care package with all sorts of different items. I pulled one out slowly, confused until I read the first item and my face slid into a huge smile.

A mug that said *I told you so.*

A mousepad that said *I told you so.*

A ring holder that said *I told you so.*

A coozie that said *I told you so.*

A bottle of wine that she'd wrapped with a label that said *I told you so.*

A candle she'd wrapped with a label that said *I told you so.*

And lastly, an oversized sleep shirt that said *I told you so* which matched the T-shirt I'd just noticed she was wearing.

"That's a big fucking *I told you so* to you."

I laughed and hugged her hard. She was the best best friend I could ever ask for.

"When do I get to buy you a pottery wheel?" I remarked. She and Logan had moved in together the month before.

"Please!" she scoffed. "I would never get engaged before a year—at least."

I wrapped my arm around Owen. "We have the best best friends ever."

"Mine's better," Owen replied. "Besides, he's my best friend, *and* he's going to be my brother."

Of course, now I like to think I gave Owen what he'd been secretly wanting all along—he'll just never admit it.

Made in the USA
Monee, IL
01 December 2023

47899496R00166